Angels Take All Forms

sequel to Surrender

Nancy Peterson Gibbs

WESTBOW
PRESS®
A DIVISION OF THOMAS NELSON
& ZONDERVAN

WestBow Press books may be ordered through booksellers or by contacting:

WestBow Press
A Division of Thomas Nelson & Zondervan
1663 Liberty Drive
Bloomington, IN 47403
www.westbowpress.com
1 (866) 928-1240

Scripture quotations are taken from the Holy Bible, New Living Translation, copyright ©1996, 2004, 2015 by Tyndale House Foundation. Used by permission of Tyndale House Publishers, a Division of Tyndale House Ministries, Carol Stream, Illinois 60188. All rights reserved.

ISBN: 978-1-9736-8087-1 (sc)
ISBN: 978-1-9736-8088-8 (hc)
ISBN: 978-1-9736-8086-4 (e)

Library of Congress Control Number: 2019919748

Print information available on the last page.

WestBow Press rev. date: 12/05/2019

Who's Who??

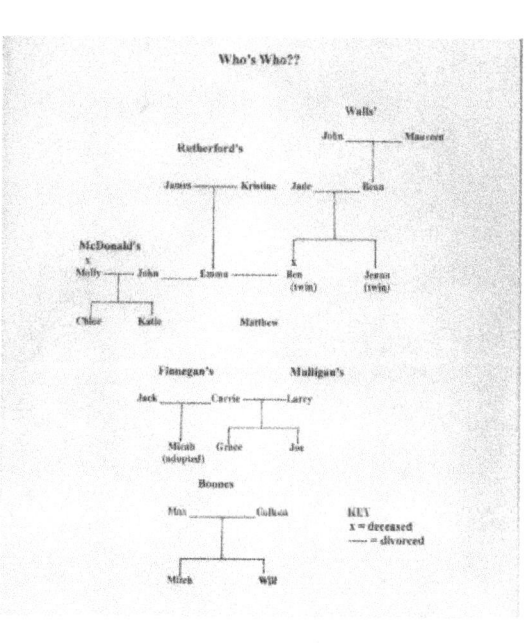

The Lord has established the heavens his throne,
from where he rules over everything.
Praise the Lord, you his angels,
you mighty ones who carry out his plans;
listening for each of His commands.
Praise the Lord, you armies of angels,
who serve Him and do his will.
~Psalm 103:19-21

1

Do not make friends with a hot-tempered person; do not associate with one easily angered.

~Proverbs 22:24

"**P**lease! Stop, Tony!"

Grace was curled up in fetal position, shielding herself from Tony's strikes.

"Why were you flirting with Will today? Do you think he's better than me?" Tony's jealousy flared. His eyes were wild with fury. He kicked Grace as he spewed his acidic accusations. Grace was sobbing as she tried to reason with him.

"Tony, I team teach with him. I'm not flirting. You know he's our friend."

"You're making me angry, Grace! If I see it again, you'll be sorry and so will your boyfriend!" Tony kicked her one more time and then stomped out of her apartment door.

Grace and Tony had been dating for almost a year. They met at the elementary school that they taught at together. Tony taught physical education and Grace taught special education. Grace was immediately smitten with Tony when he knocked on her classroom door at the beginning of the previous school year. He asked her if he could arrange a time that he could teach her class as a whole group. He told her that he knew special education teachers didn't get much down time and he'd like to give her that time a couple of days per week. He told her she could send her assistant with them, and that way Grace could do some lesson planning, phone calls, or catch up on her emails. Grace was blown away by his kindness. They started dating and fell head over heels. They met each other's families and started spending more and more time together.

Tony came from a large Italian family. He was the youngest of four children. He had an older sister, Helena and two older brothers, Mario and Francesco. Tony called himself the "oops" child, as there were twelve years between him and the oldest, Francesco. Grace loved Tony's family and cherished the time she spent with them. There were nine nieces and nephews between the three siblings, so there was always someone at the house. When you entered, you were treated like royalty; greeted with kisses and hugs, and earsplitting Italian greetings.

Tony's dad died of a heart attack a few years prior. That was the only information that Tony gave Grace of his father. When Grace asked questions, Tony dismissed them, saying, "That's the past, Grace. That's where it stays."

Tony's mother, Angela Russo, "Angie," was a stout lady, thick and strong in stature. Her salt and pepper hair, pulled back in a bun. She had an inviting smile and loving, tired, dark eyes.

Grace unraveled herself from the corner of the kitchen and held onto the counter to help herself up. She walked into the bathroom, choking on her tears. She looked into the mirror and didn't recognize the person looking back. She thought back to the episode that triggered Tony's violence.

Will Boone taught next door to Grace. He also worked with the autistic population, and their classrooms shared an adjoining door. Will was dating Melissa, an attorney, and oftentimes double dated with Grace and Tony.

Will and Grace had become close friends the previous school year. They shared classroom management strategies and planned their lessons together. They even ate lunch together in the cafeteria with their classrooms, since their students could not be left without their professional knowledge. Tony always seemed to walk into the cafeteria for a glass of tea during their lunch time. Initially, Grace thought she was imagining things, but then Tony made a comment one day about checking in on her to make sure she was "on her best behavior." She often saw him walking by her classroom during the school day. It made Grace uncomfortable, but she laughed it off with him.

This particular day Grace was heading back to the lunch table with her students' lunches, and slipped on some food on the floor. Will was sitting with the kids. He reached out to grab her, and she landed on his knee. Tony walked in and saw them both laughing hysterically, as Grace was getting up off of his lap. Grace met Tony's eyes and saw his immediate outrage. He gave Grace a death stare and walked out of the cafeteria. Will saw it too and later said something to Grace.

"Tony looked pretty upset today. I think I'll go say something to him. It really didn't look good. I'm a guy, and I wouldn't want to see Melissa in some guy's lap either."

"Don't worry about it, Will. I'll talk to him. He'll be fine." Grace was uneasy about it though and just hoped that Tony would let it go.

"No, really, Grace. You and I spend a lot of time together and I want him to know that I would never disrespect him."

So, afterschool, Will walked out to the gym to talk to Tony, and he returned pleased with his decision. "He thought it was as funny as we did, Grace. I'm glad we talked. He's a good guy."

Grace felt of sense of relief. "Thanks for doing that, Will. You are a stand-up guy."

"Thanks, Grace."

Will left right at 3:30 that day, and Grace stayed to finish up some paperwork. She got her afternoon text from Tony

Tony: are you heading out soon?

Grace: In about 30 minutes. Finishing some plans for tomorrow.

Tony: ok- I have to pick up some things for my mom from the store. I'll text you later.

Grace: Sounds good. Say hi to sweet Ms. Angie for me!

Tony: will do

Tony lived in the basement apartment of his mother's house. His sister and brothers were married; his mom lived alone since his dad died. He was a dedicated son. He was able to help her out, and he banked away his paychecks for the future- win-win.

When Grace got back to her apartment that night, she called her mom, Carrie to check in. Her mom and brother, Joe were teachers too. It was late August and school had been in full gear for a couple of weeks now. Grace hadn't talked to her mom in several days. Carrie was married to Pastor Jack. It was a match made in heaven. Her mom met Jack through her best friend, Jade. Jade's husband, Beau, had an affair several years prior and Jade took off to the beach to clear her head. That's where she met Pastor Jack. He helped Jade and Beau through their trials; and Jade introduced Jack to Carrie. And just to make the story more perfect, Jack was transferred to Carrie's family's church in Georgia- all in God's plan!

Grace's dad, Larry, left them for his mistress, and they never heard from him again. Grace and her brother, Joe went through a really tough time when he left, but Jack changed their lives. He was the father that God always meant them to have; Grace was sure of it.

"Hey Mom!"

"Hey Grace! How's your school year going so far?"

"Great, Mom. I have all of the same students as last year, less two. You never know when a new student will come in, but I love it! It's hard work but so worth it. How's your class?"

"My class is priceless! I keep saying I'm going to retire, but I don't know what I'd do without those hugs every day!"

Grace laughed. "We'll give you extras, Mom! How's Joe?"

"Haven't heard from him this week. You know your brother. Probably won't see him until church Sunday."

"I'll have to shoot him a text. We'll get into our routine soon. I'll see you sometime this weekend. Just wanted to say hi."

"Thanks, honey! Love you! Have a great day tomorrow!"

"You too, Mom. Love you!"

As soon as she hung up, there was a knock on the door. Grace looked through the peep hole. It was Tony Grace smiled, unlocked the door, and opened it.

"Hey Tone! Glad you came by. I think I'm going to order a pizza. How's that sound?"

"Seriously, Grace? You aren't going to apologize?"

Grace turned and looked at Tony. "What are you talking about?"

Tony snapped. He grabbed Grace by her upper arms and pushed her against the wall in the kitchen. Grace was horrified.

"Tony! Please! You're hurting me!"

Then he slapped her across the face. Grace felt her tooth dig into her cheek. She tasted blood.

"It's always about you, Grace! I'm hurting you? Do you think I'm stupid?"

Grace slid down the wall, cowering from the man she loved and planned to marry. He slapped her harder. Grace's head slammed into the wall. She felt dizzy.

"Your boyfriend, Will came by the gym after school. Did you send him?" Then Tony kicked her in the ribs, and continued his berating.

"Do you honestly think I would believe your cover? You slipped and landed in his lap? Really, Grace?" Another kick followed, this time to her back as Grace faced the wall in defense.

"I promise, Tony. I did slip! I would never hurt you! I love you! Will wanted to talk to you because he said it would bother him too if he saw Melissa in the same situation."

"Oh, so now you're defending him?" Tony grabbed Grace by the hair, squatting down to meet her eyes.

"You make me sick, Grace!"

~

Grace came back from her racing thoughts and found herself still looking blankly at her image in the mirror. Her face was swollen; a contusion protruding from her forehead. Her body writhed in pain, but the thing that hurt the most was her broken heart.

Grace slid back down the bathroom wall to a lowly position. She crossed her arms across her chest, and shouted to His throne room. "Please, Lord! Show me the way!"

2

A false witness will not go unpunished and he who breathes out lies will perish.

~Proverbs 19:9

Grace stumbled into her bedroom and laid down on her bed. This was the worst she had seen out of Tony. She learned after the first few months of dating that he was quick to anger. He would shout at her over little things. He didn't approve of her going out with her girlfriends. He told her it wasn't appropriate since they were in a relationship. He told her that he loved her and wanted her all to himself. At first, Grace was flattered. No guy ever loved her this much, but then she felt controlled.

Grace would tell Tony that maybe they were moving too fast, and they needed to see less of each other. That's when he started grabbing her, shaking her, and calling her names. But then he'd always cry, and apologize to her, telling her that he loved her and couldn't live without her. Grace would see his sweet, loving, compassionate side- the one she fell in love with in the first place. She would forgive him and give him another chance. It was a vicious cycle.

Grace's wails came from the depths of her soul and she prayed. "Lord, I don't know what I am doing in this relationship! I don't know how to get out! Who do I talk to, Father? I don't want his family to think less of him. Everyone loves him! I don't want him to lose his job! I am so afraid, Lord! Please show me the way, or help him to change."

Grace lay in bed and looked at the ceiling, blank and empty- just like her emotions. She knew she had to get a sub. Tomorrow was Friday so by Monday, she should be healed enough to return. She was thankful that she had done that planning after school. She called Max, her favorite sub. He did well with her students and Will liked him too. He agreed, and then she sent Will a text.

Grace: Hey! I've got some kind of stomach bug. Max is coming in for me tomorrow.

Will: Sorry! Feel better and have a great weekend! If you guys want to get together, let me know. No plans this weekend.

Grace: Thanks! Talk soon.

Grace took a hot bath and had a glass of wine. She still couldn't believe Tony lost his composure like that!

She got out of the tub, and slipped into her pajamas. She climbed into bed and took out her Bible. She was long overdue, and felt ashamed as she opened it. She had put God on the back burner.

Then, her phone beeped. It was Tony.

Tony: I love you, Grace. I am so sorry! I just couldn't stand to see you in Will's lap!

Grace started crying. She knew he didn't mean it! She texted back.

Grace: I promise! It really was an accident, Tony! Will is just my friend and co-worker. You have to believe that!

Tony: I know! I messed up so bad! I'm bringing dinner over. I'm going to take care of you tonight. I love you so much, Grace! Please forgive me!

Grace: That's okay. I'm in bed.

Tony: I insist! I'll be there soon.

Grace was so confused! *Why won't he give me time to think?* She needed to talk calmly to Tony tonight about her concerns. Maybe they could just take a little break from each other. *Time healed all wounds, right?*

Thirty minutes later, there was a friendly rap on the door. Grace walked slowly to the door, her ribs throbbing with every step. She looked through the peephole and started laughing. Tony was standing holding a bouquet of flowers, a large brown bag, and a defeated look on his face.

Grace opened the door and Tony humbly walked through the door with tears in his eyes. He put everything down on the counter and took Grace into his arms. Through his sobs, he begged Grace to forgive him. Then he carried her back to bed and told her that he was going to take care of her all weekend. He put the flowers in a vase and put them on her dresser. He served her the Chinese food that he'd brought on a tray, and delivered it to her in bed. Then he fixed himself a plate and lay beside her. He promised that he would never touch her like that again. He too secured a sub for the following day; and planned to win back Grace's love.

Grace had forgiven him. She felt sure that this was God showing her the way, answering her prayer. She knew that Tony regretted his behavior. Matthew 6:14-15 said that if you did not forgive others, your father in heaven wouldn't forgive you. Forgiveness was the way- plain and simple.

3

I will instruct you and teach you in the way you should go. I will counsel you with my loving eye on you.

~Psalm 32:8

Emma Walls stayed in touch with John MacDonald, the heart recipient of her deceased husband, Ben Walls. Ben was killed in a car accident by a sixteen-year-old driver under the influence. The driver was Daniel Bar and it was the first time he tried alcohol. He had just gotten his license. Daniel was consumed with guilt and had been under a suicide watch at the jail; refusing to eat or drink. When Jade and Beau Walls, Ben's parents, found out, they knew what their son would want them to do. They all visited Daniel in jail and forgave him. They pleaded with him to make a right out of a wrong. They appealed for a lesser charge for him. After serving his punishment, Daniel in turn, was visiting high schools across the state. He was sharing his story and campaigning against drunk driving.

John MacDonald had two young daughters, Chloe and Katie. They became fast friends with Matthew Walls, Emma and Ben Walls' son. In June, Pastor Jack had arranged a service, named 'Surrender' at the Gwinnett Braves Baseball Stadium. The service consisted of the testimonies of Emma and her son Matthew; Daniel Bar and John MacDonald. Matthew struggled after the death of his father and started having nightmares. It was after Emma's desperate prayers for her son one night, that Matthew saw heaven and his dad, in a divinely-inspired dream. This dream gave peace to all involved in the tragedy and changed many lives.

The service proved that when you surrender your lives to Jesus, He brings you through the storms. The testimonies of the widow, the six-year-old son, the drunk driver, and the heart- recipient brought many unbelievers to Christ that day. After the service, the families of Ben Walls, Daniel Bar, and John MacDonald went out for lunch. It was a joyous day for all involved. God's mighty hands!

For now, Emma and John met up only with their children in tow, for play dates. While the kids played, Emma and John would talk and share stories of their deceased partners. John lost his wife to cancer and because of the gift of Ben's heart, John was able to care for his wife through her final days. The night Ben was killed, John's family gathered around his deathbed and prayed for a miracle- and it came. John and his wife, Molly were so grateful, as their daughters would have been left parent-less. Ben's death gave John life.

John texted Emma during the week and told her that his girls needed a "Matthew fix." Emma laughed and invited them for lunch on Saturday. Emma fixed potato salad, sub sandwiches, and homemade brownies for dessert. The kids played on the jungle gym that Ben had built for Matthew. Emma remembered the day it was finished. They had spoken of more children in the future. One just never knows.

Emma spread a blanket on the grass for the kids when it was time to eat. She and John sat at the picnic table nearby and talked. Each visit became more comfortable with John. Emma even shared her nervousness in meeting him the first time- the day of the *Surrender* service. They all met Pastor Jack at his church to go over last-minute details of the service. Then, they all took the church van over to the stadium.

John had arrived at the church with his girls before Emma and Matthew had arrived. Pastor Jack had directed them downstairs to a preschool classroom so his girls could play while they waited for the others to arrive. When Emma and Matthew arrived, Jack was waiting for them in his office. They sent Matthew downstairs to play with the girls and Jack prayed with Emma. When they walked downstairs to meet them, Emma heard Matthew say, "Can I listen to it?" When Emma hit the doorway of the preschool room, Matthew was sitting on John MacDonald's lap listening to his heartbeat, his dad's heart- that saved John's life.

Emma remembered John's kind eyes and warm smile when he met her. Emma, too listened to John's heart and for a few seconds, Ben came to life. John shared his apprehension as well. He explained that it was a simultaneous feeling of joy and guilt all wrapped up in one. Emma loved listening to John's perspective on it.

"I never thought of it that way, John." She realized in talking to him that it had to be just as difficult for him, as the recipient. He gained life because of their loss.

"It's true. I was so grateful that I could care for Molly and our girls. I knew on my deathbed that Molly had fourth stage cancer. We were trying to make plans for the care of our girls *for the rest of their lives*. We cried and prayed together, constantly. And then, there was a heart for me! It was truly a miracle, Emma." John's eyes filled with tears. He was looking into the distance as if reliving every moment.

"And then when it came time to meet you, I was consumed with guilt. Here I come, alive and well; all because of your husband's death! It was just so…so bittersweet."

"Thank you for your honesty, John. You know, we never once felt resentment toward you. Ben was such a compassionate person. He worked with our youth at church. He was all about being an organ donor. He thought it was selfish *not* to donate what God gave you."

John smiled and responded with sincerity. "It truly could not have gone any better. It was definitely God's work."

Emma's eyes welled with tears of gratitude. "I totally agree."

The kids played until they got hungry again. This play date turned into an entire day together and Emma could not have been happier. She ordered pizza and then they all went out for ice cream. It was a sense of contentment that neither of them had experienced in a very long time. When it was time to go, Katie revealed her impeccable manners, without a word from her dad.

"Thank you for having us, Ms. Emma."

And then the four-year-old, Chloe, "Thank you, Ms. Emma."

"You are so welcome, girls. Let's do it again soon, okay?"

Matthew hugged both girls' goodbye, as if they were his sisters. "Bye Katie and Chloe! Bye Mr. John. Be careful driving home."

John ruffled Matthew's hair. "See you, buddy! I promise I'll drive safely."

Emma hugged both girls and then their dad. "Thanks for coming, John. I really enjoyed it."

"Me too. Next time, it's at our house. I'm grill *master*."

Emma concurred. "It's a deal."

4

And God is able to bless you abundantly, so that in all things at all times, having all that you need, you will abound in every good work.

~ 2 Corinthians 9:8

After John and the girls left, Emma gave Matthew his bath and read him his bedtime stories. He was fast asleep after the first book. Then Emma called her mom, Kristin Rutherford. She needed to talk to someone about her feelings. She was starting to have very real feelings for John and didn't know if it was appropriate. For some reason, she felt guilt.

Why do so many strange things happen in my family? Emma wondered how she could be falling for her deceased husband's heart recipient! And stranger than that was the fact that her mother, Kristin, was the one that Ben's father had the affair with for three months. She had met Beau in a county class for teacher certification hours. Kristin knew at that point that her husband, James Rutherford, was having an affair. Beau, too, was feeling distant from Jade. Jade, Ben's mom, had found text messages and voice mails on her husband's phone. She confronted her husband, but never knew the woman's identity.

Ben and Emma were dating at the time and Ben shared his anguish about the 'home wrecker' (pen name for her in the Walls' household).

While Jade was off clearing her head at the beach, Jenna, Ben's twin sister, went to the counselor at school to talk. The counselor was Kristin Rutherford, Emma's mother. While Kristin was listening to Jenna's story, she realized that Jenna was Beau's daughter. She put it all together...Beau's son, Ben was dating her daughter, Emma.

She was devastated by the trauma she had caused Beau's family. That evening, Kristin had a nervous breakdown. Emma found her staring into space on their bathroom floor and Emma took her to the hospital. Kristin spent a week there, and through counseling sessions in the hospital, she decided to come clean with the Walls' family. She needed forgiveness to move on.

Shortly after Kristin's confession, Emma and Ben announced their pregnancy. Kristin Rutherford and Beau and Jade Walls were suddenly forced into an awkward relationship. They would soon be sharing the role of grandparents. But by the grace of God, they made it work and now even shared holidays together.

"Hi, Mom"

"Hey Ems! What's going on?"

"Matthew and I spent the day with John and his girls."

"That's fantastic! How are they doing?"

"They're great, Mom. He is the nicest guy and he has the sweetest girls. Matthew adores them."

"That's amazing, Ems. Who would have thought that Ben's death could have brought about so many blessings!"

"I know, but why do I feel so guilty about it?"

"Because you loved Ben so much, Emma. This is the first guy you've felt anything for in quite a while."

"I know. It's such a weird feeling! He has Ben's heart, Mom! Why does that bother me so much?"

"Ben's heart is what brought you and John together, Ems. That's a God thing! Ben is in heaven. You have to forget about the heart and concentrate *on the person*."

"You are right, Mom. Thanks for listening. How's Dad?"

Kristin paused and smiled. "It's so nice to hear you say 'dad.' He's doing great, Ems. We're talking about getting remarried."

Emma had chills. Her voice strangled at the base of her throat, stifling tears. "Talk about God's work, Mom. That is so awesome!"

"I know. I thank God every day for all of His blessings."

Emma's dad, James Rutherford had walked out on Emma and Kristin the night that she and Ben came to discuss their pregnancy with them. Kristin had just gotten out of the hospital and James was irate. He demanded that Emma get an abortion and go to college, as originally planned. Ben stood up to James Rutherford and told him that they would never murder their baby. James walked out and they hadn't seen him for over five years. When Ben was killed, Kristin felt a relentless urge to call James and let him know. That phone call led them back together. Kristin learned that James had a drug addiction. He lost everything and found the Lord in the process. He had been sober for two years and still attended 'Narcotics Anonymous' (NA) meetings.

"When are you thinking of remarrying?"

"I'm not sure yet. I'd love Pastor Jack to do the ceremony. I'm going to talk to him soon. Maybe sometime this fall."

"I love you, Mom. I am so happy we have the new and improved James Rutherford back in our lives. He's a changed man!"

"I know. It makes me think of the scripture in 2 Corinthians: if anyone is in Christ, he is a new creature. The old things have passed away."

"I love that one. You're right, Mom! He is living proof! Are you guys going to church tomorrow?"

"We can't make it tomorrow, honey. Dad has a friend coming over in the morning. It's someone he met in NA who keeps relapsing. He's back and Dad is on a mission to save him. Come over after church if you want. I'm making lunch."

"Will do."

"Love you, Ems."

"Love you too, Mom"

5

Would not God have discovered it since he knows the secrets of the heart?

~Psalm 44:21

Sunday morning, Grace woke up to her alarm and looked in the mirror. She wanted desperately to go to church. She missed her family and always felt renewed after Pastor Jack's sermons.

Tony had spent all day Friday and Saturday with her, but returned to his mother's house in the evenings. His mother was a devout Catholic and frowned upon her son spending the night at his girlfriend's apartment. Tony respected his mom's wishes. Grace loved that quality in him.

Grace still had a visible bump and some bruises and scratches on her face; but improving. It was easily concealed with a little make-up. If anyone asked, she would blame it on one of her aggressive students. She hopped in the shower and got ready. She fixed her hair so that her bangs would cover the contusion, and put on extra make-up to cover the bruising. On the way out the door, her phone beeped. It was a text from Tony.

Tony: On my way over with breakfast.

Grace: How sweet! But, I'm on my way to church.

Tony: I don't think that's a good idea.

Grace: No worries- I'm fine. Thanks for taking care of me this weekend.

No response.

When Grace walked into church, it was the usual reunion of family and close friends. Jade and Beau were back from their trip to Charleston, South Carolina. Emma and Matthew joined them in the pew. Matthew was sitting on Grandpa Beau's lap talking non-stop. Joe and her mom were sitting in front of them. Grace felt a gush of love race through her. She slid into the pew and hugged her brother tightly.

"Hey Gracie! How's the school year going so far?" Joe was always eager to hear about his sister's class. He taught science to middle school students, so their teachings were worlds apart.

"Great, Joe! How 'bout you? I've missed you so much. Just too busy!"

"I understand! It was tough getting back in the swing of things after having off all summer. My students are good- very hormonal, as usual."

Grace laughed and looked up to see Tony slipping in the row to sit beside her. Her mom hugged Tony on the way in. Joe shook his hand.

"Great to see you, Tony."

"You too, Joe."

Grace was shocked and a little perturbed that Tony showed up. Saturday night, he said he was going to go to church with his mother. She cringed thinking about how upset her mother and Joe would be if they knew Tony had hurt her. They loved him and never saw that side of him.

Tony sat down next to Grace and took her hand. With a forced smile on his face, he said through clenched teeth, "You shouldn't be here."

Immediately, Grace felt that sick feeling take residence in her. She developed it whenever she knew that she had angered him. The service had started so Grace didn't respond. She prayed that God would speak to Tony today and cleanse him of his anger.

Jack's sermon was centered around Matthew 4:1-4: "Jesus was led by the Spirit into the wilderness to be tempted by the devil. After fasting forty days and forty nights, Jesus was hungry. The tempter came to Him and said, 'if you are the son of God, tell these stones to become bread.' Jesus answered, 'It is written that man shall not live on bread alone, but on every word, that comes from the mouth of God.'"

Jack preached on temptation. He explained that temptations were strongest when people were at their weakest. He explained that Satan waited for the perfect opportunity to tempt people to sin. Jesus had been without food for forty days and that is when Satan made his move. Jack explained that when people gave into temptation, they were selling their souls to the devil. It brought temporary happiness, but later it caused greater pain and guilt. What may be tempting for one, may not be for another; but it was no secret- Satan knew our weakness.

"Then Satan gets us to rationalize our bad behavior… getting us to reason why it was okay. God hasn't changed, but society has! God is more interested in our character, than our decisions, because if we had good character, we would make *good* decisions."

Jack ended the sermon by explaining that it was necessary to own wrongdoings and weaknesses; and repent. He explained the necessity of giving them to God. For man it was impossible, but for God *all* things were possible. "God doesn't save us from the storms of life, but He sees us through them. We were designed to need Jesus, so we need to seek Him in everything we do. God's power is made perfect in weakness."

As Jack spoke, Grace hoped and prayed that Tony was listening. If he would just repent and ask God for help with his anger issues, God would see him though the storm. *Maybe this sermon would make for good discussion today?* Grace would read Tony's mood after church. *Maybe this was God working?*

After the service, everyone congregated outside of church, while Pastor Jack and Carrie said goodbye to the guests. It was a hot, humid day with a strong, intermittent breeze. It was evident that rain was in the forecast. A gust blew Grace's hair up off of her forehead as she and Tony were talking to Joe.

"Wow, Grace! What happened to you? Did Tony beat you up?" Joe followed his comment with uproarious laughter; as if it was the funniest thing ever said. Tony didn't miss a beat. He laughed and gave Joe a high five to acknowledge his humor. Grace was sickened, but prepared.

"It was the wrath of one of my *overzealous* students. Just an accident. He doesn't realize his own strength."

"I don't know how you do it, Sis. Special Ed was definitely your calling."

And then, as if Satan was in full gear, Will Boone and his girlfriend, Melissa joined the group.

"Hey guys! How are you two feeling? Or did you have a romantic day off together on Friday? Come on, fess up!"

Grace forced a laugh and Tony joined her.

"Hey Will! Hey Melissa! Actually, we both got food poisoning, we think. We ordered pizza Thursday night and both got sick." Grace couldn't believe how quickly she could lie outside of God's house.

Tony joined in on the conversation. "Yeah, it was rough, but we're good as new now."

Then Grace looked to Will and Melissa. "I don't think you have met my brother, Joe." Grace turned toward her brother. "Joe, this is Will, my partner in crime at school. He teaches the other autism class, next door to me. And, this is his girlfriend, Melissa."

Joe shook hands with both of them.

"It's nice to meet you both. So, were you there for the attack, Will?"

Grace was horrified as she watched Will's perplexed expression.

"What attack?"

"Grace said she got attacked by an overzealous student." Joe echoed his sister's explanation.

Will looked closer and then realized what Joe was saying. "Ouch! When did that happen?"

Grace had to think fast and more lies spewed. "It was Thursday after you left school. I stayed to finish some paperwork and Eddie and his mom stopped by. Eddie forgot his lunchbox and was not handling it well."

Thankfully, Will bought the story. He knew Eddie could get rambunctious when things got off schedule. "Wow! Sorry about that!"

Melissa joined in. "You need a raise!"

Then, Matthew Walls saved the day. "Hi Grace! Hey Tony! Hey Joe!"

Everyone acknowledged Matthew and asked him about his

first-grade class. After his ten-minute dissertation, all of the adults joined the group. Will and Melissa said their goodbyes. Jade and Beau suggested they all go out to lunch together and catch up. All were in accordance, but Grace couldn't take anymore. She proceeded to tell more lies. "Tony and I are going to head over to his house. His mom isn't feeling well and we are going to stop in and check on her."

Carrie responded with sincerity. "I'm so sorry to hear that, Tony. Is there anything we can do?"

"No ma'am. Just prayers, I guess. But thanks for asking. Next Sunday, we will join you for sure."

Carrie hugged her daughter and Tony. "Love you both. Have a great week at school and we'll talk during the week." Then she noticed Grace's face.

Grace was at breaking point. "Long story, Mom. Joe will fill you in. Love you! Have a great lunch everybody!"

Tony took Grace's hand and they walked to their cars in the parking lot; like young couples in love. Grace was holding back her tears. She couldn't wait to get into the car to unload.

6

When I am afraid, I put my trust in you.

~Psalm 56:3

Jade, Beau, Carrie, Jack and Joe headed to IHOP for lunch. Emma and Matthew headed over to her mother's house. At lunch, the best friends caught up. Jade and Beau were retired now and doing lots of traveling. Jenna, their daughter (and Ben's twin) was teaching in Raleigh, North Carolina. She was engaged to her best friend, Maggie's brother, Jax Ferguson. Micah, Jack's adopted son was engaged to Maggie. They all met when Maggie's oldest brother was getting married and Jenna was invited to the wedding. Jenna introduced Maggie to Micah (who was in medical school at Duke). They hit it off, so Maggie asked Micah to come to the wedding, too. They were all inseparable from that day forward.

Currently, Micah was doing his residency and Maggie was a nurse at the same hospital. They would tie the knot as soon as Micah finished. The four of them were best of friends. It gave their families comfort knowing they had each other. Jade and Beau loved Jax and Carrie and Jack adored Maggie. Their families were sure to start growing; and there was heaps of love to go around.

After non-stop conversation, Joe made an announcement at the lunch table. "I met a really nice girl at school. She's a new teacher this year."

Carrie's heart leapt with joy. Joe had gone through a hard time in college. He was drunk one night and got involved with someone else's girlfriend. He was beaten unmercifully for it and came home. He completed his degree at a local college and when he finished, he put his life into teaching. He dated, but never found the right one. He was twenty-five years old now and had his own apartment. Carrie prayed diligently that God would put the *right one* in his path. For Joe to bring it up, she knew it was serious.

"Joe, that's awesome! Tell us about her." Carrie was ecstatic and Joe got in defense mode.

"Her name is Achara. She's the sweetest, kindest girl I have ever met. She's from Thailand. She's been in the states for about four years. She worked three jobs to pay for her master's degree. I think I'm going to ask her out."

Pastor Jack piped in. "Invite her to church. That's always innocent enough."

Joe hesitated, but responded boldly. "She was raised Buddhist. She knows nothing about Jesus."

"Well, maybe God put her in your path to teach her." Jack always looked at the glass half full.

"I was thinking the same thing, but I don't want to shove it down her throat. For now, I'm going to pray about it and see where it goes. She truly acts like the Christian I want to be. She's patient, kind and honest. She never loses her temper, hates gossip. I love being around her. She makes me want to be a better person."

Jade continued the discussion. "That is basically their culture, Joe. I taught with a guy who was Buddhist. Their way of life is very peaceful and loving. He explained to me that they believe that our problems arise from negative states of mind and happiness arises from positive states of mind. Meditation is their method of finding that positive place."

Carrie was confused, and didn't want to upset Joe with her questioning. "So, do Buddhists believe in God?"

"I was wondering the same thing. Is Buddha their god?" Jade continued.

Joe was *clearly* exasperated, wishing he'd never gone into detail. "I don't know, ladies. We haven't gotten to that conversation yet. I'll be sure to keep you posted."

Carrie and Jade both identified Joe's sarcasm. Carrie kicked Jade under the table, acknowledging their blunder, but happy she wasn't alone.

Jack ended the conversation in his very reasonable, loving manner. "We'll be praying, Joe. God will guide you."

"Thanks, Dad."

Everyone at the table smiled when they heard Joe say 'dad.' Carrie had been married to Larry and they had Grace and Joe together. He walked out on them for another woman and never returned. Carrie was bitter for a long time. She never thought she could trust again. Grace and Joe suffered too. Grace went through a period of promiscuity. Joe chose drugs and alcohol to numb his pain. It was Jade's trip to the beach, after Beau's affair, that changed Carrie's life. It was at the beach that God put Pastor Jack in Jade's path. Jack helped heal Jade and Beau's marriage, and in turn, Jade introduced Carrie to Jack. They married. Grace and Joe earned a father and a loving brother, Micah. They had all walked through the darkest of times, but never once did they walk it alone. This was the work of The Potter.

After lunch, Joe headed back to his apartment and Carrie questioned Jack in the car on their ride home. "Jack, doesn't it say in the Bible that you should not be unequally yoked with an unbeliever?"

"It does, but don't worry about that right now, okay? It's not like she's an atheist. She just doesn't know Jesus because she was raised in Thailand, which is a Buddhist nation. God doesn't see as a man sees, Care. God sees the heart.

First Corinthians 7:14 says that the unbelieving wife has been sanctified, or set apart, through her believing husband. God can definitely work through the believing spouse to bring the unbeliever to Jesus. That may be God's plan in all of this. We have to trust Him."

Jack looked at Carrie who was listening intently. "Let's pray about it. Joe is strong in his faith. God will see this through."

"I love you, Jack Finnegan. You always calm me down."

Jack smiled and grabbed Carrie's hand. "I love you too, Care."

7

A good name is better than precious ointment; and the
day of death, than the day of birth.

~Ecclesiastes 7:1

When Tony and Grace got to the parking lot, Tony got in the
passenger side of Grace's car. He had parked next to her.
Grace exploded into tears. She felt them rise from the core
of her soul; the pain like a heavy blanket.

"I told you it wasn't a good idea to come to church, Grace."

Grace was stunned and angered by his remark. "It wasn't a good
idea to beat me either, Tony!"

"I didn't beat you, Grace. I lost my temper because you were in
another guy's lap!" Tony caught himself before he blew. He took a deep,
relieving breath. "I love you, Grace, but I already apologized! How long
are you going to punish me for this?"

"I don't like lying, Tony! I just left church and all I did was make
up stories to cover up for your temper!" Grace felt safe speaking freely
in the parking lot of church. She knew her family was close by. *Would
she regret it later?*

"I said I was sorry, Grace! What else do you want me to do?"

"I don't know. I wanted to go out to lunch with my family, but I
couldn't take any more questions! I can't live like this Tony!"

Tony reached across the console and grabbed Grace's hand. "Calm down, Grace. It's going to be okay. Why don't we go by my mom's house, like you told everybody? She had a big pot of sauce on the stove when I left. We can eat lunch with her and it will be one less lie that you told."

Then Tony took Grace's face gently into his hands, forcing her to look at him and smiled. "Look into my eyes, Grace. Everything is going to be okay. I love you. Come on. Follow me to my mom's house. She's been asking about you."

Grace smiled back. "Okay, I'll go for a little while."

When they got to Tony's house, Angela Russo was sitting at the kitchen table reading the newspaper. The house smelled of tomatoes and oregano. Grace's mouth watered.

"Hi Angie!"

"Grace! Amor mio! My love!" Angie took Grace into a big hug and kissed both of her cheeks. Then she took Grace's face into her hands.

"Let me look at you! You are beautiful! *Bello, bello!*"

Then she gasped. She touched the bump on Grace's forehead and caressed her bruised face. "What happened to you, Grace?" Angie's forehead creased in concern; her eyes spoke of alarm.

Here we go! Grace wanted so badly to say, "Your son beat me!" She went in for the lie, instead. But, before Grace could utter a sound, Tony spoke up. "She got attacked by one of her special needs students, Mom. She's okay. She's used to it." He laughed and looked at Grace, to agree.

"Oh no! I am so sorry, my love! Come sit down. Let me take care of you. I made some fresh sauce and I've got pasta. Let's eat together. Oh! How I've missed you, Grace!"

"That sounds fantastic, Angie! I'm going to run to the bathroom really quick. I'll be right back to indulge."

While Grace was in the bathroom, Angie turned to her son. "Tony, are you sure it was her student?"

"Yes, Mom! Why are you asking?" Tony was visibly defensive. He felt his face flush. He was tempted to raise his hand to her, *but it was his mother;* he told himself this *over and over.* It lessened the urge.

"You promise me you're not following in your father's footsteps?" Angie had urgency on her face and purpose in her tone.

"No, Mom! Grace works with severely autistic children. They can get very aggressive!"

"Okay. I am just checking. She's a beautiful girl, Anthony. You treat her like a queen, now- you hear me?"

"I will, Mom. Don't worry!" And with that, Tony took his mom into a hug and waited for Grace to return.

When Jade and Beau got home, Beau checked his cell phone. He had it charging when he left for church. There were three missed calls from his dad within the hour. He left one voicemail.

"Hey Son. Give me a call as soon as you can."

Beau called him back immediately. "Dad, everything okay?"

There was a pause and then John Walls responded. "Well, yes and no, Son. Your mom went to see Jesus this morning."

Beau sat down on the bed. His heart twisted and he swallowed a lump in his throat. A numbness took him over and it came in a rush that stunned him. Jade came out of the bathroom and knew by her husband's expression that something was wrong. She sat down on the bed beside him, her heart thumping to the pulse in her neck. It brought back vivid memories of the phone call they received the night their son, Ben, was killed.

Jade gently took his hand and whispered. "Beau, what's wrong?"

"It's my mom, Jade. She's gone."

Jade and Beau left immediately for the assisted living residence to be with Beau's dad. When they arrived, the apartment door was open. John Walls was kneeling by the bed in prayer. Maureen Walls' body was already taken. Beau felt heartsick that he wasn't there for his father. Jade and Beau knelt on either side of him and held his trembling hands. Beau's dad prayed aloud:

"Heavenly Father, I know Maureen is with you right now and it gives me peace. Thank you for allowing me sixty-eight years with her, Lord. You are so very generous. I can't imagine life on earth without her, Father, so please see me through, until we meet again." He turned to Beau as a pool of tears flowed down his anguished face. Beau took his dad into his arms. Jade wrapped her arms around both of them; and they cried together.

8

Fathers, do not provoke your children to anger, but bring them up in the discipline and instruction of the Lord.

-Ephesians 6:4

When Grace returned to the kitchen, Angie had bowls of pasta and sauce already placed on the table. Grace took a seat next to Tony and Angela led them in prayer. She started with the sign of the cross. "In the name of the Father," touching her forehead with her right hand, "the son," touching her chest, "and the holy spirit," touching her left and right shoulder, "Amen." She brought her hands together in prayer. "Bless us, oh Lord and these, thy gifts, which we are about to receive, from thy bounty, through Christ, our Lord, Amen." Grace joined in with Tony and Angela. Over the past year, she learned the prayer by heart. She loved Angie's unpretentious nature and her undying loyalty to her Catholic faith. Grace always felt a warm, rush of love when she was around her.

"Dig in!" Angela chuckled as she reached for the red wine, which was a staple at every Russo meal.

"Grace? Would you like some?"

"No ma'am. I have to drive home and wine makes me sleepy."

"Si Si" Angela understood and poured herself and Tony a glass.

"This is delizioso, Angie!" Grace tried her hand at Italian.

Angela laughed. "Grazie! Grazie!"

Moans were sounding across the table. Angela Russo was an impeccable chef. She always had a pot of something, in or on the stove, as her children always seemed to pop in unexpectedly. She always wanted to be prepared.

"How is your beautiful family, Grace?"

"They are doing great, Angie. Thank you for asking."

"You usually eat with them after church on Sunday? No?"

Grace winced thinking of the fiasco outside of church. "Yes ma'am, but today I wanted to see *you* for a change."

"Oh, grazie, grazie!" Angie reached over and patted Grace's hand. As they were talking, the kitchen door that led to the driveway flew open.

"Hi Nona!"

Tony's eldest brother, Francesco, and his six and eight-year-old sons, Dominic and Angelo came full force through the door. Angela turned her chair to take both boys into her comfy lap.

"My angioletto!" She kissed them both. Grace knew that meant 'angel' and smiled. Angie was such a loving grandmother. Her children and grandkids adored her.

"Hi Mama!" Francesco entered after his boys and Angela stood to greet him. Francesco took his mom into a tight embrace. Angela came up to his chest. Francesco, like Tony, fit the description of tall, dark and handsome. They had pearly white smiles and were of lofty, husky stature; much like younger versions of Sylvester Stallone. Then Francesco moved to Grace. Grace stood and squeezed him tight.

"Grace, you are beautiful as always. I hope my little brother is treating you right."

Then both brothers wrapped each other up in a hug, slapping their backs as they released from each other.

"Frannie! How are you, man? Where's Clara?"

Clara was Francesco's wife. Grace loved to be around her. She was a calm, loving, wife and mother. She never had a negative word to say about anyone; and she was a wonderful listener.

"My other half is out with the girls today. I've been working a lot of overtimes lately and she needed a break."

Francesco was a detective in the police department. He did a lot of security jobs on the side to save for family vacations. Clara was a stay-at -home mom. She had a nursing degree, but decided to stay home with her kids. She planned to return to the field when they got older.

"Well sit down and eat, Fran. Where are the boys? Are they hungry?"

"No, Mama, I took them to McDonald's for a Happy Meal, but I would love some pasta. Why do you think I came over here, huh?" Francesco chuckled.

"I hope you came to see your mama- not just to eat!" Angie lovingly shook a fist at him.

"You know I'm kidding, Mama. Let me check on the boys quick. I'm sure they're in the yard."

Angela Russo's backyard was the neighborhood hang-out for years. There was a swing set, a sandbox, and a cement slab with a basketball hoop. Angela loved having kids over. She liked to know where they were and that they were safe; and they brightened her day. It made her husband crazy, but she didn't care. Antonio Russo, her husband, was a difficult man to be around; but she had loved him just the same.

Francesco returned and sat at the table with them. After a few minutes, the boys came running into the kitchen.

"Uncle Tony! Will you play basketball with us? Please?"

Tony smiled and looked to Grace. "Want to join us?"

Angie intervened. "No, Tony. You go. Grace came to see me. You see her all the time. Now, go!"

Grace giggled. "That's right. You go ahead, Tony. I'll hang out with your mom and help her clean up."

Then Francesco piped in. "I'll be right out, Tony. We'll play HORSE. How 'bout that boys?"

"Yessss!" The boys were squealing with excitement and instinctively ran to grab their Uncle Tony's hands. As Tony was pulled outside by his elated nephews, Angela turned to Francesco.

"You're a good father, Fran. I'm very proud of you."

"Thanks, Ma." Francesco finished his pasta, kissed his mom and headed to the backyard. Angela yelled behind him. "You digest before you play now!"

Then Angie turned to Grace. "God blessed me with good kids, Grace. My boys always watched out for their mama."

Grace smiled. "You are blessed Angie, but they are too. You are a pretty awesome mom and grandma, you know."

"Oh, Grace, I've made my share of mistakes too." Angie stared ahead, reminiscing with hurt in her chocolate eyes.

"Everyone makes mistakes, Angie. We have to learn from them."

"Very true, Grace." Angela took Grace's hands in hers and looked in her eyes. "I need to ask you something, Grace. I've wanted to ask you for a long time, but *especially* today. God is talking to me."

"Okay, Angie. Please, ask me anything." Grace felt a little uneasy, but she loved this woman so much. She trusted her decisions.

Angie looked deep into Grace's eyes, squeezing her hands lovingly. "Does my Tony treat you with respect?"

Grace felt electrical currents spreading through her body. A dizziness took her by surprise. She averted her eyes from Angie, not wanting her to read them. It was too late.

"Oh no, Grace. Tell me the truth, please. Does my Tony put his hands on you in a bad way?" Angela was staring at her and Grace could see fear take over Angie's demeanor. Tears welled in her dark eyes, her inner light fading quickly. She looked with obligation to Grace, as she broke out in a sweat. "Tell me, Grace."

Grace felt queasy. *How could she betray Tony and break this sweet lady's heart? But she was sick of the lies!* "Just a couple of times, Angie… but it was understandable. I did some stupid things."

"No, Grace! Don't you blame yourself! My whole life I did that with Tony's father! He had a very bad temper and he beat me up." Angie wiped tears as quickly as they fell. "Tony took the brunt of it because he was the youngest. The others were much older. They were away at college or living on their own. They didn't see as much as Tony." Angela stared blankly ahead, as if in the moment. "Tony used to fight Antonio when he saw him hit me. I started seeing a counselor, Father Tom, at my church right before Antonio died. I should have done it much sooner.

Father Tom told me that divorce is okay if your husband is hitting you. He said that a husband should be patient, kind and slow to anger! He should love you like Jesus loves. It's in the Bible, Grace."

Grace was crying now and nervously looking toward the door to make sure Tony didn't hear.

"He did that to you, didn't he?" Angie gently touched Grace's face, using her thumbs to absorb her tears. "It wasn't your student, was it, Grace?" Angie held Grace's gaze. "You need to tell me."

"Yes ma'am." Grace felt a flood of emotion rush over her. She felt guilt for talking about Tony, but felt a simultaneous sense of relief that she had someone to confide in. *How could anyone hurt Angela Russo?*

"Please don't say anything to Tony, Angela. Please! It will make him so angry." Grace found herself panicked. *Why did I tell her?*

"Oh, how well I know." Angela was crying too. She took Grace into a healing embrace. Grace felt an odd sense of rejuvenation.

"You tell him, Grace! You tell him *no more* or you are gone! You call me. Father Tom said the best thing I could have done for Antonio was to leave him, call the police! He said that I enabled him when I kept letting it happen!" Angela took a napkin from the table. She wiped her tears and blew her nose.

"I am so sorry, Grace. Father Tom told me to watch my boys, especially Tony, because he saw so much. He said kids mimic the behaviors they see."

Then, the door flew open and two sweaty boys came running into the kitchen. "Nona, can we have a drink, please?"

Both ladies got up from the table, snapping out of the emotion they were sharing. Angela opened the fridge to get drinks and Grace started clearing the table, as if nothing happened. Francesco and Tony entered next and helped themselves to a cold can of coke from the fridge.

Tony came behind Grace while she was washing dishes at the sink. He put his arms around her shoulders and whispered an 'I love you' into her ear and kissed her cheek. Grace forced a smile and kept on with what she was doing. Her mind was flooded with waves of emotion. Right now, she felt an odd sense of courage, knowing she had Angie on her side. Tony and Francesco sat back down at the kitchen table while the women finished cleaning up. Angie joined her sons at the table.

When Grace finished with the dishes, she turned toward the table. "I'm going to head out. Thank you for an incredible lunch, Angie."

Tony responded with agitation in his tone. "Why are you leaving so early?"

"I've got to get ready for tomorrow. Being out Friday set me back a day. The sub used all of my plans."

Tony was persistent. "Oh, come on Grace. It's only 2 o'clock!"

"Tony! Give her some air, man!" Francesco was shocked by Tony's control.

Tony's face reddened. "I'm not sure this is any of your business, Fran."

Angela calmly rose from her seat at the table and took Grace into her arms. While squeezing her tight, she said, "You run along now, Grace and get your stuff done. I'm going to spend some time with my boys."

Tony stood with confrontation on his face, clearly losing control. "I'll walk you out."

Grace took charge knowing she had Angie to protect her. "No, no, I'm fine. Please, don't get up. Enjoy your family."

Then Grace blew kisses across the table. "Good to see you again, Francesco. Say hello to Clara for me. See you at school tomorrow, Tony." And then Grace peeked into the living room and said goodbye to Dominic and Angelo, who were watching a movie, curled up together on the couch.

"Bye Grace!"

And then Grace walked out to her car and drove off, wondering if Tony mentally recorded her early departure for future warfare.

9

For just as we share abundantly in the sufferings of
Christ, so also our comfort abounds through Christ.

~2 Corinthians 1:5

Emma and Matthew arrived at her mother's house and found her
parents and their guest sitting around the kitchen table.

"Hi Gram and Gramp!" Matthew charged into the kitchen
for his usual hugs.

"Hey Em! Just in time to eat." Emma could smell her mom's chicken
pot pie baking.

"Smells heavenly! Hi everybody!" Emma kissed her mom and dad
and then extended her hand to the guest. "Hi, I'm Emma."

The handsome, salt and peppered haired gentleman rose to greet
her. "Nice to meet you, Emma. I'm Mulley."

"Nice to meet you, Mulley. Interesting name."

"Yep. You can thank your dear ole dad here for it. We go to NA
together." Then he paused and continued, "Well, when I show up. Your
dad has been very persistent and I'm back, *once again*."

"Well, good for you. I hope it lasts this time. I'll keep you in my
prayers."

"Thank you, Emma. I appreciate that."

"You're welcome. My dad is a changed man. If he can do it, *anyone* can."

James laughed. "She's right, Mulley. I told you!"

"Well your dad has been a life saver. We have very similar stories and he's taken me under his wing. It gives me hope."

After lunch, Mulley left and promised that he would see James at the NA meeting the following evening. That's when Kristin told Emma the good news.

"Your dad and I have some good news, honey. You know I told you we were ready to remarry?"

Emma smiled and looked at both of them with a wink of approval. "Yes?"

"Well, we were saying fall or winter, but then we decided, why wait? We are ready to do this. So, I called Pastor Jack this morning and he agreed to marry us in three weeks, after the church service. Whoever can make it, fine. If they can't, that's fine too. But usually the whole gang is at church anyway. It will give us enough time to send out a quick invitation this week."

"That is awesome! Congrats!" Then Emma laughed. "It sounds so funny congratulating my parents on their *engagement*."

James smiled. "Yeah, it's a little different this time around, isn't it? No engagement rings, but we're going to pick out promise rings for each other to give at the ceremony. It will be our promise of commitment to one another for the rest of our lives." James fought back his tears. "I love your mom so much, Ems. I'm going to make it right this time. I am a different man, I promise."

"I know you are, Dad. I'm so thankful you are back in our lives. You are new and improved. I thank God every day for it." Emma hugged her dad. "I love you, Dad."

"I love you too, Ems."

When Grace got back to her apartment, she already had three texts from Tony.

Tony: You seemed weird when you left. What's going on?

Tony: Is everything ok?

Tony: Grace, text me back please!

Grace looked at her phone and shook her head. She could have guessed this would happen! Whenever Tony felt out of control, it made him uneasy. Grace poured herself a glass of wine and sat on the couch. She couldn't stop thinking about the conversation she had with Tony's mom. His dad abused her! That's why Tony never wanted to discuss his dad! *That's the past, Grace. That's where it stays.*

Grace texted him back: Everything is fine, Tony. I'm just tired and I have to get ready for tomorrow. I'll see you in the morning.

Tony: ok

Grace sensed anger in his simple response and it bothered her. *Why do I always have to worry so much about what he is thinking? This relationship is so much work!* Grace was mentally exhausted! She decided she would go to work early the next morning to get her lesson plans done and instead grabbed her IPAD. She googled "children of abusive fathers."

Grace read every website available and had cold chills all over her body. Tony fit every description. *In their intimate relationships, they used intimidation and violence to get their way. They disrespected women the way their fathers did. They believed violence was an effective way to resolve problems and conflicts.* After several hours, Grace shut down her computer. She felt sorry for Tony. He learned it from his dad. It wasn't his fault!

Grace decided that she would talk to him. She would suggest getting counseling. Her own step -father was a pastor with a doctorate in psychiatry. Jack could help him! Grace set her alarm for 6:00 a.m. She fell asleep in prayer.

Grace got to school at 6:45a.m. Her students didn't arrive until 9 o'clock, so she had time to prepare. When she unlocked her classroom door, she realized Will's light was on next door. She put her purse on her desk and walked through the adjoining door to Will's classroom.

"Good morning! Good minds think alike. Are you always here this early?"

Will looked up and Grace knew something was wrong. He wasn't his cheerful self.

"What's wrong, Will? Are you okay?"

"It was a bad day yesterday, Grace. Melissa broke up with me. It seems she's hooked up with a fellow lawyer from her firm."

Grace sat down across from him at his reading table.

"I'm so sorry, Will. I just saw you at church with her yesterday! What in the world happened?"

"Well, I guess she needed the Lord for repentance after cheating on me." Will looked defeated- like he hadn't slept all night. Grace's heart ached for him.

"She had texted me that morning to see if I was going to church. She met me there and said she was treating for lunch afterwards." Will paused. His eyes darted back and forth, remembering every moment. "After a nice lunch, she asked if I wanted to take a walk with her at the park. That's when she broke it to me. She was crying. She said she loved me and didn't want to hurt me, but she had to give this guy a chance. She said she had a feeling with him that she never felt before- like he was *the one*."

"Ouch! I'm sorry, Will. God must have another plan for you. You just have to believe that she wasn't *the one*."

"I know. It just hurts the ego a little bit." Will forced a smile. "You can't help but question what he has that I don't."

"Don't do that, Will Boone! You are a great guy. It's *her* loss! I wouldn't be surprised if she comes back in a few months, begging your forgiveness. That's when you have to be strong. I mean, you have to decide if you can trust someone again after such a betrayal. Honestly, it's good that you found out now. I'll be praying for you."

"Thanks, Grace."

"I mean every word," Grace admitted. "I can't believe you are here today! I would be home wallowing in self-pity!"

"Not me- I have to keep busy. It's wasted energy thinking about it." Will was black and white. Grace was all of the gray matter in between- sensible to her sensitive.

"Good for you, Will! Let me know if you need anything. I'm going to get some lesson plans done." Grace headed through the adjoining door, feeling Will's hurt as if it were her own.

Grace and Will made it through the day. Their students seemed unusually tired today, so their behaviors were lessened. They got their students on the bus and Will headed out. He told Grace he was exhausted and he would see her in the morning. Grace hadn't seen or heard from Tony. He usually sent her a text at some point during the day. He didn't come into the lunchroom during their lunchtime either. *Maybe this is a good thing? Maybe he is giving me some space?* Grace sent him a text.

Grace: Hey! Did you have a good day?

She set her phone aside and got busy at her paperwork. She decided she would finish her plans for the next couple of weeks since she had the urge.

After a while, Grace looked up at the clock. It was 5:30 p.m. and the hallways were quiet. She hadn't heard from Tony. *Creepy.... Is he playing games with me?* Grace quickly dismissed the thought. She packed up her stuff and started heading out. She felt pleased that she got everything done. She turned off her classroom light and headed out the door... only to meet Tony's crazed eyes in the hallway outside her room.

10

The one who does what is sinful is of the devil because the devil has been sinning from the beginning. The reason the son of God appeared was to destroy the devil's work.

~1 John 3:8

Grace gasped, but then composed herself. "Hey Tone. Did you get my text?"

Tony walked toward her, forcing her back into her classroom. He shut the door and locked it behind them. He kept the light off. "You know, I really thought I could trust you, Grace."

Grace was terrified. He had that look in his eyes. He flipped that demonic switch.

"What are you talking about, Tony? You can trust me." Grace kept backing up, talking calmly. She maintained eye contact, hoping to calm him.

"I knew you were up to something, Grace. You came in early to see your boyfriend today."

"No, Tony. I got here early to do my lesson plans. He was already here."

Tony paced. He wasn't listening. The only thing he heard was his own lies. "You were in his room this morning- sitting across from him. It looked like you were having a pretty intimate conversation."

"Melissa broke up with him, Tony. He was telling me about it." Right when the words left her mouth, she knew it was a mistake.

Tony put her up against the wall. He punched her in the stomach. "Oh good! Now he's *really* available." Tony was seething. "Do you think he's a better man than me, Grace?"

"Of course not, Tony. I love you. Please stop. Someone is going to hear you. You'll lose your job. You don't want that."

"No one is here, Grace. Harry gave me the key to lock up when I left." Harry was the custodian who loved Tony. *Everyone loved Tony! No one would believe this!*

This time, he grabbed her by the hair, bringing her down to the floor. "And don't tell me what I want, Grace! You left my mother's house yesterday saying that you were going to do your lesson plans. Why did you come in early? Admit it Grace!" Grace felt his spit hitting her in the face. He was out of control, the look of an unrestrained animal.

"Tony, please. I'm not going to admit to something that I didn't do. I was on the computer looking up information on children of abusive fathers last night. I want to help you, Tony." Grace desperately looked into his eyes, trying to tame his fury.

"Tony, I love you so much. Please don't imitate the sins of your father. We can get you help."

"My father! What do you know about my father?" Grace's comment made his frenzy escalate. He landed a blow to her nose and it started to bleed. Grace took fetal position, shielding her face from more strikes.

"Tony, please! It's not your fault! Jack can help you!"

Tony paced the room like a caged animal, then returned to Grace and kicked her. With a demonic laugh, he bellowed, "Jack? Your holier than thou step-father? What a joke!" He continued to pace as if hunting prey.

"I know it's not my fault, Grace! It's your fault! You are the problem! I just keep giving you more chances, but you just don't listen!" Tony started kicking over desks and chairs. Grace prayed that someone would come to her rescue.

41

"My mother told you about my father, didn't she?" Tony looked venomous, spittle shooting from his vile mouth. Tony walked toward Grace and kicked her again. "Didn't she? Answer me!" Tony's voice escalated. It sounded unfamiliar- hollow and soul-less.

Grace felt nausea overcome her. *I should not have mentioned his father!* Grace didn't want Tony to hurt Angie. "Tony, your mom wasn't being mean. She loves you so much! She just questioned me about my face. I couldn't lie to her! I'm sick of lying, Tony! I want to help you, but you won't let me!"

Tony kicked Grace one last time, a visible vein bulging from his forehead. The pulse of his temples was in harmony with Grace's pounding heart. He grabbed her purse and emptied the contents, taking her phone and putting it in his pocket. Before he walked out, he callously warned her. "If you say one thing about this Grace, you will be sorry." He stormed out, slamming the door behind him as if on a mission from Satan.

Grace sat curled in a ball of shame. She felt numb and drained of any value. She tried to lift herself and couldn't. She fell back down and howled, "Lord! Help me! Please!"

God answered her. Grace saw the light go on under the adjoining door. She heard someone. With every breath that she could muster, she called for help. "Help me!" The door opened and Will appeared, looking around the dim room.

"Grace! What happened? Who did this to you?" Will was unnerved. He turned on the light and bent down in front of Grace. She was humiliated for Will to see her in this condition. She looked toward the floor.

"Was this Tony, Grace? Tell me! I just saw him walking out of school when I was pulling up. He looked angry about something!"

Grace couldn't look Will in the eyes.

"Grace! Answer me. You have to call 911. Don't let him get away with this!"

Grace whimpered back. "He took my phone."

Will shot up as if remembering something. "I've got mine! That's why I came back to school. I left it on my desk." Tony ran next door and grabbed his phone. "I'm calling, Grace."

"Will, he's going to kill me!"

"I'll get to him first!" Will dialed 911.

11

The Lord will rescue me from every evil attack and save me for his heavenly kingdom.

~2 Timothy 4:18

Francesco was sitting at his desk at the police station when he heard a call come in on the police radio. It was an assault on a female teacher at his brother's school. Francesco immediately grabbed his keys and headed out the door to join the responding officers.

Will left Grace and waited at the front door of the school for the officers to arrive. He knew the custodian locked the door behind him when he left. You could get out, but not back in. Will filled the officers in as he led them to Grace's classroom. When they arrived, Francesco was sickened.

"Oh no! Grace! Who did this to you?"

Grace was equally horrified. She never thought about Francesco responding to Will's call. In response, Grace put her head in her hands and sobbed. Francesco knelt down in front of her as the two other officers took a report from Will.

"Talk to me, Grace. I am here for you."

Grace couldn't look him in the eyes.

Will answered instead. "His name is Tony Russo. He is the physical education teacher here."

A repulsion took over Francesco's stunned body. He looked to Grace. "Did Tony do this to you? I have to hear it from you, Grace."

Then Grace remembered how angry Tony was when he left. She feared that he was on his way to his mother's house. Grace looked up at Francesco with panic in her eyes.

Grace surrendered and responded. "Yes, it was Tony. And I'm so afraid he is heading to your mother's house!"

Francesco responded instinctively and took Grace gently by her arms. He looked into her terrified eyes. "Grace, what are you talking about?"

Grace had no choice but to answer him. "Your mother questioned me about the bump on my head the other day, while you guys were playing basketball. She wondered if it was Tony who did it to me. She admitted to me that your father abused her. I made a comment while Tony was attacking me today. I begged him not to imitate the sins of your father." Grace gasped as she realized the certainty. "He knew it was your mom that told me, Francesco!" Grace wept out of control. "He was so angry! Fran, you have to make sure he's not hurting your mom!" Grace's sobs echoed off the classroom walls.

Francesco snapped into detective mode immediately. He turned to the other officers and directed them to his mother's address. "Go now! I'll meet you there."

The officers raced out and Francesco turned back to Grace. "You have to go to the hospital, Grace. You have to press charges. This has to stop!"

Meanwhile, Will was putting the pieces together, realizing that Francesco was Tony's brother. There was an uncanny resemblance. "I've got this, sir. I'll make sure she gets to the ER." Francesco was calling for the ambulance as Will spoke. He thanked him and headed out the door to his mom's house, praying Grace's intuition was wrong.

When Francesco left, Will knelt down in front of Grace and without saying a word, took her in his arms. She was broken and Will hurt for her.

"What have I done, Will? This is such a mess!" Fear and emptiness were her only companions.

Will held her tightly. "Grace, you have made the best choice and the *only* choice you could. Tony's behavior is *not okay.*"

Grace choked on her tears as thoughts of Tony's arrest raced through her mind. "He's going to go to jail, Will. He's going to lose his job!" Alarm rang through Grace's body as the realization took residence. Her heart raced along with the hollow, dull ache that surged through her.

Will pulled away from her and gazed into her eyes, as if examining something under a microscope. His eyes were soft like a caress. He used reassuring words. "Grace, you've done *nothing* wrong. Tony *deserves* to lose his job *and* be in jail. You are doing him a favor. He needs help and you deserve a life of love."

Will saw the ambulance pulling up outside the classroom window. He let them in and waited for them to load his shattered friend into the back. All the while, Will held Grace's hand and assured her that she did the right thing. Then he followed the ambulance to the hospital.

12

Fools give full vent to their rage, but the wise bring calm in the end.

~Proverbs 29:11

Tony's fury raged as he drove toward his mother's house. He shook as he thought of his mother disrespecting his father. *Why would she tell Grace about my father? Why can't he just rest in peace?* His anger was controlling him, masking the pain he felt deep inside. *My mother betrayed me! She betrayed my dad!* Tony's thoughts made him want to punish her!

The growl of his engine ceased in the driveway of his childhood home. Tony looked in the rearview mirror. A vein in his forehead was clearly visible, pulsating in beat with his heart. He laughed demonically, secretly looking forward to confronting the woman who caused all of this. He walked toward the kitchen door. It was locked so he took out his key. He smirked, feeling in complete control. The light over the stove was on and he could see the lights from the television flickering on the walls in the living room. He walked through the kitchen, remembering how he sat around the kitchen table with his mom, Fran and Grace; playing HORSE with his nephews. *Why did you have to go and blow it, Mom? Why didn't you mind your own business and keep your mouth shut?*

Tony walked into the living room. His mom was asleep in her

recliner. He was at war with himself. He wanted to hurt her. *She is no better than Grace!* Tony heard the arguments between his parents. His mom was flirtatious- *just like Grace.* She was friendly to all the guys. Deep down she wanted someone besides his dad. He knew the truth. No wonder his dad hit her. She deserved it... *just like Grace did.*

As Tony drew closer to her chair, he accidentally kicked the magazine rack. Angie was startled out of her slumber. She tried to focus on the face above her, coming out of sleepy confusion. "Tony, is that you?" She reached for her glasses on the end table next to her chair. Tony came back to reality, away from his vicious thoughts, as he realized his close proximity.

"Hey Mom." Tony feigned a kiss on his mother's cheek, not wanting to look suspicious.

"How was work today? Are you hungry? I have some lasagna in the fridge."

Tony paused and thought of work. A wave of reality rushed over him as he recalled the condition that he left Grace. He started pacing the floor as if released from captivity. He started to sweat and panic came over him.

Angie sensed that something was very wrong. "Tony, what's wrong, honey? Talk to me."

Tony's vehemence took him over. He rushed toward his mother screaming, "*You* are what's wrong, Mom!" He grabbed her by her arms and shook her violently. Angie's glasses flew off of her face, hitting the end table and bouncing to the floor. A blessing in disguise, blurring the vision of her outraged son.

"Why did you dishonor Dad?" Saliva shot onto Angie's face. Memories rushed back to her. Her son resembled her deceased husband to a tee; stained souls- hardened by generational sin.

Before she had time to react, Francesco had Tony down on the floor in the living room, hand-cuffed and delirious. The two other officers read Tony his rights, as Francesco knelt before his grief-stricken mother. Angie reached for her glasses. Francesco watched his helpless mother, with trembling hands, try to compose herself.

"Mama, are you alright?"

"I'm okay, Francesco. Please, Tony doesn't need to be locked up. He needs help!"

Tony had the eyes of a pursued animal; round and alarmed. He was shouting as he was led out of the house. "You are my brother! What are you doing, Fran? Why are you sticking up for her? She's bad news, Fran! She's been cheating on me with that Will scum she teaches with!"

Francesco ignored him and held his mother in his arms. Angie was sobbing. "Give him a chance, Francesco. He didn't hurt me."

"Mama, listen to me." Francesco peered into his mother's chocolate eyes. "He beat Grace again, Mama. She's in the hospital. We have to do this. He has to stop!"

When Grace arrived at the hospital, she called her parents from her room. She was relieved when Jack answered. He asked no questions. He simply assured her that they were on their way. She knew it was too much to explain over the phone. She told him she was fine, but that they needed to come. She had been hiding something that she reasoned too shameful to disclose, even to the ones she loved the most. They were the ones who loved her deeply, the ones she could trust. She could not wait to be set free from her secret. A momentary, warm rush of relief washed over her.

Will stayed in the waiting room while Grace was examined. He called Max, Grace's favorite sub to cover for her the next week. The police had contacted the principal of the school to relay the incident. They would have to find a replacement for Tony. Will was sure the event would be on the news that evening. He was so grateful that he had forgotten his phone and was there for Grace. God worked in mysterious ways.

13

Then you will know the truth and the truth will set you free.

~John 8:32

After Jack and Carrie got over the shock of their daughter's appearance and admitted abuse, they prayed together. Grace explained everything from the time she started seeing signs of Tony's control, to the final demise. Carrie was sickened over the fact that she never saw any signs. Jack, as always brought clarity and peace to the situation. Grace felt like a weight was lifted from her, but still struggled with God's part in it. As Jack and Carrie sat by her bedside holding her hands, Grace asked Jack a pressing question. "Why did God let this happen to me?"

"God is never the author of evil, Grace. But He does allow others to *choose* evil. The amazing thing is God uses those evil choices to work for the good. That is His ultimate purpose, His righteousness and justice."

Grace started crying. "I loved him for a year, Dad! I put him in jail! I humiliated his family!"

Jack squeezed Grace's hand and calmly replied. "Grace, Tony made those choices. You were beautifully and wonderfully made by God. All those doubts that you aren't good enough are lies. When your biological dad left you, you felt abandoned. You lost that male figure in your life.

Your broken self-image led you to make bad choices in your life. You let the criticism from an abusive man decide your path."

"You're right. He was always so suspicious and jealous. I could never relax in our relationship. You know, I can handle the body pain, but it's my heart that hurts the most."

Jack's heart ached for her.

"You protected Tony's secret for so long, Grace. You got disconnected from God. Every time he hurt you, your soul died a little more. When you are connected to God, you have a healthy soul. We take our soul to eternity, Grace. It's never too late to feed your soul."

"I'm so angry with myself. Why did I allow that? I am as much to blame as him!" Grace covered her face and wept.

Jack nodded in understanding. "You were trying to cage something that needed freedom, Grace. And you finally did that. Tony's demons had nothing to do with you. God gives peace, not fear. If life was all good, we wouldn't need God. Just give it to The One who can and will carry it all for you."

Grace laid perplexed listening to her beloved step-dad. He was always without judgment, using God's promises to heal. Carrie held Grace's hand and quietly praised God for putting Jack in their lives. He always knew the right things to say.

"I love you guys so much. I don't know what I would do without you." Grace looked lovingly to each of her parents.

Carrie looked into Grace's swollen eyes. "Take one day at a time, Grace. Nothing is too big for God. He wants us to trust Him. God is giving you another chance. Move on with gratitude and know that there is nothing you need that He cannot provide."

Jack smiled as he listened to his wife. "She's right, Grace. We all need to come to the awareness that the One who is in charge of our lives is totally trustworthy."

Then there was a rap on the door. Will appeared. "Excuse me for interrupting. I'm going to head out, Grace. I got Max to cover your class this week. He said to take as long as you need."

"I can't thank you enough, Will. I truly don't know what I would have done if you didn't forget your phone." Grace wiped tears from her inflamed face.

Will smiled. "It was definitely a God thing, Grace. I'm convinced of it. I'll be in touch tomorrow. You rest and take care of yourself, okay?"

Carrie got up from her chair and hugged Will. "Thank you for taking care of our daughter. I'm adding you to my praise list."

"You are welcome, ma'am. Your daughter is very special to me."

Jack shook Will's hand. "Thank you, son. And you are right. It was definitely a God thing."

As Will was leaving, the doctor came in. He introduced himself while he shook Carrie and Jack's hands. "Well, you have a very lucky girl here. She has several broken ribs, but she's going to heal up just fine. Since we have her here, we'll keep an eye on her. Let her have a good night's sleep. You can take her home tomorrow. There's not much we can do for fractured ribs. You can ice them for relief and I'll prescribe some pain reliever."

"When can I return to work, doctor?"

"I'm afraid you'll have to take off for *at least* a couple of weeks. You will experience some pain for a while. I'll see you in my office in a couple of weeks, and we'll go from there."

As the doctor was leaving, the nurse entered the room. "We have a Francesco and Angie waiting to see you. I just wanted to make sure you were up for more company."

Grace looked to Jack and Carrie for support. "Do you think they are mad at me?"

Jack took Grace's hand. "I doubt that very much, Grace."

Grace looked to the nurse. The nurse sensed her fear and reassured her. "I don't think Angie is leaving until she can give you a hug."

Grace smiled. "Send them in."

Angie came through the door, gripping a handkerchief in her hand. She was less boisterous than usual, a contriteness taking over her demeanor. Carrie rose to greet her and took her into her arms. A silent sob was apparent through the convulsing of Angie's body. When she looked to the hospital bed, her sobs were audible. She took Grace's marred face into her hands. "Grace, I am so sorry! This is my fault."

"Angie, *please*, no! This is not your fault!"

Jack gave up his chair and led Angie to it. "Angie, sit. It's going to be okay."

Francesco moved toward the group, a look of remorse and exhaustion etched on his face.

Angie continued. "No, Grace. Listen to me. I waited too long. If I had gotten help sooner with Tony's dad, Tony would be different. He saw too much!"

Jack chimed in, sensing Angie's pain and wanting to calm her. "Angie, don't be haunted by the what-ifs of life. It's wasted time. See your mistakes as a blessing, instead. You saved Grace, Angie. You gave her the confidence to confront Tony. God turned all of this into good. He is giving everyone, even Tony, a second chance. The past is gone. Grasp these second chances and move forward. Make your life what God intended it to be."

Angie listened intently and her crying subsided. "What if I don't know how to move on?"

Jack knelt down and looked Angie in her remorseful eyes. "You have to trust God to see you through. If suffering was good enough to teach God's son, it's enough to use as a lesson in our lives too. Jesus' experience with suffering and resurrection made Him perfectly suited to be the Savior of our lives.

"All of the sufferings we go through, Angie, eventually lead to glory. Hebrews 4:13 says that nothing in all creation is hidden from God's sight. Everyone has a prideful side- one too broken to admit to, but God knows it. Jesus knows and feels what we go through. Satan wants us to think that Jesus is not there for us, but nothing is farther from the truth. We can't hide anything from Him. He's our Father."

Francesco joined in the conversation. "Jack's right, Mama. We have to trust God to get us through. None of us saw Tony's sin. But by the grace of God, he's where he needs to be, as hard as it is."

"What's going to happen to Tony, Francesco?" Grace asked with an ache in her heart.

"He'll be charged with aggravated assault. He'll most likely be fined and will probably serve at least a year's time in prison. We plan to arrange for a good psychiatrist to treat him while he is there."

Jack responded with his usual loving spirit. "I plan to visit him weekly, too."

Angie looked at Jack with tears in her eyes. "You don't hate him?"

"Absolutely not, Angie. Tony is broken. God wants Tony to come out of hiding and come to Him. We are all sinners, Angie. God loves us just as we are. He keeps no score of wrongs, just endless forgiveness. We all need to pray for Tony to surrender himself to God with all of his sinfulness. God wants to take it from him. God forgives and forgets our shameful ways when we repent. We have to turn to Him. He is so much bigger than our weakness."

Angie was sobbing. Francesco moved to her side and took her hand. "Thank you, Jack. I think Tony is lost. I don't think he understands or believes any of that. Could he be too far gone?"

"No, Angie. God never gives up on us. He wants to save all sinners. James 1:5 says that if anyone lacks wisdom, we should ask God who gives generously to all, without finding fault and it will be given to us."

Angie wept. "Oh, Jack, I want that for him so much!"

"Angie, I am going to teach him these promises. God wants to heal Tony, but it's up to Tony to repent and accept God's forgiveness. Apart from God, Tony can do nothing. As hard as this experience seems, I know God is working. It may take some time, but prayer is a powerful thing."

"I am so grateful to you, Jack. Thank you! Thank you from the bottom of my heart."

Francesco rose and extended his hand to Jack. "You are an amazing man, Jack. You have given us so much hope. Thank you."

Jack discounted his hand and took Francesco into a warm embrace. "We are going to get through this together."

Jack, Carrie and Grace assured Angie and Francesco that Tony would be in their daily prayers. Before Francesco and Angie left, Jack led them in prayer and they promised to stay in touch.

14

May your fountain be blessed and may you rejoice in the wife of your youth.

~Proverbs 5:18-19

Maureen Walls was cremated and the funeral service was held the following Saturday at Jack's church. This allowed time for Jenna, Jax, Micah and Maggie to travel from Raleigh. The church was filled with all of the family and friends that congregated at Jade and Beau's house on Thanksgiving, with numerous more. John Walls was a Methodist pastor for fifty plus years and he and Maureen were well-loved. Jack led the celebration in the standing- room- only filled church. John Walls sat in the front row, deep in thought. He looked down at his once shiny wedding band that was worn to a dull finish. His years of marriage to Maureen were evident in every scratch and ding, a beautiful memory of their life together. He thought back to their wedding day and smiled.

When it was time for the eulogy, ninety-year-old John Walls walked with the self-confidence of a seasoned pastor to the pulpit. John's tribute to his wife was a message of unconditional love. The only sound in the church was sniffling as John shared their love story:

"Sixty-six years ago, I was fresh out of the seminary and I was assigned to my first church. I was nervous as a turkey on Thanksgiving, but I should have known that God had it all planned out." John nodded his head slowly, acknowledging His mighty Savior's work. "You see, Maureen was my secretary. I was a faithful man and I didn't want to gawk, but boy was she beautiful!" Laughter filled the church. John smiled and looked into the distance as if remembering every instance. Then he continued.

"She was beautiful inside and out. Maureen answered phone calls, did clerical tasks and quite frankly, kept me in line. I'll never forget the first time I met my congregation and had to give my first sermon to them. I was working in my office and Maureen came by before she left. She asked me if I needed anything. I said, Maureen, I want you to pray for me because I am a little anxious about Sunday." He paused, staring down at the floor in thought. "And then, she looked at me with those kind eyes and said very simply, 'Cast your anxieties on Him because He cares for you, John. God would not have led you here if He didn't plan to lead you thorough.'"

John wiped a tear from his face. "She said, 'John, God put you in this church because He had confidence in you. Just trust Him and do it for His glory.' And it was that day that I knew I was going to marry Maureen Murphy. She worked hard and never grumbled. She provided and protected for those she loved. She was reliable, trustworthy, respectful, and had good judgment. She was wise to the ways of the world. She served others with a gentle and loving spirit. She was an amazing and nurturing mother to Beau and she trained him in the way he should go. She looked out for my interests and supported me in everything I did." His words flowed like warm syrup, smooth and sweet. John paused. He closed his eyes and allowed Maureen's memory to fill him. "I just described a Proverbs 31 wife from the Bible. You see, Maureen's beauty came from Jesus. She put God first and loved Him with her whole heart. She followed His ways and strived to do only things that pleased Him."

John looked up and made eye contact with every area of the sanctuary. He continued, speaking from his heart with God's perfect word. "Maureen was a wife of noble character, worth more than rubies.

I had full confidence in her and I lacked nothing of value. She did me good, not evil, all the days of her life."

John walked back to the pulpit and grabbed the sides as if to give him strength. "I don't know what I'm going to do without her, but one thing I know for sure is…" John wrestled with the cry lodged at the back of his throat. He took a deep breath and smiled as he visualized the reality. "Maureen is with her Savior. She went to heaven in her sleep and when I woke to find her gone, she had a smile on her face. I will cherish the time I have left on this earth, but I can hardly wait to see that beautiful smile again."

Then John took his seat in the front pew, next to his weeping son.

15

You cannot serve two masters at the same time. You will
hate one master and love the other. Or you will be loyal
to one and not care about the other. You cannot serve
God and money at the same time.

~Luke 16:13-15

Two weeks after Maureen Walls' celebration of life service,
Kristin and James Rutherford remarried. Surrounded by friends
and family after the Sunday morning service, Jack Finnegan
led the ceremony and used James' testimony for his message to the
congregation.

He read from Romans, chapter eight. "Those who live according to
the flesh have their minds set on what the flesh desires, but those who
live in accordance with the Spirit have their minds set on what the Spirit
desires. The mind governed by the flesh is death, but the mind governed
by the Spirit is life and peace. The mind governed by the flesh is hostile
to God. It does not submit to God's law, nor can it do so. Those who
are in the realm of the flesh cannot please God."

Then Jack closed his Bible and shared his message. "We are gathered
here today to celebrate the marriage of Kristin and James Rutherford.
For those of you who don't know, James and Kristin were married for
the *first* time 25 years ago. The difference between then and now is that

Christ wasn't the center of their life then. Today, by the grace of God, they are re-entering life with Jesus as their center. You see, James lived in the flesh. The flesh, as Paul calls it in the letter to Romans, is the *worldly* ways, not the *Godly* ways. Flesh is the outer man and our soul and spirit are the inner man. When we choose people by what we see on the surface, or when we put our jobs before our family, or when we choose other women over our wives; drugs over prayer..." Jack hesitated, letting the Spirit move him. "When we do these things, we miss the mind of God.

"God's grace changes our lives. Anytime we sin, we are allowing these desires to take priority over God. If your soul desires something more than God, it becomes your idol. When we allow our flesh to direct our thoughts and actions, it leads to spiritual ruin every time. Because man-made things will die, but Godly things will remain. Eventually, the world will disintegrate and *only* God's kingdom will last."

Jack paused to let God's words sink in. The sanctuary was silent. Mulley, James's friend from NA wept in the back pew. He knew so well what it meant to live in the flesh. He lost his family over his choices. He was sick of relapsing and turning to drugs and alcohol. He was so grateful that God put James Rutherford in his path.

Grace sobbed holding her mother and brother's hands. She knew that her relationship with Tony lacked God. Grace was ready to reconnect with God and vowed to pray for Tony's spiritual healing. It wasn't until she was brought to her knees that she realized she needed her Savior. She couldn't do life without Him.

Jack continued. "These are the facts, folks. Those who follow Christ are part of God's unshakeable kingdom. No matter what happens on this temporary earth, our eternity is built on a rock, solid foundation that cannot be destroyed. Don't put your confidence in earthly things. These things are temporary! Set your sights on eternity! Build your life around Christ and His unshakable, indestructible kingdom. Concentrate on your inner man- your soul and Spirit."

Jack paused again and said a silent prayer that God would change hearts. The peacefulness in the sanctuary indicated that God was surely in that place. "Jesus died for our sins and left all of us an inheritance- a free gift! And He lives today on the right hand of His Father, making sure we receive this gift. So, say *yes* to Jesus! Don't try to write your own book and do it your way. Jesus is the only author of your life."

Jack was being fueled by the Holy Spirit. The words flowed from his mouth. "The ironic thing is that we are all sinners! We sin every day, whether it be a judgmental thought, a feeling of dislike for our neighbor, gossip, envy… the list goes on! Some sins are bigger than others, but the truth is that *every* sin separates us from God. But the most amazing thing about all of this is that we have an awesome Creator! We have a loving, forgiving, compassionate, patient and gracious Father who gives us a clean slate when we repent. Jesus frees us!"

Jack paced the altar wanting to make his point, his mind racing with thoughts. "You know, James Rutherford told me the other day that he felt a surge of wholeness and freedom that he knew only God could give. God led him back to the woman he fell in love with the first time… but this time, *God* is in charge of their marriage. God's grace changes your life. Make God your idol and it will change your life. James and Kristin are perfect examples of it."

Kristin and James exchanged their vows before God, friends and family. Both of them cried tears of joy, as Jack introduced them to the congregation. They knew this renewal of their love was God's flawless will.

After the ceremony, the guests congregated outside of the church. Grace, Joe and Carrie made their way outside feeling renewed by Jack's sermon and the miraculous reunion of Kristin and James. While they were standing and talking, a man approached them. Solemnly, he met each of their sets of eyes and simply called them each by name. With tears in his eyes… "Carrie, Grace, Joe. Hi."

Carrie felt her knees buckle and backed up to the bench behind her. "I have to sit down." Joe was speechless, but Grace displayed hope.

"Dad? Is that you?" There stood Larry Mulligan, their estranged husband and father, who left them six years prior for his mistress, without another word.

"It's me, Grace."

Grace embraced her estranged father, both of them weeping. "I knew you'd be back! I have been praying for you!"

Carrie was still reeling from the unexpected reunion and with cold curiosity acknowledged him. "What are you doing here, Larry?"

Jack was watching from a distance and sensed Carrie's disapproval. He calmly entered the situation. "Everything okay over here?"

Larry looked Jack in the eyes and extended his hand. "Hi, I'm Larry Mulligan."

Jack knew immediately who he was and felt uneasy. "Wow. Well, good to meet you, Larry. I'm Jack Finnegan, Carrie's *husband*."

16

Be kind and compassionate to one another, forgiving each other, just as Christ forgave you.

~Ephesians 4:32

Larry hesitated for a moment but felt a peace come over him… a peace that surpassed all understanding. "Well, thank you, Jack. All I can say is, God is good. Your sermon touched me in ways I can't even explain. I know what I have done to Carrie, Joe and Grace. It was inexcusable, but I have repented and I am ready for God's grace to change my life."

Jack smiled and patted Larry's back. "I guarantee that He is already working. How about we all go to lunch?"

Carrie was flabbergasted by Jack's hospitality. "Jack, I'm not sure I am ready for this."

Joe agreed. "Me either! Where have you been, Dad? Not even a phone call? Really?" Joe's emotions engulfed him. He swallowed his tears and wiped his eyes. He turned his back on his father, composing himself, as he sucked in his sobs.

"I understand, Joe. I would love to have lunch with you and tell you the whole long, sad story. I don't blame you for hating me. I have hated myself for so long."

Then James Rutherford walked up. "I see you met my buddy, Mulley."

Confusion took residence over the group and Grace investigated. "How do you know my dad?"

James returned the confusion with a look of horror. "Your *dad?*"

"This is the family I left, James." Larry "Mulley" Mulligan looked remorseful in his candid response. "God has definitely brought me to my knees."

James was visibly shaken. "Oh wow. I had no idea." He looked to each of them and explained. "We met in Narcotics Anonymous and I …" James fumbled with his words, not knowing how much to divulge during this very fresh reunion.

Larry sensed James's discomfort. They had confided in each other with their similar stories, but Larry never shared names. "James, it's okay. I'll explain. You go enjoy your wife and thank you for everything. If I hadn't met you, this day may have never come. God is definitely at work."

James smiled awkwardly, still in shock. "No doubt, Larry. No doubt."

Jack intervened as he always did. His pastoral and psychiatric roles came naturally; clearly, his spiritual gifts. "Listen Larry. We will meet you at IHOP in about twenty minutes. It's right down the road to the right. Are you familiar with the area?"

"I know right where it is. I will see you there." And Larry Mulligan humbly walked away, feeling crushed, but grateful for his chance at forgiveness.

For the first time in their married life, Carrie felt incensed. "What are you doing, Jack? That man ruined our lives! He walked out on us and never looked back!"

"Let's go," Jack responded with a calm sternness.

The four of them walked to the parking lot, not speaking. On the way to the restaurant, Grace spoke up. She was shocked by her mother's outburst. "Mom, you told me that I needed to forgive Tony in order to move on and have the life that God intended me to have. How is this situation any different?"

Carrie was crying out of frustration and anger. "You're right, Grace. I'm just so angry! He left me without any money and with two children, that just happened to be his! It was the hardest time of my life!"

Jack put his arm around Carrie for comfort and calmly joined in the conversation. "Care, your life wasn't ruined. You had tough times but God saw you through. God brought us together through it all. This is coming full circle and God is in the driver's seat. Larry needs this time and so do you guys. Forgiveness frees us, Care. Remember Matthew 18:22… God forgives without limit… Seventy times! We have to forgive to be forgiven."

Carrie knew Jack was right but still harbored bitterness. The ride to the restaurant was silent. Everyone was lost in their thoughts. Jack prayed silently for this reunion to bring about the peace and love that only God could bring.

When they arrived at IHOP, Larry was entering the restaurant. Jack parked the car and suggested they pray before going in. Without a word, Carrie, Joe and Grace bowed their heads and Jack led:

"Heavenly Father, I know this is your work. You brought the lost back. Again, you are showing us how you make good out of every dishonest situation. Lord, fill us with your love and forgiveness while we meet with Larry today. Help Grace, Joe and Carrie open their hearts and be free from the anger that they harbor for him. In Jesus' name. Amen."

They all exited the car without speaking. While they walked into the restaurant, Carrie took Jack's hand. "Thank you, Jack. I love you."

Jack kissed the top of Carrie's head. "I love you too, Care. You can do this."

Grace and Joe walked behind them, listening and smiling as they felt God's love between them. Joe put his arm around his sister and took her into a side hug, "Let's do this, Grace."

"I'm ready, Joe."

When they walked in, Larry motioned for them in the back room of the restaurant. Jack waved back and they walked toward him. "I thought we'd have more privacy back here.

Jack agreed as they all took a seat around the table. "Good idea."

"I can't thank you enough for giving me this opportunity." Tears streamed down Larry's face. "Pastor Jack, I felt the Holy Spirit today. Your sermon touched me to the core of my soul." Larry picked up a napkin and wiped the moisture from his face. "I lived in the flesh my whole life! Until now. While you were preaching, I looked around, embarrassed by my tears. I was making sure that no one was watching me. It was *then* that I saw Grace, Joe and Carrie sitting there. I knew at that *very moment* that God had put me there. I wasn't going to come to church today, but James Rutherford has never given up on me, not once! He was there for me every time I relapsed. He kept telling me that if he could do it, anyone could."

Larry laughed thinking of the day James had said that to him. "I didn't feel worthy to walk into church today. I was ashamed. I've been praying, but I couldn't bring myself to enter God's house. And when I did, He blessed me. Go figure."

Grace, Carrie and Joe were weeping. They felt his sincerity. They felt his shame. They all knew shame, but God forgave them. Carrie reached across the table and took Larry's hand. "I forgive you, Larry. God blessed us after you left. It wasn't an easy time, but He saw us through. Jack has brought us back to the gospel. Finding God is going to change your life, just like it did ours."

Larry choked back his tears. "I want you to know everything. I want you to believe that I was a completely different person then."

Joe couldn't take his father's pain any longer. "It doesn't matter, Dad. I forgive you too! I made horrible choices in college, but God brought me back too. You have a clean slate."

Larry looked his son in the eyes. "Thank you, Joe. You have no idea what that means to me."

Grace was next. "Dad, we are all sinners. We have so much to catch up on. Let's not waste another minute. I forgive you. Welcome back."

Jack was speechless. He looked around the table, smiling and knowing that God was surely in their presence. Lunch was relaxed, like old friends catching up on lost memories. Grace and Joe spoke of their teaching experiences and Larry shared his good memories of being their dad. As they were leaving, they all exchanged phone numbers and Larry thanked Jack for the amazing job he did helping to raise his children. He told Jack that he had a lot to learn from him, and that he was ready and willing. He asked Joe and Grace if they could meet for lunch once in a while. He promised that he would take it slow, but that he didn't want to miss out on another moment of their lives. Grace and Joe agreed.

Jack told Larry that he was there for him any time he needed to talk. They all embraced before heading back to their cars. The day proved to all of them that true joy and forgiveness only comes from knowing Jesus.

17

Come to me all who are weary and burdened and I will give you rest.

~Matthew 11:28

Before church services on Sunday, Jack and Carrie were sharing a cup of coffee on their back deck. Jack was feeling sad about the fact that he and Carrie hadn't been spending much alone time together. Carrie understood the part of being a pastor's wife, but sometimes the ones you loved most got put on the back burner.

"Care, after church this morning, how about you and I slip away to the mountains. We can sit in my favorite spot and have a picnic. How's that sound?"

"That sounds fantastic, Jack. It's a plan!"

"We've been so busy lately, Care. We've had Maureen's service, Kristin and Jack's service, Grace's situation, Larry's return...." Jack looked into their yard as he spoke. Carrie noticed his exhaustion. She lost track of their relationship, too. Teaching and Jack's work on the weekends took up their days.

"I'm not complaining. It's all good and I love my service to God." Jack paused and then looked to Carrie, "But I am tired, Care and I miss you. I haven't even been to the doctor or dentist in well over a year. I'm forgetting to take care of myself."

Carrie listened and smiled. She got up from her seat across from him and sat in his lap. "Sounds like the life of a minister." They laughed together and Carrie continued the conversation. "I miss you too, Jack. I hope I've thanked you enough for all that you do for our family and friends. I feel so blessed to have you."

"And I feel just as blessed having you guys."

After church, Jack told the usual lunch bunch that he and his beautiful bride were escaping to the Georgia Mountains to spend some much-needed time together. They stopped at Publix, got fried chicken and chips, packed their cooler with waters, and they were off. It was fall and the colors were majestic. They had the car windows open and Jack held Carrie's hand. No words were necessary. The landscape and fresh mountain air replaced the chat. 'A picture paints a thousand words' proved factual.

Less than an hour later, Jack pulled into his favorite spot. It was the spot he came to when he had to clear his mind and find answers. It was here that Jack prayed, seeking guidance from God after the death of Ben Walls. It was here that the Holy Spirit spoke to him and where he came to the decision to rent out the Gwinnett Braves stadium to do his service. It was here that God made it clear to Jack that he had to invite the drunk driver, Daniel Bar; the heart recipient, John MacDonald; and Emma Walls to speak at Ben's service. It could not have gone any better. Many came to Christ that day.

Jack and Carrie sat on their blanket, looking out at the glory of the mountains. Jack shared with her how the answers just came to him that day and how a yellow butterfly landed on his Bible while he was praying. They reminisced about how Matthew Walls, interrupted his mother during the service and said he wanted to share his dream about heaven. He had been experiencing nightmares over his father's death. Emma had dropped to her knees and begged God to take away his nightmares and bring her son peace. God answered her prayer through this dream and many lives were changed after that service.

Jack and Carrie spent three hours just sitting and talking. They prayed together before they left, thanking God for their time together and all of the blessings He had given them. And when they were finished, a yellow butterfly sat atop the fried chicken box between them. An indescribable peace came over both of them. Jack gave Carrie his hand to pull her up. As Carrie folded the blanket she looked her husband in the eyes. "God is so good, Jack. He truly is always with us."

"I have no doubt, Care. Always."

18

I can do all things through Him who gives me strength.

~Philippians 4:13

Grace returned to work after four weeks. She felt restored. She spent that time off healing physically and spiritually. She stayed at her mom and Jack's house during that time. She wasn't ready to be alone with the memories so fresh in her mind. She prayed a lot and studied her Bible- the channel to her soul. God's book of promises.

Jack was an amazing teacher. In the evenings, Grace would often sit and pick his brain about the questions she had written down in her scripture readings. Will kept in touch with her via texts and assured her that Max, her sub had everything under control. She also got to see him at church on Sundays. Grace was so grateful for Will's friendship.

After the incident, cards and flowers flooded in from fellow teachers and parents of present and previous students; all offering their prayers and well wishes. Will had given all of them a heads-up that Grace was at her parents' house. Sweet fragrance and colorful blossoms adorned their living room.

Her first day back at school, Grace arrived early to a welcome back sign above her classroom door and a vase of fall flowers on her desk. The card read, "So happy to have my partner back. You have been missed. Thankful that you are okay. Love and prayers, Will."

Grace sat down at her desk and wept happy tears. God had blessed her with amazing people in her life. She read notes from Max about what he had covered with her students. Then Grace followed up with her lesson plans for the week. After doing it for several years, it came naturally. She shot Max an email thanking him for all he had done.

Will came in shortly after and greeted her with his pearly white smile and a big hug. "Gracie! Welcome back!"

Grace squeezed him tightly in return. "Thank you, Will... for everything!"

Her eyes filled with tears and her voice cracked. "Thank you for the flowers, your friendship- just for always being there! I just can't thank you enough."

"Grace, please stop thanking me. You would do the same for me. That's what life is all about."

"Well, I am glad you are in my life. It's great to be back and I can't wait to see the kids!"

Her classroom aide, Rosie arrived next with additional hugs and kisses. She was an older woman with grandkids of her own. She came back to work fulltime when her kids were married. She had lost her husband three years prior. She had an autistic grandson and lots of love to give out. She worked between both classrooms, as Grace and Will had eight students between them.

The bell rang and they all headed down to the buses to get their students. As each student got off the bus, each had a sparkle in their eye when they saw Grace. They each showed their affection in their own unique way. Grace felt their love and it filled her up.

Grace fell right into her routine. The only thing that pricked at her conscience was the fact that the PE teacher was now a woman- a fresh out of college, bundle of joy. Will noticed her preoccupation at lunch when Grace saw her walk into the cafeteria to get a glass of tea at the teacher's lunch bar. It brought back disturbing memories of Tony coming into the cafeteria to check on her.

"Are you okay? You seem quiet."

Grace came back to reality. "I'm okay. It's just a weird feeling knowing where Tony is and knowing that I caused it."

Will bit his lip to hide the sudden irritation that raged in him. He collected himself and responded calmly and in a matter of fact manner… "Tony caused it, Grace. Tony did."

Grace could tell by the look on Will's face that she had struck a nerve in him. "You are right, Will. It's just going to take time to grasp."

"I know and I'm praying for you, Grace. I'm here whenever you need to talk. Time truly does heal all wounds." Will took a sip of his drink. "Remember, Grace. Don't look back. You're not going that way. That door is closed."

Grace returned to her apartment after work for the first time. Carrie had come by after work previously to collect her mail and get the things Grace needed. When she walked in to the apartment, the memories flooded back. She visualized being in fetal position in the corner of her kitchen. She remembered Tony caring for her that weekend after he attacked her. *Why did I allow him to treat me that way?* Grace came back to the moment to the sound of her phone beeping. It was her mom.

Carrie: Remember, we are here for you. Come back to the house if you don't feel ready.

Then her brother, Joe: I love you, Gracie. Call if you need anything and I will be there.

Then Jack: Praying for you! Joshua 1:9 Love you!

Grace smiled. Joshua 1:9 was her favorite scripture: Be strong and courageous. Do not be afraid; do not be discouraged, for the Lord your God will be with you wherever you go.

Grace felt so grateful for all of the love and support she had. She had a TV dinner and a bottle of water for dinner. She made a mental note to stop by the grocery store afterschool the following day. She was exhausted and climbed into bed with her Bible and responded to her texts. Before she fell asleep, her phone beeped one more time… it was Will:

Thinking about you. I hope your first day back to the apartment went well. I'm here if you need to talk. See you tomorrow. It's great having you back.

Grace felt a flutter in her heart. Every day was looking a little brighter.

19

You will be hated by everyone because of me, but the one who stands firm to the end will be saved.

~Matthew 10:22

Jack, as promised, visited Tony religiously once a week. His first visit was met with total obstinacy. "Well, if it isn't the holier than thou Pastor Jack Finnegan!" Tony applauded Jack and laughed heartlessly.

Jack smiled and responded humbly. "I'm a sinner just like everyone else in this world, Tony. I'm just thankful that we have an amazing Savior who gives us lots of chances."

Tony laughed in Jack's face. Jack saw the anger in his eyes and it gave him chills.

"If there really is this loving, forgiving God that you talk about, then why does he allow bad things to happen at all?"

"That's a great question, Tony. The truth is that God doesn't cause bad things to happen. He gives all of us a free will. We live in a fallen world because of the sin of Adam and Eve. *We* are the cause of our own problems, but God is there to give us a way out." Jack saw the fury rise on Tony's face. His eyes wrathful, yet empty; his voice shallow and hurtful.

"I can't listen to this garbage! Get me out of here, guard!" Jack was disappointed, but it was a start.

The second visit, Jack brought Tony a Bible. He asked him to at least accept it as a gift. He told him to read it when he was lonely or feeling angry. Jack showed him that he had written down some hopeful passages on a sheet of paper and placed it in the front of the Bible. He told Tony that this was a good place to start.

"Tony, these are God's words. Rely on Him. Write down any questions you have and I will answer them the next time I come." Tony walked out again, but he took the Bible with him. Progress.

The third visit started with one question. "Why is God allowing me to suffer if he loves me so much?" Tony sat slouched in his chair. His arms crossed over his chest. Jack felt a chill in the air as he spewed out the question.

"God is letting you suffer the consequences of *your* decisions, Tony. We all make poor choices and they impact everyone around us. You have to ask Him forgiveness and mean it. You have to turn to Him. You need a Savior, Tony. We all do. It's how we are wired."

"Oh really? And why did this mighty Savior bless me with an abusive father?"

"We have to forgive our earthly fathers, Tony. Maybe it was the best that he could do. More than likely, your dad learned the behavior from his father. It's called generational sin. We have to break that cycle."

Tony made no eye contact. He sat with his head down and Jack prayed that he was listening.

"God loves the wayward too, Tony. Luke 15:7 says that there is more joy in heaven over one lost sinner who repents, than ninety-nine righteous people who don't need to repent."

Tony looked up with vehemence. "So, you think I'm wayward, huh?'

"We are all disobedient at some point in our life, Tony. The only way out is to accept Jesus. He wants to lead you. I promise that if you do, you will find peace."

"This is ridiculous!" Tony walked out once again.

As he walked through the door, Jack shouted a request. "Tony, at least read the scriptures I wrote down for you. You have nothing to lose!"

One step backward.

The fourth visit was more of the same. Tony looked as if he had aged ten years. He had bags under his eyes and he moved lifelessly. When he sat down at the table, he looked up at Jack with distant eyes and without expression. "When are you going to realize that you are wasting your time?"

Jack smiled and responded honestly. "Probably never, Tony. I never feel like I'm wasting my time when I'm serving God."

Tony scoffed and slammed his cuffed hands on the table. "Don't you see that this Bible is a fairy tale? You seem like an intelligent man, Jack! Why do you believe these lies?"

"Tony, that is purely your opinion. These are not just interesting stories. They are accurate, historical accounts written by people who experienced God. The Bible is pure. Over 24,000 manuscripts of scripture were found across continents and they all line up. We have more documentation on Jesus than any other person in history." Jack paused in frustration and said a silent prayer.

"Tony, just surrender to Him. You have two choices in life. You can live with Him forever in eternity or live without Him forever in torment. If God isn't real, nothing matters. But if God is real, he's the only thing that matters! Why not, Tony? You have nothing to lose and everything to gain! Just exchange the truth of God for the lies in your head!"

Tony stood and stared Jack down. "You are the liar, Jack! You are a fanatic!" Tony kicked the chair back and walked out the door shouting, "Waste your breath on someone else! Leave me alone!"

Jack sat, feeling defeated. He was physically and mentally exhausted. He was starting to wonder if he'd ever get through to him.

20

But as for you, be strong and do not give up, for your work will be rewarded.

~2 Chronicles 15:7

Grace's life was falling back into place. She and Joe had lunch with Larry, their biological dad a couple of times. He was staying clean and sober and they were sharing a lot with each other. She prayed for Tony's healing daily and kept in touch with Angie, Francesco and his family. They had confided in Grace that their visits with Tony were agonizing. He harbored a lot of anger toward them for "putting him in prison and taking Grace's side." And although they knew it was not true, Tony had convinced himself that Grace and Will had betrayed him.

Grace went by her parents' house afterschool one day to talk to Jack. She texted before she came by to make sure they were home. She had something pressing on her mind. Her mom had responded that it was perfect timing. Joe was visiting, too. When she arrived, they were all sitting on the back deck. Grace had a fluttering feeling of joy when she saw them all sitting there. She loved her family so much and didn't know what she would do without them. Grace went around the table and hugged all of them. She took a seat.

"Okay, Grace, spill it. I can tell just by looking at you that you have something on your mind." Joe smiled as he was thinking the same thing that his mother just said. They knew Grace like the back of their hands.

"Don't mess with Mom, Grace. Let it all out."

Grace smiled in accordance and spoke. "I feel like I have to visit Tony."

Grace read her mother's expression immediately, as she turned to her husband for support. Joe looked down, hoping Jack's answer would be an irrevocable "no!"

Jack responded without thought. "I just don't think that's a good idea, Grace. I need you to hear me out."

"Okay, I'm listening."

"His sin has destroyed him. His perception is distorted and his connection with God is completely broken. I look in his eyes, Grace and it's…" Jack paused, searching for the right word… "emptiness… darkness. It is very sad to see, Grace." Jack paused and looked at Grace, reading her reaction. Tears spilled down her cheeks.

"Honey, I just think you being there, will just fuel his fire."

Carrie handed her daughter a napkin to wipe her face, as Grace tried to explain her reasoning. "Angie and Francesco see the same thing. He thinks Will and I betrayed him! I just want him to understand that I *never* did anything with Will." Grace helplessly ran her fingers through her hair. "I want him to know that!"

Carrie reacted immediately. "Grace, we know that. But even if you did, Tony's behavior was still not acceptable. Convincing him of that will solve nothing."

Joe agreed. "Mom's right, Grace. That is a minor detail in all of this."

Grace cried out in frustration. "Why can't he see that he was wrong and repent?

Jack answered her calmly. "His soul is dead, Grace. Our souls were made to love and do the will of God. First Peter 5:8 warns us to be sober and vigilant because the devil walks about like a lion, seeking whomever he can devour. Satan is always looking for weakness and he found Tony."

Grace was moved to sobs. "This is awful! What do we do for him?"

"All we can do right now is pray for him. Tony's soul will never be satisfied without God. God is the only one who can heal him, but Tony is the one who has to make that choice. I just don't think it's a good idea to visit, Grace. Please just trust me on this."

Grace respected Jack's request but had a sense of fear. "Are you going to keep visiting him?"

Jack nodded. "I am."

"Why, Dad? Doesn't scripture say to walk away if you are getting nowhere?"

"It does, Grace. That's Matthew 10:14. That is when Jesus sent his disciples out to spread the good news of Jesus. He tells them if anyone did not welcome them, or listen to their words, to leave that house and shake the dust off of their feet. It basically is telling us to move on when we feel we've done all we can do. But I'm not ready to give up yet."

"Why?" Grace asked with hope in her voice.

"I feel like I am breaking through a little bit. He's accepting my visits. He accepted the Bible I gave him and he's starting to ask questions… angrily, but he's asking."

Grace reached across the table and grabbed Jack's hand. "Thanks for not giving up. I'll keep praying."

Joe reassured his sister. "We are all praying, Grace."

Then Jack changed the subject. "I think we should sit right here and I'll order some pizza. How's that sound?" It was unanimous.

Carrie followed Jack inside to get drinks and find coupons. "It's nice having just the four of us together, isn't it?"

Jack responded with a hug. "It sure is, Care. We are blessed."

While their parents were in the house, Grace was able to catch up with her brother.

"So how is everything going, Joe? Are you still dating Achara?"

"I am. I've coined her nickname… it's Char." Joe smiled and looked at his sister.

"How cute is that? I want to meet her, Joe! I can see it in your eyes. This is getting serious!"

Joe blushed. "I like her a lot, Grace. She's so sweet. Not like anyone I've ever dated before."

Grace was thrilled for her brother. "Okay, then let's get together this weekend. How about dinner Saturday night? I'll ask Will to come with me so it doesn't look like I am your overprotective sister."

Joe laughed. "She wouldn't care anyway, but go ahead and ask Will. He's a lot of fun. I'll check with Char tomorrow at school and I'll let you know."

"It's a plan. I'm looking forward to it."

21

Trust in Lord with all of your heart and lean not unto your own understanding. In all your ways submit to him and he will make your paths straight.

~Proverbs 3:5-6

Jack walked into his family doctor's office the next morning. He had made his appointment the week before and got right in. It happened so quickly that he hadn't even mentioned it to Carrie. The nurse called two days later and told Jack that the doctor wanted to run some more tests. He had ordered additional bloodwork and some x-rays. Jack had lost ten pounds without trying and he was experiencing lower back pain and extreme fatigue. He decided not to mention the second round of testing to Carrie or the kids. He knew they would jump to conclusions. He was meeting with the doctor to go over the results.

When Dr. Mitchell entered the room, Jack rose to greet him and extended his hand. They shook hands. "Pastor Jack, I thought you would have your wife with you."

"No, not today, doctor. She's a teacher, and getting a sub and lesson plans together for a sub takes an act of God. I didn't want to bother her with a routine checkup. She doesn't even know I'm here."

Dr. Mitchell pulled up a rolling chair across from Jack and faced him. His solemn face moved Jack's heart to skip a beat. "Jack, I'm afraid

I have some bad news. All of your tests came back indicating kidney cancer. I'm referring you to one of the finest oncologists in the state. He can see you today at 1o'clock to go over your options."

Jack was silent, staring deep into the doctor's eyes. *Options?* "How bad is it, doctor?"

"Well, Jack, based on the majority of cases of this particular stage of cancer, I've seen longevity of up to two years, with treatment."

Jack was shocked. Reality was hitting him fast. "*With* treatment?"

"Yes. It appears that you are at a stage four, Jack. The cancer has metastasized to your lymph nodes and liver."

Jack sat back in his chair and ran his fingers through his hair. "Wow. I visit cancer patients all the time. I never anticipated being on the other side of the table."

"I'm sorry, Jack. Can I call someone for you? Are you okay to drive?"

"I'm really fine, doctor. I'm not afraid to die. I just never thought about *how* it would happen. I trust God completely with my life. It's in His hands."

Dr. Mitchell handed Jack the oncologist's card. "I've seen plenty of miracles happen in my life, Pastor Jack. I'll be praying that you are one of them. A positive attitude is half the battle and you've got that hands down."

Jack stood up again and shook the doctor's hand. "Thank you, doctor."

"Good luck to you, Jack. If you have any questions, please call me. I think you'll be pleased with the oncologist. He's a fine man and an awesome physician."

Jack sat for a moment after the door clicked shut behind the doctor. He thought of how often he preached to his congregation that whether they were having good or hard times, they needed to stop, pray and then allow God to take over for them. He needed to practice what he preached. Jack bowed his head and prayed:

"Lord, I got my faith from you, and the reality of my faith is that, I can do all things with you as my power source. I am surrendering this to you right now. You are so much greater than this diagnosis. I am putting my complete trust in you. Please, Lord, give me the strength, peace and guidance to make the right decisions and please give me the words to tell Carrie and the kids. Amen."

Jack walked into the parking lot. The sky was a sapphire blue and a warm breeze scattered the withered leaves across the pavement. Musical chirps filled the air and a yellow butterfly fluttered past Jack's face. An immediate and very uncanny peace came over him. He was certain that God was in the lead.

Jack called the church office to make sure he had no pressing issues. His secretary assured him that his calendar was clear. Jack went to the grocery store and bought four ribeyes and salad makings. He went home, marinated the steaks, made the salad and headed to his 1 o'clock appointment. Joshua 1:9 played in his mind, *Be strong and courageous. Do not be afraid. Do not be discouraged for the Lord your God will be with you wherever you go.*

The first thing Jack noticed when he walked into the oncology office was that these workers were created by God for a reason. Every one of them was living to the potential that He gave them. He was greeted with an inexplicable loving kindness and he felt the compassion of every one he came in contact with. He didn't feel alone. No fear.

Dr. Jollie, pronounced "Jolly," came into the examining room and he represented his name's expectation. He was bald with a round, plump face and sparkling blue eyes that radiated love. Jack smiled as he visualized him with a white beard and red suit. Jack stood and greeted him when he entered. "I have to know, doctor. Do people tell you very often that you resemble your name?"

Dr. Jollie chuckled. "Actually, no, Mr. Finnegan. Most people are so distraught when they meet me that they barely look me in the eyes. You are certainly an exception to that rule and your attitude will be on your side through this journey."

"Well, my journey so far has been a blessed one and I plan on it continuing."

"Well, you are certainly a blessing to our community, Pastor. I was at the Gwinnett Braves stadium for your *Surrender* ceremony. It was life changing."

Jack smiled and thought back to that day. "It really was an amazing day, doctor, and it was all God inspired."

"I believe that with my whole heart, Jack. God called me into this field, too. I love my job."

"Well, your outlook is contagious, doctor. Your staff is remarkable as well."

"Thank you for sharing that, Pastor. I interview and hand- pick each and every one. I tell them at the interview that if they don't feel that they can come to work with love in their eyes and heart, then they needed to stay home that day. These patients are going through so much emotion. They need us. So far, so good."

Jack smiled. "I like that concept, doctor. I feel the love and now I'm ready to hear my options."

"Okay, but before I start, I want you to know that whatever you decide, we'll get through it together. We will be here for you."

Jack knew that God was already working.

22

We can confidently say, "The Lord is my helper, I will not fear. What can man do to me?"

~Hebrews 13:5

J ack left Dr. Jollie's office with a clear picture of his choices. He sent a group text to Carrie and the kids when he got in the car.

Jack*:* It's Friday night and you deserve a nice dinner. Steaks are marinating. I think another family night is an order. I won't take no for an answer.

He got responses from all of them within 10 minutes:

Carrie: Well, I'm in, but you have no choice. I live with you☺

Grace: Steak? That's a no-brainer. Be there about 4:30.

Joe: I'm in. I'll help man the grill.

Jack grinned with every beep from his phone. This was going to be rough, but he was ready.

The evening was flawless. Everyone was in a great mood. The food was great and conversation flowed. Grace, Joe and Carrie shared stories about their students and the ups and downs of teaching as Jack took it all in. He was so grateful that his family was so close. In ministry and counseling, he came across so many families that didn't get along. It was difficult to watch how lives were destroyed by lack of forgiveness and hidden secrets.

Jack was preoccupied as the night went on. He knew he had to share his news and more than anything he didn't want them to worry. He silently prayed for God to give him the right words and that his family would feel peace. He would call Micah over the weekend. Micah had been through the death of his mother from breast cancer. He had been a rock through all of it and Jack hoped he would have the same strength.

"Well, it's been great having all of this time with just the three of you- twice in one week! I was just talking to your mom recently about how I had gotten so caught up in funerals and weddings that I was missing that alone time. God made it loud and clear to me that it was time to pause and take that time."

Grace reacted in gratitude. "And you were such an amazing help in my situation with Tony. Thank you for that, Dad."

"You are so welcome, Grace. You know, the older I get, the more I realize that every letdown we go through in life always seems to succeed in some way. It either leads you to humble yourself, or turns you to God more completely. I don't try to figure things out or analyze things like I did before. I've learned that God's ways are perfect and He directs us when we surrender to Him."

Grace knew that surrendering everything to God was her weakness. She still found herself questioning and regretting her past decisions, rather than letting them go and moving on. If she surrendered something to God, she always seemed to take it back. "I'm working on that, Dad. You give me hope."

Jack continued. "One of the things I had put off was my annual doctor appointment and I did that finally."

Carrie chimed in, relieved. She had been meaning to ask him that. "Oh good, Jack. When is it? I'll take a sick day and we can make a day of it."

"I already went, Care."

"You did? That was quick. Why didn't you tell me?"

"Well, when I called they fit me in quickly. I really didn't have time to tell you and then I forgot."

"No worries. How'd it go? Good to go for another year?"

Jack hesitated but pushed himself to finish. Carrie saw the hesitation and felt a sudden heaviness in her heart. "Well, not exactly. I wanted to talk to you about it while we were all together; and I don't want you to worry, because I'm not."

Carrie's heart sank deeper. A blanket of fear covered her. Her heart pounded…she heard it in her ears. "Jack, you are scaring me."

Grace was her mother's clone. She thought just like her. "Me too! Dad! Please! What's going on?"

Joe, more pensive, listened hopefully.

"I've got cancer." Jack knew he had to get to the point. He suffered the rising tension. *Please, Lord, I need your peace.*

The only sound on the back deck was the chirping of crickets in the distance. Jack continued through the palpable hush. "It's called Renal Cell Carcinoma, which is a cancer that affects the cells of the kidney. It's the most common kidney cancer."

Carrie's mind raced in beat with her heart. "Jack, what are you saying? How do you know for sure? They could be wrong! Let's get a second opinion."

Jack reached across the table and took Carrie's hands in his. "Care, calm down. We will get through this."

Joe was stunned and needed some answers. "How serious is it, Dad? What's your prognosis?"

Jack took an audible breath and answered. "This is what I was told… it is a stage four cancer, which means it has metastasized. It has spread to my lymph nodes and liver."

Carrie and Grace were sobbing as Joe continued his questions. "Is it treatable?"

Overwhelmed and saddened by their reactions, Jack lost his focus on Joe. He wanted them to be comforted. "Please. Grace and Carrie, look at me." Jack spoke calmly and emphatically. Both of them looked up at Jack as they wiped their tears on their shirt sleeves.

"I am not afraid to die. I'd like more time on earth, but this is in God's hands, not mine. The doctor told me that there were treatments that I could go through, but they would be to prolong my life, not save it. The treatments have side effects that can impact the quality of my life. I would prefer quality to quantity any day. I don't want to be sick.

I want to make this decision together, but right now I want all of us to pray about it and trust God. He is ultimately the one that will save me, if it is His will. Can you all do that for me? Please?"

All of them nodded, sensing Jack's urgency. "I have to talk to Micah too. We'll talk about it again, but for now, let's pray about it. And starting tomorrow, I want us all to live every single day that God gives us like it's our last. Okay?" Jack smiled and looked each of them in the eye. All of them got up and hugged him.

Whatever the journey, they would walk it together.

23

So, we fix our eyes not on what is seen, but what is unseen, because what is seen is temporary and what is unseen is eternal.

~2 Corinthians 4:18

Saturday morning, Jack got up to see Tony in prison. Two weeks had gone by and he hoped he would be more receptive. He had sent Micah a text and asked him to give him a call when he had a chance. Micah was finishing up his residency at a hospital in North Carolina. Jack never knew a good time to call.

Carrie and Jack prayed together the night before and lay in each other's arms until they fell asleep. Carrie felt numb the next morning but promised Jack that she would keep a positive attitude and trust God. She planned to visit her best friend, Jade, while Jack was at the prison. Grace and Will had plans with Joe and Achara for dinner that night. They wanted to cancel, but Jack made them promise that they would live life.

When Tony entered the room, he sneered. "I thought you gave up on me."

Jack laughed. "I'll never give up on you, Tony. I've just had some stuff going on in my life."

"Does it have anything to do with your promiscuous step-daughter?" Tony let out a malicious laugh.

"Tony, I will not sit here and listen to you talk negatively about Grace. She's done absolutely nothing wrong and deep down you know it too." Jack wanted to evade the Grace conversation so he added, "I have been diagnosed with cancer, Tony. I've been given one to two years to live."

Tony was silent for a minute but held eye contact with Jack. He sat back in his chair gloating as if he'd won a card game. "Wow. So, have you changed your feelings about your warm and fuzzy God?"

Jack looked back at him perplexed. "What do you mean?"

"Your remarkable Savior, Pastor Jack. If He loves you *so* much, why would he give you cancer?" Tony held up his questioning arms in the air. He laughed as if he'd won the argument even before Jack answered.

Jack answered calmly. "God didn't give me cancer, Tony. God is for us, not against us. Jesus told us in John chapter 16 that we would have trials in this world, but we didn't have to fear because He has overcome the world."

"So, you think He's going to cure you, huh?" Tony hid his mouth as if covering up a laugh.

"I don't know what is going to happen, Tony. I believe in miracles, but I don't know what God has planned for me. Whatever happens, though, I know He is right there with me. I have nothing to be afraid of with God on my side. Earthly things are temporary, Tony. I plan to die with joy in my heart because I know where I'm going."

"What about your perfect little family, Jack? You're not going to see them again." Tony was relentless in his sarcasm; it fueled Jack to teach.

"That's where you are terribly wrong, Tony. Earthly life is quick, but eternal life is forever. When you accept Christ, you gain everlasting life. When God calls me home, it's a temporary separation. We will all be together again."

Tony let out an uproarious laughter and then looked at Jack with utter disbelief. "You really believe that, don't you?"

"It's the facts, Tony. Romans 8:18 says that our present sufferings are not worth comparing with the glory that will be revealed to us. Our source of comfort isn't only that we'll be with Jesus, but we'll be with each other too. It's a promise. Death is merely a doorway to eternal life."

Jack looked to Tony for a response. He sat staring into space with a smirk on his face. "What are you thinking, Tony? Talk to me."

"I was just thinking about how disappointed you are going to be, Jack. Death is the end."

"No, Tony. Death is the beginning of eternity. It is life's greatest certainty. For God's children, death isn't the worst thing, it leads to the best. The best is yet to come. Tony, before I die I want you to understand that."

Tony listened, shaking his head the whole time. "And the unbelievers go to hell, right? This conversation is ludicrous!" Tony got up angrily from his chair. "I'm ready, guard!"

Before he walked out, Jack got in one last thought. "Tony, it's a free gift! Just pray about it! For believers, this life is the closest we get to hell, but for an unbeliever, this life is the closest thing you get to heaven. Do you want to settle for this life, Tony?"

And then the door clicked shut behind him.

Will picked up Grace at her apartment Saturday night. They had made plans to meet Joe and Achara for dinner. In the car, Will sensed Grace's uneasiness. "Are you okay?"

"Jack has fourth stage cancer." That was the first time that Grace had spoken those words aloud and it hit her like a ton of bricks.

Will pulled the car over in front of a house in her neighborhood. "What?"

Grace was choking back her tears. "He's dying, Will. He told us last night."

"Grace, I am so sorry. Are you sure you want to do this tonight?"

"We promised Jack that we would live our life. He wants life to go on. He wants us to live every day like it's our last."

Will grabbed a napkin out of the glove box and handed it to Grace. "Wow. That is an incredible testament to his faith. He lives God's word, Grace. It should be a lesson to all of us."

"I know. He's really not afraid to die, Will. He said he is moving heaven-ward." Grace laughed and wiped her eyes. "He truly is an amazing man. I wish I could be more like him. I guess it's selfish of me because all I can think about is how difficult life on earth will be without him."

"That's not selfish, Grace. That's love." Will met Grace's eyes and smiled.

"I know. Thanks for listening. Telling you just made it so real."

"I'm sure it did. I'm here for you to talk, any time. But tonight, I think you should fulfill your promise to Jack and enjoy life. What do you think?"

Grace smiled. "I think you are right. I feel better already." And Will headed to the restaurant.

They met at Willy's Wing Hut. It was a family owned, local restaurant with wooden floors. Movie and sports memorabilia adorned the walls. Joe and Achara already had a table. Joe flagged them down. Will and Joe shook hands and Joe introduced them. "Char, this is my sister, Grace, and her teacher friend, Will."

Char stood to greet them. She started to bow her head in greeting and then stopped herself and laughed. "Oops! Sorry! It's a habit."

Will and Grace laughed. "No problem! I think it's beautiful." Grace went in for the hug and Char reciprocated. "It is so nice to finally meet you, Char. I've heard so much about you! I feel like I know you already."

Char giggled. "I feel the same about you. I'm so happy you could make it tonight."

"Me too!" Grace and Will took a seat at the table and then Char shared her condolences. "I'm so sorry to hear about your step- dad. Joe was telling me about it before you came. He sounds like a very positive man."

"Thank you, Char. It was tough news, but with God's grace, we'll get through it together."

"Of course, you will. You are so lucky to have family and friends around. My parents live in Thailand. I miss them very much."

"I bet you do! But please, consider us your American family, okay?"

Char sensed Grace's warmth and it made her feel so special and welcomed. She felt so grateful to have met Joe. The evening went great.

Achara had Grace and Will's seal of approval and it delighted Grace to see her brother so happy. On the way home, Grace admitted to Will that she felt guilty having fun when she knew her dad was sick. When she got home, she gave him a call. He answered the phone. "Is this my girl?"

Grace's eyes welled with tears. "It's me, Dad. Are you doing okay?"

And with the typical Jack Finnegan attitude, he responded, "I couldn't be better, Gracie. Life is good and God is great."

"I just wanted to tell you that I love you, Dad."

"I love you too, Grace."

24

Consider it pure joy my brothers and sister whenever you face trials of many kinds, because you know that the testing of your faith produces perseverance.

~James 1:2-3

Thanksgiving was fast approaching. Jade and Beau Walls were the annual hosts and every year the guest list grew. This year Kristin would be there with her now husband, James. Jade thought back to the past Thanksgivings at their house. The very first one was just after they found out that their son Ben's girlfriend, Emma was not only pregnant, but her mother, Kristin was the woman that had been seeing her husband, Beau for three months. That first year, Jade couldn't bring herself to invite Kristin, but time eventually healed *most* wounds.

It was also at this first Thanksgiving that Jack asked Carrie to marry him. Jade smiled as she remembered... then her heart sank. *And now he's got cancer.* The following year, Matthew was born and they had all been brought together by the grace of God, as they shared grandparent responsibilities. The first Christmas was at Carrie's house. Kristin and her parents were invited to that and it was there that Jack and Carrie invited all of them to their wedding on Sanibel Island. This was where Jack's previous church was located and where Jade met him. She later introduced him to Carrie and the rest was history.

And the following Thanksgiving, Matthew Benjamin Walls was baptized at a morning service led by Jack. Jade shook her head in amazement as she thought back. She had come to the realization that all things truly did come together for the good, when you loved God.

Kristin was always the one to pick up John and Maureen Walls (Beau's parents) and George and Alicia King (Kristin's parents) from the assisted living facility. Kristin's parents met John and Maureen Walls through the blessing of Matthew. Emma, their precious granddaughter always included them in the family celebrations. This year they decided to stay at the retirement home. Since Maureen's passing, John decided to stick to their routine. He knew this was what Maureen would have wanted. John was a retired Methodist minister and led a Thanksgiving service at the retirement home. Jade, Beau, Jenna, Emma and Matthew visited him that morning. It gave all of them peace to know that they were making great friendships at their newfound home, even at their age.

This year Emma invited John MacDonald and his two daughters. She had been spending lots of time with them. They were like family. Joe had also invited Achara for her first American Thanksgiving feast. Grace came single. Will flew back to Tennessee to spend it with his parents and brother. Micah, Jack's son and his fiancée, Maggie were traveling from North Carolina. Jenna flew in early to spend time with her parents, while Jax stayed in North Carolina. Jenna's heart was heavy.

Jade and Beau picked up Jenna from the airport on the Sunday night before Thanksgiving. Jenna taught school and had the week off. Jade knew that something was wrong when her daughter called and said she was coming alone. Jade couldn't wait to put her arms around her and find out what was going on. Jenna was already at the baggage claim when her parents walked into the airport. Jenna ran to them. She met her dad's embrace first and then wept in her mother's arms. Jade whispered in her ear calmly. "Whatever it is, Jen, we'll get through it."

"I know, Mom. I need you guys so badly."

Small talk followed as they waited for Jen's luggage. Jenna asked how Pastor Jack was doing and they filled her in on what they knew so far. When they got in the car and headed back to the house, Jenna confided. "I need you to pray for Jax, Mom and Dad. He's been acting really distant lately, short-fused and irritable. He didn't want to go out to dinner or to the movies anymore and if we did, I always paid. He never even offered. He started borrowing money from me, saying that he didn't have time to cash his check. I could tell he was lying about where he was some days." Beau and Jade listened attentively, hoping there was a happy ending.

"Last night, he came over. I bought steaks and while we were grilling outside on the patio, I put his jacket on because I was cold. When I put my hands in his pockets, I found my 14-carat gold bracelet and necklace that you got me last Christmas. He stole from me!"

Jenna started sobbing. Jade looked to the back seat and put her hand on Jenna's knee to comfort her. Jade felt dizzy. She was trying to take it all in. It was all too hard to believe!

"Did you confront him about it?" Beau tried to stay calm, but there was resentment in his question.

"I did. I asked him why he had them and he said he took them so he would know what size jewelry I wore. I could tell he was lying."

Jenna pulled Kleenex from her blazer pocket and wiped her nose. "I told him he needed to leave. I told him I couldn't live with dishonesty and that I didn't know who he was anymore!"

Jade continued the questioning. "Did he leave?"

"No! He started crying! He told me he was so messed up! He told me he maxed out all of his credit cards and owed lots of money to people! He even said he pawned some of his mother's jewelry!"

Beau was putting it all together. "He's got a gambling addiction?"

Jenn's tears flowed. The truth suffocated her. "Yes! I'm so scared for him, Dad! He is telling his family tonight."

Now Jade understood why Jenna called so abruptly Saturday night and said she was coming.

"Why tonight, Jen?"

"Micah and Maggie are leaving Wednesday to come here for our Thanksgiving get- together. Mr. and Mrs. Ferguson are having their Thanksgiving dinner tonight."

Jade and Beau were speechless. Jenna continued to clear her mind. "I feel terrible that I left him, but I just couldn't handle it! I just couldn't bear to see the hurt on his family's face! I hurt to the core, so I know how they are going to take it. I can't believe I didn't see the signs any sooner."

Beau remembered Jack's sermon on foundations and felt moved to respond. "Sometimes it's hard to see how secure a person is on the inside when looking from the outside, Jen. Stress just pushes you to your limit…to cave." Beau could relate and felt a deep sadness for his daughter. He could feel her hurt and it brought back memories of the night that he told Jenna about his affair. Beau suffered "broken heart syndrome" over the trauma that he caused his family.

Jade was still reeling from the conversation. Her mind raced with questions. "Did Maggie or Micah notice a change in his behavior?"

Jenna nodded. "Yes, just a few days ago, Mags asked if everything was okay with Jax and me. She said he was so hard to get along with. She thought we had an argument or something. I told her I was worried about him too. She said she was going to talk to Micah and her parents about it."

"Does Maggie know that you won't be there tonight?" Jade was always concerned about people's feelings.

"Yes, I called her last night after I talked to you. I told her that I wanted to get some alone time with you and Dad since I haven't been home in a while. I couldn't tell her I knew anything."

Jade smiled and reached for Jenna's hand. "Well, we are glad you are here. I'm sure Maggie will be in touch. I just hope that Jax doesn't lose his nerve."

Jenna agreed. "I know. He promised me, so I am taking his word for it. Please pray."

Beau wrapped up the conversation. "We have to take one day at a time, Jen and trust God to lead us through. He hasn't let us down yet."

Jenna smiled. "I know, Dad. Thanks for listening. It feels so good to be home."

Maggie texted Jenna late Sunday night: "Jax told us. We are in shock, Jen. We have to pray! I love you! We'll talk when we get there."

Jenna: "I'm praying, Mags. I'm scared but trusting God. Love you too! Drive safely."

Before she fell asleep, a text came from Jax: "I told them, Jen. I am so sorry I hurt you! I am so ashamed. Please don't give up on me. I am going to get help."

Jenna: "I'm here for you, Jax. We'll talk when I get back."

25

The Lord is my rock, my fortress and my deliverer. My God is my rock in whom I take refuge; my shield, and the horn of my salvation; my stronghold.

~Psalm 18:2

Thanksgiving

The guests started arriving around 2 o'clock. The aroma of roasting turkey filled the house. The chatter got louder as each guest arrived. Carrie, Jack, Grace, Micah, Maggie, Joe and Achara came at noon to help set up. Micah and Maggie hugged Jenna tightly when they arrived, assuring her that they would get through Jax's addiction together. They moved the living room furniture to the peripheries of the room to allow for comfortable seating. The dining room was no longer able to fit them. Instead, the dining room table decked the desserts that were brought. The Thanksgiving dinner was set up buffet style across the kitchen counters.

About an hour later, everyone filled their plates and found a place at the make shift, 10-foot table. Jack, as tradition had it, started the celebration. He stood and faced the guests.

"I can't tell you what joy it brings me to see you all here. This is our eighth annual celebration and we have been through so much together."

A murmur of agreement rippled through the room. Many reminisced to the death of Ben and the miracles that followed the tragedy.

"Some of you have been here from the start, some have passed on to the other side, and still some of you are new to this motley crew." Laughter exploded through the room. "But whatever your situation, we are grateful for God putting you in our path. Before we pray, I wanted to address my diagnosis. I know that you have heard that I have cancer. I wanted to thank everyone for their prayers and to tell you that life goes on. Our life is fragile and we live only by the permission of our precious Savior. So, I depend on Him.

"Carrie, Micah, Grace, Joe and I have agreed to let God decide my outcome. The treatment available to me will possibly prolong my life, but not save it. The side effects of the medicines and procedures can destroy my quality of life and I don't want to be held down. We choose quality over quantity. I want to enjoy every day on this earth that God gives me and when He calls me home, I will be ready." Jack looked around the table making eye contact with each one of the guests.

"Death has no age limits. We all will go through it, but it is merely the gateway to eternal life. Quite frankly, that gets me excited! It is our ultimate destination and I look forward to being in eternal perfection with my Lord and Savior. And for that, I am so thankful. Please don't feel sorry for me. Let's be joyful, okay?" Jack looked to each of the nodding faces. "Now, let's bow our heads and pray:"

"Heavenly Father, thank you for this wonderful group of people here today. Though Maureen and Ben have passed on, we know that they are in eternal joy and peace with you. We look forward to being together with them again one day. Thank you for our continued friendships and for our new ones. Thank you for John and his girls, Achara, and the reunion of Kristin and James. Lord, you make it clear to us every day that everything is done according to your perfect will and timing. Bless this food before us and let it bring nourishment for our bodies. Amen"

As everyone ate, the table was opened to anyone that wanted to share praise. John MacDonald and Emma Walls announced their plans to marry. They both shared that they had never felt it was possible to move on after the death of their spouses, but they had learned that all things were possible with God. They asked if Jack would marry them. They wanted to do it on New Year's Eve and then after the ceremony, ring in the New Year together at their house.

Jack agreed happily and shared that he felt the same way when his wife, Mary died of cancer. God too, had led him to Carrie. Joe joined in the conversation, remembering back two years prior. It was Ben's final Thanksgiving before the accident. They had gotten into a conversation about death and heaven. Ben and Emma had just completed a Bible study on the book of Revelation. Joe had asked Ben if he would want Emma to remarry when he died. Ben without hesitation had responded, "Absolutely! I would want them to be happy." Emma thanked Joe for sharing that memory. She and John assured everyone that although Ben and Molly would never be forgotten, they had surely found love again.

Micah and Maggie were next. They announced that they planned to marry over Spring Break at their church in North Carolina. The reception would follow at the Ferguson house and of course they wanted Jack to marry them. Micah and Maggie had discussed it with her parents. Micah knew that his dad's cancer was fast growing and wanted to make sure they planned it within six months. If he showed any regression before that time, the Ferguson's agreed to come to Georgia for the wedding. More than being certain that Maggie was the one, Micah knew he wanted his dad to perform their wedding ceremony. Maggie couldn't agree more.

26

For God so loved the world that he gave his one and only son that whoever believes in him shall not perish but have eternal life.

~John 3:16

After dinner, everyone did their part cleaning up. After desserts and coffee, the guests scattered to different areas of the house continuing their conversations. Joe, Char and Grace were enjoying their dessert at the dining room table. Achara was still in thought over Jack's dialogue.

"May I ask you guys something?"

"Sure, Char, what is it?" Grace looked to Char as Joe responded.

"Christians believe that you go to a *forever* place when you die?"

Grace's mind raced. She didn't realize that Char wasn't a Christian. She wanted to respond so that she understood completely, but didn't know where to start. Joe, thankfully beat her to it.

"We do. Heaven is a real place whose builder is God. Jesus, His son, is there now preparing for our arrival." Joe smiled quizzically at Char, trying to read her expression.

Char listened intently, wanting desperately to understand. "So, if you do good, you go to heaven and if you don't you go to hell?"

Joe paused. He knew this was a lot to take in, having been raised a

Buddhist. Joe wanted Char to just accept Him, but he knew she needed to know Him first. "Well, it's more than that, Char. Actually, accepting and trusting Jesus as your Savior is what gives you eternal life. It is a free gift. By believing in Jesus, we automatically want to do good works because of all He has done for us. Our good works earn us rewards in heaven."

Char looked confused but interested. "What is sin?" Does sinning make you go to hell?"

Grace was getting uneasy. She tried to help Joe out and joined in. "We believe sin is anything that separates us from God. God is love. He wants us to love Him and our neighbors. That pleases Him because the very nature and essence of God is love. He created us out of love, for love. We are his children and he wants to be in a relationship with us. We were created for an eternal relationship with him. He loves us so much that when we ask forgiveness and really mean it, he gives us a clean slate. He wants all of us in heaven with him."

Grace was on a roll. "Does that make any sense at all, Char? I know I am rambling, but I just want you to understand everything! It is 100% real! I promise you!"

Char laughed. "I believe you!"

Matthew heard the conversation about heaven when he walked into the dining room to get his dessert. "My dad is in heaven, Char."

And then Chloe ran in and hopped into a chair next to Matthew. "My mom is in heaven, too. No more cancer. She's with Jesus and so happy."

Char was mesmerized by the conviction of these young children. She turned to Grace and Joe. "I want to learn more."

Joe smiled. "I would love to teach you more, Char. It will change your life."

Maggie, Emma and Jenna came into the dining room and sat down. Achara asked Joe to show her to the restroom. The kids ran off to play and Jenna addressed Grace.

"Grace, I just wanted to let you know that I've been praying for your peace and Tony's healing. I'm so sorry that you had to go through all of that."

"Thank you, Jen. I feel the prayers. Jack's been visiting Tony but he's still struggling spiritually. I'm trying to trust God in all of this, but it is so hard!"

Maggie spoke up next. "I've been praying too, Grace. Everyone has a story. Jen and I just found out that Jax has been struggling with a gambling addiction. Please add him and our family to your prayers."

Grace was moved to tears. "Thank you, Maggie. I am so sorry. I will pray."

"Thank you, Grace. The world is so broken. I don't know what I would do without my faith."

Grace thought of Tony and responded. "Tony is a perfect example. He is so filled with anger and distrust that it has hardened his heart. It's so sad!"

Emma responded, sharing hope. "Don't give up girls. If you told me that my dad, James Rutherford would not only show back up in our life, *remarry* my mom, find Jesus, *and* give up drugs, I would have said 'impossible!'" Emma paused and shook her head in disbelief and continued. "The last words he spoke to us before he walked out, was for me to have an abortion! But look what happened! He is completely changed by the grace of God *and* has a loving relationship with the *very* child he wanted me to abort!" Emma quieted for a second, taking in the reality of God's perfect love. "Just keep praying and trust God to answer your prayer in His perfect timing. It will happen."

Jenna grabbed a napkin and wiped her tears. "Thank you, Em. I *so* needed to hear that today."

Grace smiled and glanced triumphantly toward Emma. "Me too! Thank you for sharing that Emma."

"You're welcome. I've been there. Just know that His mighty hand is at work in all of this. Jack used to tell me to read Job in the Bible. He reminded me that Job was a better man at the end of his suffering and more blessed than before. Just don't lose heart. It will all come together in God's time. I promise."

27

And we know that in all things God works for the good
of those who love him, who have been called according
to his purpose.

~Romans 8:28

Christmas departed as quickly as it arrived. Carrie and Jack's party was another success with family and friends celebrating the precious gift of Christ. Jack had frequent visits to Dr. Jollie and miraculously the cancer had not progressed. Jack took on a ketogenic diet which eliminated carbohydrates and replaced them with healthy proteins. Cancer cells needed glucose to thrive. Since carbohydrates turned to glucose, the belief was that cutting out the carbs would starve the cancer. Jack's mantra was his diet and complete trust in God.

Family and friends waited in eager anticipation for Emma and John's New Year's Eve wedding. The day finally arrived. Kristin hired caterers and the sparkling lights and hopes of Christmas encased the house. God's love filled the air. The church service was at 7:00 p.m. It was a perfect evening. The sky was ebony and the stars and moon illuminated the sky. God's light shining down from heaven.

Nervous excitement filled the church. John McDonald's parents came, along with Molly's parents. They were thrilled for John and the girls and knew that only God could work out this flawless plan.

As the wedding song played, three attendants walked down the aisle of church. First came Katie, dressed in red velvet, smiling a toothless six-year-old grin. She gripped her small bouquet of white roses. Next tromped Chloe, slightly bashful, but proudly dropping rose petals in her emerald green dress. Wreaths of baby's breath adorned their heads like halos. Both girls climbed the steps of the altar and stood beside Pastor Jack, whose thinning face radiated joy.

The best man followed, dressed in a black tuxedo and patent shoes. He carried the rings on a white satin pillow. Matthew Benjamin Walls strategically balanced the pillow with one hand while he furiously waved to the guests in their pews. John McDonald stood next to Jack on the altar wiping tears of joy from his ecstatic face. Jack joined him. There was not a dry eye in the congregation. Sobs of elation echoed throughout the church.

Then the music changed tempo, announcing the soon-to-be Emma McDonald. She wore antique- colored lace and was on the arm of her transformed father. A man who was lost but found his way back. Kristin Rutherford wept in the front row, praising God silently for this absolute miracle.

At the foot of the altar, James pulled his daughter's veil back, kissed the top of her forehead and said, "I love you, Ems."

Emma choked back tears. "I love you too, Dad. Welcome back."

James joined Kristin in the pew and John met Emma. They walked hand-in-hand up the steps of the altar, while Matthew innocently and honestly yelled out, "You look beautiful, Mommy!"

The congregation shared in a moment of laughter and tears as Jack told them to be seated.

"I don't know about you, but I need a minute to compose myself!"

The audience laughed and murmurs of affirmation filled the room. Then Jack continued the service. "Really, if any of you know this story and don't believe in miracles, see me after church. We need to talk!"

More laughter erupted.

"Truly, these two individuals met and fell in love through tragedy... are you hearing me? Through tragedy!" Jack paused to let his words sink in. "Think about that for a minute. Ben was killed in a car accident.

John was on his deathbed waiting for a heart. His wife was dying of cancer and they had two little girls they were worried about."

There was a deafening silence, as the words took heart in the congregation.

"But what does our loving Father do? He gives Ben's heart to John McDonald. Ben's death brought John life and he was able to care for his wife in her final days. And today, their families are united in God's perfect love."

Jack looked out to the guests and continued. "You see, God is all-knowing. He is all- powerful. For those who love God, we can trust in his righteousness. He has a master plan for all of us. His plan always works out as He sees fit. Ephesians 3:20 says, 'Now to him who is able to do immeasurably more than all we ask or imagine, according to his power that is at work within us, to him be the glory in the church and in Christ Jesus throughout all generations forever and ever.' Even when your life seems out of control, God is in charge. God knows what's best for us. We have to trust him no matter what and wait patiently for him. He will bring about glorious results no matter what our circumstances.

"Romans eight, verses 37 and 38 says that we are more than conquerors through Him who loves us. Neither death nor life, angels nor demons, present or future, nor any power, neither height nor depth, nor anything else in all creation can separate us from the love of God. No one… nothing can ruin God's plan for us if we love him! He is our constant companion. Trust Him and you will be rewarded, just as Emma and John have been."

After the sermon, Emma and John exchanged vows and Jack introduced them to their family and friends as Mr. and Mrs. John McDonald. They walked down the aisle man and wife, holding the hands of their beautiful children.

The celebration continued at the Rutherford house and they rang in the New Year together, praising God for His promises.

28

Bear with each other and forgive one another. If any of you have a grievance against someone, forgive as the Lord forgave you.

~ Colossians 3:13

Spring Break

A few months passed quickly by. Spring break arrived, as did Micah and Maggie's wedding. Jack's cancer had progressed, but other than a loss in weight, no one could tell, based on his attitude. As promised, Jack got up each and every morning with joyful acceptance of another day,

Carrie, Jack and their families arrived Thursday night in North Carolina. Carrie, Joe and Grace were enjoying their week-long rest from teaching. They would be attending the rehearsal at the church Friday evening, with dinner following at a local restaurant. The rest of their family and friends would be arriving late Friday evening or early Saturday. They were all staying at the Marriott Courtyard in town. Jack met the pastor of the church before the rehearsal. He welcomed Jack and told him he was praying for his healing and complimented him on raising a fine son. Jack would be leading Micah and Maggie's wedding service.

When Micah and Maggie arrived at the church, the first thing Micah noticed was Jack's coloring. He knew that as the cancer progressed, the skin took on a yellowish tone. It saddened Micah that his dad's earthly days were numbered, but the melancholy never lingered when he saw his father's loving spirit. Joe was Micah's best man and Jenna was Mag's maid of honor. Maggie's brothers and her nursing friends completed the attendants.

Jax and Jenna were still dating, but not as often as before. Jax was receiving cognitive behavior therapy for his gambling addiction. He was developing coping skills and tools to help him resist the urge to gamble. He also attended Gambler's Anonymous (GA), modeled off of Alcoholics and Narcotics Anonymous. He was assigned a sponsor he could turn to for support. Jenna was very supportive, as well. She loved Jax and wanted their relationship to work.

The groomsmen walked the bridesmaids down the aisle of the church. Each girl was dressed in a different color pastel dress. The guys wore khaki suits and ties corresponding with the color of the bridesmaid's dress. The spring colors filled the church with a freshness of new beginnings. Their smiles filled the room with bliss. Mags wore white lace and carried a vibrant bouquet of pastel flowers. Micah waited with tearful excitement as he watched his bride- to- be walk toward him. Jack's heart was full of joy for his son. He knew that Maggie was the one and they would be together forever. He knew once again that this was God's spotless plan.

The congregation was seated as Jack spoke. "As I was thinking about Micah getting married, all I could think about was our incredible Savior. Adopted children are often referred to as *chosen children*. Mary and I had so much love to give, but we weren't able to have our own children. God had a different plan. He had chosen Micah for us.

"We had a poem hanging on our refrigerator for years. It said, 'not flesh of your flesh, nor bone of my bone, but very remarkably all my own. And never forget for a single minute that you weren't born under my heart, but in it.'" Jack paused and let the words sink in. "I always used to ponder on that poem being a minister because it's the same story with all of us and God. Our biological mothers gave birth to us, but we are all sons and daughters of God; brothers and sisters of Jesus.

"Ephesians 1:5-6 says that God predestined us to adoption as sons of Jesus Christ, according to his pleasure and will, to the praise of his glorious grace, which he has freely given to us in the One he loves. The meaning of adoption is that we receive a new relationship with God because He chose us to be full members of His family. His great love cleansed us and clothed us and promises eternal life with him. Our heavenly Father delights in pouring out his blessings on his chosen, adopted children. We are number one on his priority list.

"And God chose his son, Jesus to be adopted as well. God chose Joseph to raise Jesus. This act alone gives honor to raising another's child. Biology is the *very least* of what makes us parents. It is purely God's love. And today, we officially welcome Maggie into our earthly family, as the Ferguson's welcome Micah. And we are all gathered here together as witnesses to this love before God. Marriage is an intimate union and partnership between a man and a woman. It comes to us from God who created male and female in His image so that we may be one flesh.

"One flesh means that just like our bodies are a whole and can't be divided into pieces, so God intended marriage to be. Micah and Maggie are no longer two entities. They are one entity- a married couple, emotionally, spiritually and intellectually. Each partner in a marriage is to care for the other. It is no longer *mine*, but *ours*. They are also to serve Christ as a unit and raise their children to serve God. And as they love God as a couple, their marriage will be filled with joy.

"As Creator of the marriage relationship, God becomes your support. He gives you wisdom and His continued love to protect you. God's intention for marriage is for it to be permanent and exclusive. Biblical love thinks first of the other person. It isn't what you get out of a marriage that brings glory to God, but what you put into it. The strongest love *ever* was when Christ suffered on the cross to save us."

Jack looked to his son and Mags. "Micah and Maggie, you are to make the love that God had for us, the model for your relationship." He looked Micah and Maggie into the eyes and concluded. "When you do this, your marriage will flourish."

After the ceremony, the guests headed to the Ferguson's house. It was a perfect day of sunshine and blue skies. The smell of fresh cut grass filled the air. Tents of white adorned in spring flowers completed the yard.

Jax found Beau, James and Jack sitting at a table together. He sat down humbly to join them. He was met with warm smiles and handshakes. "I know this is probably not an appropriate time to do this, but I wanted to apologize to all of you for my behavior. I assure you that regardless of my addiction, I love Jenna very much. I am getting the help that I need. God has brought me to my knees and I am ready and more than willing to change."

James Rutherford spoke first. "Jax, I have a drug addiction and I still attend NA meetings. I understand completely what you are going through. I know that we are states apart, but I am only a phone call away if you need to talk." James pulled a pen from his jacket pocket and wrote down his number on a cocktail napkin. He handed it to him. Jax's heart warmed. He felt a rush of emotion come over him.

"Thank you, Mr. Rutherford. That means so much to me."

Beau spoke next. "Jax, I have no doubt that you love our daughter and the feeling is mutual on her part. We all have weaknesses. It's our human sin nature. We are praying for you, buddy. We are here for you if you need us." Beau patted Jax's back for reassurance.

"Thank you, sir."

Jack sat back and smiled while he listened. When there was a lull, he joined in. "Romans 3: 23 says that we all have sinned and fallen short of the glory of God, Jax. You've been forgiven and have a clean slate. Let the past go and you'll open up a space for something better. Put your focus on God and trust him. He is always there for you."

Jax felt humbled and blessed at the same time. A conversation that he dreaded turned out to be a sense of healing. Jax walked away knowing that he had the love and acceptance of Jenna's family and friends. He knew he was covered up in prayer, not judgment.

29

Be still and know that I am God

~ Psalm 46:10

The morning after the wedding, Jack and Carrie got up early and took a road trip to the mountains. They stopped by a Publix on the way to get fried chicken and drinks. It was a three-hour drive to Boone, North Carolina, the city of Daniel Boone. They drove along Blue Ridge Parkway, taking in the breathtaking views of the lush green, mountainous terrain. The higher they went, the more picturesque the views. Like the beach, the mountains separated them from the world and its problems, like being closer to heaven.

They stopped at one of the parks along the way and set up their blanket, overlooking God's magnificent handiwork. They sat in complete silence for a while, taking in the stillness. Then Carrie spoke.

"Jack, are you really okay?"

Jack looked at his wife puzzled. "What do you mean, honey?"

"I mean, are you acting this joyful so we don't worry about you? Or do you *really* feel peace?"

Jack reached over and took her hand. "It's real peace, Care. I promise. I know I'm dying and I know where I'm going. My life is God's, Carrie."

Carrie started crying. "Why are you so brave? I hate that you are dying!"

"Everyone has to die, Carrie. It's just my time. Second Corinthians, verse four tells us that outwardly we are wasting away, yet inwardly we are being renewed day by day. Our light and momentary troubles are achieving for us an eternal glory that far outweighs them all. So, we fix our eyes not on what is seen, but what is unseen, since what is seen is temporary, but what is unseen is eternal."

Carrie was blowing her nose in a napkin. "You are making that up! That's not really a scripture, is it?"

Jack laughed out loud. "Of course, it is! Would I lie to my beautiful wife?"

Carrie laughed and Jack kept on trying to convince his distraught wife that he was fine with his death. "Carrie, Philippians 1:21 states that to live is Christ and to die is gain. Paul wrote this while he was facing execution in prison. It's his epistle of joy! He knew his life was in the hands of God. He was ready to go home. Heaven is our permanent home, Care. Death means more of Christ and He is better than anything life can give us."

Carrie smiled but broke down. "I am going to miss you so much, Jack! You are one of the best things that ever happened to me!"

Jack took his wife into his arms. "It is temporary, Care. You just have to hold on to the promise that we will be together again. You can do it."

"I know I can do it, but I just don't want to do it!"

"You have to promise me something, Carrie, please. When the time comes, promise me that you won't mourn. I want you to celebrate my union with our Savior. I get to see my parents again. And Ben!"

"Okay, I promise. I'm sorry. Sometimes it's just too big! Thank you for listening."

And then, Carrie stared in disbelief at a yellow butterfly sitting atop the fried chicken box between them. "You are a yellow butterfly magnet, Jack Finnegan!"

Jack smiled. "Angels take all forms, Care."

30

The Lord God said, "it is not good for man to be alone.
I will make a helper suitable for him."

~Genesis 2:18

Summer vacation was in full gear and Grace and Will were inseparable. There was nothing romantic between them, but they were clearly kindred spirits. Both of them wanted the other to be exclusive, but it was never discussed. During school, they team taught together and afterschool they shared dinners, movies and get-togethers with mutual friends. Achara and Joe were also growing closer and they spent time together, as well.

One afternoon on the way to Lake Lanier Islands to spend the day on the beach, Will broke the silence. "Okay, I'm going to get right to the point."

Grace laughed. "Thanks for the warning."

"Are we a couple or just friends?"

Grace felt herself blush and put it back on Will. "Good question. What do you think?"

"Well, I'm thinking we are just friends, but there's nothing I'd love more than to call you my girlfriend."

Grace felt moved to tears. "That is so sweet, Will. I would love to call you my boyfriend too and I've wanted to discuss it, but I guess…" Grace paused, trying to find the appropriate words. Will finished for her.

"But you feel guilty about Tony because he thought it all along."

Grace couldn't believe he had taken the words right out of her mouth. "Exactly. And when he gets out, he's going to think he was right all along- that we really did betray him."

Will listened but responded with frustration in his voice. "Grace, you have to stop worrying about what Tony thinks. We know the truth and that is all that matters. Sometimes you have to go through the storms to find your anchor. I don't know about you, but this is the happiest I have ever been. I can't imagine my life without you."

Grace wiped tears from her eyes as she hung on every word he spoke. "I totally agree. I was talking to Jack about it the other night. He was saying that it was fantastic that we could become friends first and really get to know each other. He told me he thought it was just a matter of time before we had this conversation."

Will smiled and took her hand. "Jack is a wise man, Grace. You have an amazing family. Which brings me to my next point… how would you like to go to Nashville, Tennessee with me for a few days? I'd love you to meet my parents and my brother. I've talked enough about you to them."

Excitement surged through Grace. "I would love that, Will! I've always wanted to go to Nashville! When are we going?"

"Well, I was hoping next Saturday. We are going to meet my parents at a concert. And then we can spend a few days there. I'll show you the sights."

"Yes! What concert?" Grace asked excitedly.

"I'm not saying, Grace Mulligan. I can't give all my secrets away. I am a man of surprises."

Grace laughed. "You are the best Will Boone! I can't wait!"

Friday night, Joe, Achara, Grace and Will cooked out hamburgers and hot dogs with Carrie and Jack. Jack had lost a tremendous amount of weight and still had a yellowish cast to his skin, but his attitude was victorious. Jack was so comfortable talking about death. It gave Grace, Joe and Will so much comfort. Achara, on the other hand was confused.

She would always have questions for Joe when he was driving her home. All of them prayed that she would one day understand and accept Jesus as her Savior. It was clear to all of them that God put her in Joe's path for a reason.

Dinner was wonderful and Will and Grace said their goodbyes for the next few days. Carrie and Jack were thrilled for Grace. They worried that she would never trust another man after Tony, but God always has a different idea.

Will and Grace left early Saturday morning for Nashville. Will planned to show Grace the sights along the way. They were going to meet Will's parents for dinner at six o'clock. They had things to discuss before heading to Grand Ole Opry for the concert.

Chattanooga, Tennessee was a half way point to Nashville from where they lived in Georgia. Will took Grace to the Chattanooga Choo- Choo for lunch and then Lookout Mountain. They climbed the mountain tower and saw the panoramic view of Ruby Falls. Grace was amazed.

They met Will's parents at Mitchell's Deli, home of the best sandwiches in the city... according to the Boone family, anyway. When they arrived, his parents already had a table. Max and Colleen Boone greeted Grace as if long, lost friends. Will was a younger version of his dad. It warmed Grace's heart to see their honest love and affection with each other. Grace saw immediately where Will got his good looks and kindheartedness. Will's mom was an attractive lady with a bright smile. Grace immediately felt right at home with them. Dinner was enjoyable. His parents were easy to be with and took an honest interest in Grace's life and family.

About halfway through dinner, Grace expressed her exhilaration. "This has been an amazing day! Thank you for dinner, Mr. and Mrs. Boone."

"You are so very welcome, Grace. We are so grateful to be able to put a face with a name. Will talked about you quite often." Mr. Boone smiled as he responded. His deep voice resonated love as he spoke.

"Well, I feel the same. I am excited about meeting Mitch too. Is he coming to the concert?"

Mr. and Mrs. Boone looked to Will and smiled. Mitch was their son, Will's older brother.

Will laughed nervously and responded. "Well, Grace, that is part of the surprise. Actually, Mitch *is* the concert."

Grace was baffled and expressed it. "What do you mean?"

"My brother is Mitchell Boone."

Grace started laughing and looked around the table hoping for someone to join in. All of them looked back with expressions of honest humility.

"It's for real, Grace. My brother is Mitchell Boone, the newest heart throb of country music."

"Wow. I don't know what to say. I never put the names together. How have you kept that a secret for so long?"

"Well, living in a different state helps. It is what it is. He's just my big brother with a good voice."

Mrs. Boone joined in on the conversation. "Will and Mitch used to play together in all of the bars around Nashville. Will is just as talented as Mitch. He just chose a different path."

Will smiled and acknowledged his mother, "Thanks Mom." And then he addressed Grace. "I got sick of the bar scene and the inconsistent pay checks. I just always wanted to teach. I'm proud of Mitch, though. His hard work and perseverance have paid off."

"Well I am so excited to meet him! Thank you for having me!"

Mrs. Boone reached over and squeezed Grace's hand. "It is a pleasure having you, Grace. You are the first girl that Will has confided this to. You must be special. Will is a pretty private person."

Will smiled and agreed. "She's right, Grace. I never wanted to be known for my brother's accomplishments. I knew you were different."

"Thank you, Will. That means a lot to me."

Mr. Boone paid the bill and they headed out. Will left his car in the parking lot of the restaurant and they drove with his parents.

31

So that I may come to you with joy, by God's will, and
in your company, be refreshed.

~Romans 15:32

This was a special night. It was Will's first appearance at the Grand
Ole Opry. Mitchell Boone's name flashed on the marquises
outside. People stood on corners selling shirts, programs and
CDs. The Boone's had their own parking spot that led to a backstage
door. It was a surreal moment for Grace, but she kept telling herself that
this was just Mitch's job.

They walked the backstage hallway that led to Mitch's dressing
room. It was just like the movies, only Grace was present. Mrs. Boone
gave a friendly rap as she opened the door.

"Mitch, are you decent, honey?"

Laughter came from the other side of the door. "I'm dressed, Mom.
Come on in."

Several people sat around an oversized dressing room. Mitch and
his band sat around on the couches, while others worked effortlessly on
their hair and makeup.

When they entered, Mitch put his guitar down and excitedly
approached his family.

"Hi Mom!" Mitch hugged his mother tightly, kissing her cheek and then moved to embrace his dad. Then he spotted Will and his eyes filled with joyful tears.

"Will! You are the best thing I've seen all day! Thank you for being here!"

Both brothers wrapped their arms around each other.

"I wouldn't miss this for the world, big brother! I am so proud of you! Grand Ole Opry? *Just you?* Your dream came true, Mitch!"

"I know. I am blessed, Will." Then Mitch spotted Grace and smiled. Grace felt the same warmth that she did from Will and his parents. They were real people.

"Mitch, this is Grace Mulligan."

Mitch went in for the hug. "Grace! It's a pleasure meeting you. Thank you so much for being here!"

"It's great meeting you, Mitch! And an honor to be here!"

They all joined Mitch and his gang on the couches. It was like sitting around a family room. They talked, laughed and shared stories. Then there was a knock on the door interrupting their conversations. An attractive, middle-aged man entered.

"Showtime in fifteen minutes, Mitch!"

"Thanks Billy!" Billy Madison was Mitch's agent. He gave Mr. and Mrs. Boone a hug and shared niceties. He gave Will a hug next and shook Grace's hand, welcoming her.

"I'll show you to your seats. Go get 'em Mitchy!" He gave Mitch a hug before heading to the door.

Mr. and Mrs. Boone hugged their son and wished him luck. Mrs. Boone whispered in her son's ear. "We are so proud of you, Mitchell!"

Will was next. "How are you feeling, Mitch?"

"Major butterflies, Will. They never go away."

"You are awesome, Mitch. Just go do what you do best."

"I love you guys," were Mitch's final words. His family headed to their seats.

Billy walked them down the side steps of the stage to the front row. Grace had butterflies, so she couldn't imagine Mitchell's. They thanked Billy and took their seats. Will took Grace's hand. "What do you think?"

"I can't think! This is crazy!"

"I am so proud of him, Grace. He never gave up. This has been his dream since he was two years old! I'll have to show you pictures of him in his diaper with a guitar strapped around his neck."

Grace laughed, picturing it. "Please don't forget! Did you play guitar too?"

"I did but I haven't picked one up in a while."

"You'll have to bring it to school. Our kids would love a music time! It would be so good for them!"

"Let's do it! I'll get practicing this summer. I have to wipe the cobwebs off of it. It's been at my parents' house."

About that time, the lights blinked, warning people to take their seats.

Then Billy appeared at the microphone. The stage lights were on him as he spoke. "Good evening Nashville!"

The spotlights circled the arena as the crowd clapped and cheered their response.

"Are you ready for some good music?"

The crowd's cheers resonated throughout, sending chills up Grace's spine.

Grace looked at Will's parents, trying to gauge their emotion. Both of them had permanent smiles on their faces. Will put his arm around Grace and brought her ear to his mouth. "I am so excited for him!"

Before Billy called the band out to perform, he spoke. "You know, folks… not only is Mitchell Boone and his band talented, but they are some of the nicest guys I have ever met. I knew it was just a matter of time before their music was heard. They worked day and night to be the best they could be and they were victorious. The good Lord gave them gifts and they are using them for His glory."

Billy paused and then fired up the crowd. "Are you ready?"

The crowd chanted.

"Are you sure?"

They got louder. A rhythmic clapping filled the space.

"Then let's welcome to the stage…The Mitchell Boone Band!"

Out of the darkness, Mitch and his band found the light. Mrs.

Boone sat down, overwhelmed with emotion. Grace sat down and put her arm around her. She spoke into ear, "Are you okay?"

Mrs. Boone wiped tears from her eyes and laughed. "I'll be fine. The introduction gets me every time."

Grace smiled and stood back up. Then Will confirmed, "She does that every time. You'll get used to it." Grace acknowledged with a laugh and joined in on the excitement.

32

Be devoted to one another in brotherly love; honor one another above yourselves.

~Romans 12:10

After several songs, Mitch stopped to talk to the audience. He thanked them for being there and supporting their music. And then he introduced his family and Grace.

"Before we go on, I want to introduce to you some very special people in my life. Right here, born and bred, from Franklin, Tennessee are my parents, Max and Colleen Boone." The spotlights moved to the front row. Mr. and Mrs. Boone smiled and waved to the crowd. Mrs. Boone blew her son a kiss.

"And next to them is my best friend, who just happens to be my brother, Will Boone- and his girlfriend, Grace. They came all the way from Dacula, Georgia to see our concert tonight. They both teach special needs kids there. Can you give them a hand, please?"

The spotlight moved to Will and Grace as they waved to the crowd. Grace felt her face change color. Will was his reserved self.

"You know my brother Will and I used to do gigs around Nashville. Is there any one here who followed us back then?"

There was a deafening roar.

"That is so awesome. Thank you! So, you know how talented Will is, right?"

More whistles and cheers filled the coliseum.

"Well, how'd you like to hear him again?"

The crowd went wild. They chanted, "Will, Will, Will!"

Grace couldn't believe what was happening. She looked over at Will and he was laughing, shaking his head telling his brother, "No, no! This is all you tonight!"

"Come up here, baby brother! Show Grace what 'cha got!"

The crowd cheered louder, "Will, Will, Will!"

"I even brought your guitar from home. It has been collecting dust since you started teaching. What's up with that?"

The crowd laughed and continued their rant.

Will finally relented and ran up the stage stairs. He embraced his brother and shouted in his ear, "Revenge is sweet."

They shared a private laugh and Mitch handed Will his guitar.

"I thought we'd sing one of our all-time favorites together. Do you know which one that is, Will?"

Will walked to the microphone. "Would that be, Country Roots?"

"You've got it! This is the first song that Will and I wrote and sang together. Let's do it!"

Will and Mitchell Boone sang together, enjoying every second. They harmonized beautifully and their stage presence together was uncanny. Their love for each other radiated during their performance.

After the song, the brothers embraced and Will humbly bowed before the roaring crowd.

On the way out of the concert, paparazzi were at their peak. They were waiting outside the backstage exit. Camera flashes blinded Will and Grace as they climbed into the backseat of his parents' SUV.

Will looked to Grace when they got into the car, "Are you okay?"

Grace was shaking. "Yeah, I'm fine. I just wasn't expecting that."

"Me either, actually. It's usually not like this, but that was the first time he called me up on stage, too"

"Well, you were awesome!" Grace grabbed Will's hand. "You are so talented, Will!"

Mr. and Mrs. Boone listened from the front seat, smiling. "I agree with you, Grace. I am a little biased being his mom, though."

The camera flashes continued out of the parking lot. Mr. Boone drove without flinching.

"You are obviously used to this, Mr. Boone." Grace was in disbelief of his composure.

"We are, Grace. It seemed to calm down for a while, but like Will said, that was the first time they performed together in several years." Mr. Boone looked into the rearview mirror, "And you didn't miss a beat, son. Way to go."

"Well, thanks Dad. It was a lot of fun."

Mr. Boone drove Will and Grace back to the parking lot of the restaurant to get their car. "We'll see you back at the house."

"Be careful," Mrs. Boone reminded.

"We will, Mom."

When they got into the car, Grace looked at Will. "I am star struck!"

Will laughed. "With my brother?"

"No, crazy man! *You!* I love that playful side of you! You guys were awesome together."

"Well, thank you, Grace. It was a lot of fun! I miss it sometimes, but teaching is my thing."

"Well I am really happy you went the teaching route, or I would have never met you."

"Very true." Will leaned over and kissed Grace before starting the car. "Did I tell you my parents are retired teachers?"

"You did, but you never elaborated on your brother!" Grace laughed and Will joined her.

"True! But do you understand why? Can you imagine being harassed by reporters and cameras all the time? Mitch can handle it, but it would drive me nuts!"

"Yeah, I see what you mean. That would be tough, especially if you were married with kids."

"Exactly! No privacy! I love my quiet, little life."

"Is Mitch dating any one?"

"No one serious. He's being cautious. You know, you have to find out who likes you for who you are, not your fame and fortune."

The Boone's lived in Brentwood, along with other famous entertainers. They drove into a magnificent gated community with lush, rolling hills and stately mansions. It amazed Grace that Will had never shared his brother's notoriety. She felt honored that she was the first one he confided in.

Grace was speechless when they pulled into the driveway. She had never seen a house this size, let alone stay in one. Then Grace asked innocently but curiously, "Do teachers get paid more money in Nashville?"

Will laughed out loud. "No! Mitch bought this house for them. He lives in the basement. There is a recording studio down there, so he and his band practice here too. Win-win."

They pulled into a six-car garage. Will popped the trunk and grabbed their bags. "Follow me. I'll give you a tour. The Boone house is your house whenever you visit." Will looked at Grace because she wasn't responding and then laughed uproariously when he saw her expression.

"Okay, Grace. You can close your mouth now. It's just a house."

33

Each of you should use whatever gift you have received
to serve others as faithful stewards of God's grace.

~1 Peter 4:10

Will gave Grace a tour of the house and led her to the guest wing where she would be staying. It was the size of her house in Georgia. After she was settled, Grace and Will joined Mr. and Mrs. Boone by the pool for a night cap. Mitch's music played in the background. When Grace sat down, she shared her gratitude.

"Your home is beautiful, Mr. and Mrs. Boone. Thank you so much for having me. This will be a forever memory."

Mrs. Boone smiled and responded, "Thank you, Grace. God blessed us with two very talented sons. You know that Max and I are retired teachers, don't you?"

"Yes ma'am."

"Well, we lived very simply in Franklin, just about 15 miles from here. When Mitch's music started to soar, his accountant recommended that he invest into something, so he got this house. It's perfect for Mitch's band and wonderful for company. There are days that go by that I don't even see or hear Mitch and he's right downstairs."

Grace giggled. "I can see how that could happen, *and* you do have very talented sons. I know you are proud parents and rightfully so."

Mr. Boone added, "And you know the best part about it, Grace?"
"What's that, sir?"

"It's that they've stayed humble through it all. Our pastor, Kevin did a sermon a few months ago on the value of man and it stayed with me. He said that God doesn't judge us by success. He loves each of us the same. Our value doesn't come from what we do, what we have, the kind of home we live in, or the kind of car we drive. Our value comes from the fact that God made us and Christ died for us. So, whether or not we have *things*, we are just as valuable to God. That's why we need to put Him first in all we do. Not only did he give us the greatest gift of all- his son, he gave us gifts of the Holy Spirit- God in us. Your gift and Will's gift are teaching and Mitchell's is singing. Plain and simple."

Grace listened and smiled. She felt so at home here. Jack had the same conversations with them often. "I agree, Mr. Boone. My step- dad, Jack says that the most important thing is to be content with your gifts and use them for God's glory."

"Exactly, Grace," Mr. Boone continued. "When you lose that humility and forget *who* those gifts came from, your life starts to crumble. James 1:17 says that every good and perfect gift is from above and comes down from the father of lights. The money we make, big or small, is essentially God's money. Without Him, we would have and be nothing. We need to feed His sheep, not only in spreading His word, but giving to the less fortunate. Now's the time to give what we can't keep. We're investing in eternity."

Then Will added, "And when you give to the needy, don't let your left hand know what your right hand is doing."

"That's right, son. You are not out to impress anyone. You're just doing God's work. So, what I'm saying Grace, is that Mitch is still just our oldest son. He just makes a whole lot more money than we ever did! And when that final curtain drops, Jesus will outperform all of the famous, powerful people who have ever lived!"

They all laughed and Will continued. "I can remember waiting for hours at Open Mic night and getting paid nothing. I couldn't take it any longer. I am so proud of Mitch's determination! That was *not* an easy life, but it paid off for him."

Then Mitch walked up. "Are you talking about me?" He joined them at the patio table and looked at Will. "You were awesome tonight, Will!"

"You weren't so bad yourself! I was just saying how your hard work and persistence have paid off. You just keep getting better and better, Mitch. I am so proud of you."

"Thanks, Will. Those teaching genes of yours are pretty special too."

"I can vouch for that." Grace piped in and patted Will's hand.

"He's amazing with our students. I told him that he needs to bring his guitar to school and have a music time with our kids."

"That's a fantastic idea, Grace. Why didn't you think of that, Will?"

"It takes a village, Mitch."

Mitch laughed. "That is fact."

Mr. and Mrs. Boone got up and excused themselves. "We are beat and we have to get up early for church tomorrow," Max explained. "Grace and Will, we'd love you to join us for church and lunch."

"I would love that, Mrs. Boone. Will said you sing in the choir."

"Max and I both do. That's as far as we get with our voices."

Mr. Boone laughed as he got up to join his wife. "Yep. Our sons' voices are a gift from God. A *divine* gene!"

Max and Colleen hugged everyone goodnight and walked hand-in-hand into the house.

"Your parents are precious," Grace mused.

"Thanks Grace," Will acknowledged with grateful pride. "We are very fortunate."

"That we are," Mitch agreed. "That's why I got this house. They have been such a support system for me. I know they wanted me to go to grad school, but they were always there for me. They never gave up on me."

"That's awesome. My mom and step-dad are the same. I just recently reconnected with my biological dad, too. God is good."

"All the time, Grace," Mitch responded with a heartfelt tone.

Grace got up and said goodnight. "I am going to head to bed, too. Your brother and I saw the sights in Chattanooga before we came to your concert. It has been an amazing, but *exhausting* day!"

Mitch looked to Will. "Let me guess. You took her to Lookout Mountain and Chattanooga Choo -Choo for lunch?"

"You've got it."

Then Mitch looked to Grace. "That was our yearly family vacation when we were young. I still love that place!"

"I loved it too, Mitch. But your show was the icing on the cake. I'm still in awe."

Mitch rose to hug Grace. "Awe, thanks Grace. I'm so glad you were there. I can get you front row seats anytime. Just ask."

"It's a deal. See you in the morning."

"Goodnight Grace."

Grace headed to her private wing and Mitch and Will talked to the wee hours of the morning. Will told Mitch about his relationship with Grace.

"I am so happy for you, Will. She seems like a great one. Does she have any sisters?"

Will laughed. "No, sorry, Mitch. She has a brother, Joe, and a step-brother, Micah. She comes from an amazing family with a great community of friends." Will yawned and continued, "Can we continue this tomorrow? I need some shut-eye."

"Me too. Thanks for our talk, Will. I really miss you. I hope you didn't mind me calling you up on stage like that."

"Actually, I loved it! It brought back some great memories for me."

"Me too. I love you, Will."

Both brothers embraced and headed to bed. Their hearts were full.

34

Humble yourself before the Lord and He will lift you up.

~James 4:10

Sunday morning, the Boone family, along with their famous son, headed to church in Mitch's Hummer. Grace wondered on the way if people made a big deal out of Mitch at church.

Mr. and Mrs. Boone joined the rest in the choir room and Mitch, Will and Grace took a seat. People greeted them with warm smiles and friendly banters, but left Mitch alone. Grace sat between Will and Mitch in the pew. Grace had to ask- and so she did, "Do people leave you alone at church?"

Mitch laughed and whispered back, "Pretty much everywhere around Nashville. I was raised in this church so I'm still just Max and Colleen's son. I love it that way."

The church service was beautiful. Grace loved sitting between Mitch and Will. Their voices were as deep and beautiful as their faith. After church, they all headed to Noshville for lunch. It was one of the local favorites with a New York flair. They ate grilled pastrami sandwiches and cheesecake for dessert. And like Mitch alleged, they were respected and allowed to eat in peace.

After lunch, they stopped by the store for groceries. Grace planned to cook dinner for them a couple of nights. At the checkout, Will picked up the Sunday newspaper. On the front page of Headline News was the title, 'Mitchell Boone and His Brother Reunite at the Grand Ole Opry.' Under it were two photographs. One picture was of Will and Grace in the front row with the caption, 'Will Boone, teacher from Dacula, Georgia and girlfriend, Grace watch his brother perform.' The second picture was of Mitch and Will jamming on the stage together. The caption read, 'Mitch calls his brother on stage to perform with him.'

Will handed the paper to Grace. "I wonder how long it will take Georgia to get the news."

Grace looked at the headline in shock. "This is crazy, Will. I'm just little ole Grace from Georgia." She looked up at Will and laughed. "I feel so significant."

They were both laughing as Mitch walked up. Will handed his brother the paper next. "Thanks, Mitch."

Mitch laughed. "You're welcome. Great photos. You're both very photogenic!"

When they got back to the house, Will and Grace put the groceries away while Mr. and Mrs. Boone changed out of their church clothes. They were going to relax around the pool. Grace and Will planned to cook dinner. Grace checked her phone. She had it turned off during church. The face of the phone read: three missed calls. One was from Jack, one from her mom and the third one from Francesco, Tony's brother.

35

Cast all your anxiety on Him because He cares for you.

~1 Peter 5:7

Grace told Will that she had to return her mom's call. She walked out onto the massive front porch and took a seat in an oak rocking chair. Mammoth ferns swayed from the porch's eaves. A large stairwell and columns adorned the entrance to the front door. Grace took in its grandeur as she dialed her mom's number. Carrie answered on the first ring.

"Hi sweetie. How's Nashville?"

"Amazing, Mom. I have so much to tell you." Grace ranted on about the surprise concert and the weekend's happenings. Carrie listened actively, dreading the conversation that had to follow.

"Wow! That is fantastic, honey. My daughter knows a celebrity!"

"Sorry I just rambled on like that, Mom. We just got back from church and I saw three missed calls. One was from Francesco. What's going on?"

A few awkward seconds of silence followed before Carrie responded. "We don't want you to worry, Grace, but we wanted you to be aware."

Grace's heart sped up. "What is it, Mom? You are scaring me. Is Jack okay?"

"Yes, honey. Jack is doing fine. He's taking a nap as we speak.

He's gets tired more easily, but he's the same Jack." Carrie paused, but courageously disclosed. "Actually, Grace, it's Tony. He's getting released from prison next week."

Bile burned in her throat. "How Mom? He hasn't served all of his time yet."

"I know, honey. I agree. Evidently, since it was his first offense and he had good behavior in prison, he earned an early release."

"Where is he going to live, Mom?" Grace felt panic come over her. Her voice escalated.

"Well, Francesco called Jack. He's not allowed to live with his mother because of his attack on her. So, Jack set up residence for him in a parishioner's home. You know Ken Smith? He's the retired minister that owns that landscaping company?"

"Yes."

"Well, Tony is going to work for his company in exchange for room and board. Until he gets back on his feet."

"Has Jack seen him lately, Mom? Has he changed?"

"Jack tried the past couple of weeks and Tony refused his visits. He felt like he was making a little progress, but he's not sure."

"What does Francesco think?"

"He's concerned, Grace. That's why I called. We think you should stay in Nashville for a few weeks until we see what's going on. Jack and I will rent a condo for you."

"No, Mom. That's not a problem. The Boone's have plenty of room here. Thank God it's summer vacation and I have the time!"

"Well, I don't want you to wear out your welcome. I'm sure everything is going to be fine, but it's probably not a good idea for him to see you and Will together right now."

"I know. I was telling Will the same thing!"

"Don't worry, honey. Just have fun. He is going to have to report to a parole officer weekly, so he's being watched. Talk to Will and his parents and get back to me."

"I will, Mom. Thanks. Pray that he has changed. This is so scary!"

"We are praying, Grace. Go enjoy your day. I love you."

"I love you too. Tell Jack and Joe the same."

Grace hung up the phone and started crying. Suddenly all of her old feelings of fear and insecurities came rushing back. Then the front door opened and Will found her. He sat beside her and took her hand.

"Is it Jack?"

Grace met Will's eyes. "No. Jack is okay. It's Tony, Will. He's getting out next week."

Grace told him the whole story. Will assured her that spending the summer in Nashville would be awesome and he would be with her every step of the way.

Grace and Will made dinner that evening and served it poolside. Mr. and Mrs. Boone and Mitchell gave Grace their full attention as she explained to them her poor choice in her relationship and all that stemmed from it.

Graciously, Will's family displayed only love and acceptance. They prayed together for Tony's healing and guidance for Grace and Tony's families as they dealt with his release.

36

Do not worry about tomorrow, for tomorrow will worry about itself. Each day has enough trouble of its own.

~Matthew 6:34

A couple of weeks passed and Grace kept in touch with her family on a regular basis. Tony was out and seemed to be adjusting and keeping up with his parole officer. Grace felt better about the situation and was enjoying her time in Nashville with her newfound family.

One night they went to a Nashville Sounds game, the minor-league team of the Milwaukee Brewers. Mitch sang the National Anthem. Another evening, they went to Santa's Pub, the ultimate dive with cheap food and drinks. Mitch and Will sang karaoke. Grace embraced her new life!

Nevertheless, the tides turned. The Atlanta newspaper featured pictures of Will and Grace at Mitchell Boone's concert. The picture caption read, "Local teacher sings on stage with his brother at the Grand Ole Opry while his girlfriend looks on." Jack and Carrie refrained from telling Grace because they didn't want to worry her, but they knew they had to make the phone call to Nashville.

Grace was drinking coffee out by the pool one morning when her phone rang.

"Hi Mom!"

"Hi, honey"

An eerie silence followed. "Grace, The Atlanta News got ahold of the story of Mitch and Will being brothers."

"Really? What did it say?"

"Well, that Will taught in Dacula, as did his girlfriend, and …"

"Wait, Mom. They mentioned my name as Will's girlfriend?"

"Yes, Grace. With pictures. It's the buzz around town."

Grace felt nauseous.

"And Tony knows, honey. He saw the paper and didn't take it very well. He hasn't shown up at work for a week and skipped out on a meeting with his parole officer."

Grace was silenced. The pause was deafening.

"Grace, it could be nothing… we just thought you should know."

"Mom, do you think he'll come to Nashville?"

"I don't think so, honey. The police are on it. There is a missing person's bulletin out and his picture is everywhere. I'm sure he will turn up. He'll get over it. It's probably good that he found out."

"This is horrible, Mom! I *knew* this was going to happen!"

"Grace, calm down. This is not the end of the world. Tony got what he deserved and so did you. You met Will out of all this mess. It is clearly God's work."

"I know, Mom. I am so happy, but I just want this nightmare to end!"

"I know, honey. Keep praying. And say a prayer for Joe. I guess Achara has been acting very stand-offish the past few days. She's not answering his calls or texts. He's really down."

"That's terrible, Mom! I just talked to him last week. I invited them to Nashville. He sounded like everything was great."

"I know. He is as confused as any of us."

"Well, thank you for telling me. I'll call him."

Grace hung up and prayed. Will joined her with his cup of coffee. "What's wrong, Grace? It's written all over your face."

"The word is out in Georgia. The news posted an article and pictures of us at the concert. Tony saw it and he's missing."

"Grace, this could have nothing to do with us. And he's not coming to Nashville if that's what you think. He'd never find us. Our residence and phone number are unlisted and Mitch is on tour in Ohio, Pennsylvania and New York next month. Let the police take care of it. There is nothing we can do about it."

"And Joe thinks Char is breaking up with him and he is devastated. I feel so disconnected from my family! I miss them, Will. I want to be there for Will and I want to see Jack!" Grace started to cry. Frustration took charge.

"Then let's go see them, Grace. I'm not letting Tony Russo run our lives! One wrong move and he's back in prison- and for much longer next time."

"I know! I am sick of it too! I'm angry, Will! He abused me and I allowed it. And now he's silently controlling me again!"

"Don't allow it, Grace! Let's go to Georgia. Maybe news of our being home will bring him out of hiding."

"Really, Will? Would you go with me?"

"Of course, Grace. I am not afraid of Tony Russo. He picks on women! He's a coward!"

37

I sought the Lord and He heard me. He delivered me from all my fears.

~Psalm 34:4

Grace and Will headed out the next morning for Georgia. When they arrived, Carrie was out shopping. Jack was sitting at the computer working on his Sunday sermon. Grace came up behind the chair and hugged him. She noticed his bony structure.

"Grace!" he said looking up. "Welcome back! Hi Will!"

"Hi Jack! How are you feeling?"

"Couldn't be better, son." Jack rose from the chair slowly, holding on to the sides of the chair for support. "How was Nashville? I hear you have a pretty talented brother."

"Yes, sir. He's incredible. A spiritual gift from God for sure."

Then Grace chimed in. "It was awesome, Dad. Have you ever been to Nashville?"

"No, I haven't, Grace. It's on my bucket list, but I'm not sure I'll get to cross that one off." Then Jack started laughing, amused with himself.

Will started laughing out loud. Grace looked at Will horrified and yelled, "Dad! That's not *one bit* funny!"

Jack took Grace into a hug. "Life is but a mist, Gracie. We're all dying. I just might be going sooner than later."

Grace squeezed him back. "Ugh! You are impossible! Where's Mom?"

"At the grocery store. You know your mom. She's going to cook a feast for you guys."

Grace continued with the questioning. "How about Joe? How's he doing?"

"He went for a run. He's struggling, Grace. He doesn't understand Char's behavior. Quite honestly, we don't either. It happened so abruptly, with no rhyme or reason."

Grace was pensive. "Do you think she met someone and was afraid to hurt him? She is just so kind, Dad! It doesn't make any sense that she wouldn't explain herself!"

"I have no idea, Grace. We just have to pray about it. He was so grateful that you were coming home. You are a great sister. You know that, don't you?"

"I love him so much! I want to figure this out!"

"We will, Grace. God's in charge."

Carrie cooked her famous chicken enchiladas that night. They all sat around the table and talked. Joe was not himself; broken and confused. It broke Grace's heart.

Later that evening, Jack and Carrie went to bed. Jack tired easily and Carrie always joined him, savoring every moment she had with him. Their unconditional love for each other was a beautiful testament of God's love.

Grace, Will and Joe sat on the back deck and talked. Grace questioned Joe about Achara. "When did you notice the change in her behavior, Joe?"

"It was drastic, Grace. One day we were fine and the next she was cold. It's been about a week. She won't answer my texts or calls. The last correspondence was a few days ago. She said she was going to Thailand for the summer. It's so strange!"

"Do you think the Christianity thing is getting to her? I know she's been confused."

"I don't think so. She would have told me. I love her so much, Grace. This really hurts." Joe's eyes filled with tears as he stared into the distance.

Will joined in the conversation. "Has she left for Thailand yet?"

"I don't know."

Will continued. "Fight for her, Joe! Go to her apartment and talk to her."

"I don't want to scare her off. If she needs space, I want to give it to her."

"Will is right, Joe. This is ridiculous! We are going there tomorrow! I'll go with you."

Joe looked up with a glimmer of hope in his eyes. "Really? You don't think that's being too pushy?"

"No! You love her and you want answers!"

"What if she's with another guy?"

"Then you find out! Not knowing is torture!"

"You are right, Will. This is killing me. I have the key to her apartment. She went to a conference for a couple days and she needed me to water her plants. I could always say I was returning the key."

Grace was hopeful. "There you go, Joe. It's a plan."

Will headed back to his apartment to spend the night. Joe headed to bed. Grace called Francesco. "Fran? Hi, it's Grace."

"Hi Grace." Fran sounded tired. Mentally exhausted, to be exact.

"I just wanted you to know that I am back in town. I can't live my life in circles, constantly scanning my surroundings."

"I understand, Grace. My whole family understands. We love you and want you to feel safe."

"Thanks, Fran. That means a lot. I love you guys too. I just want this nightmare to end!"

We do too, Grace. Do you know of anyone or any place that Tony might want to go? Think hard."

"I have thought long and hard, Fran. I keep coming up blank."

"Okay. Well, try not to worry, Grace. Just enjoy your life. You deserve it. We'll find him."

"Thanks Fran. I am praying."

"Us too, Grace. We love Tony. We need to get him some help. He has a lot of good deep down in him."

"I know he does. That's what I fell in love with."

38

Peace I leave you; my peace I give you. I do not give as the world gives. Do not let your heart be troubled and do not be afraid.

~John 14:27

The next morning, Carrie made a big breakfast for everyone. The four of them spent time around the table together, just like old times. The thought of Jack's vacant chair one day made Grace's stomach turn. She dismissed the thought immediately.

Later, Grace and Joe headed over to Grace's apartment to pick up mail from her neighbor. Next stop was Char's apartment. They stopped by McDonald's drive- thru for some comfort fries and Grace gave Joe a pep talk, as they approached the apartment complex.

When they pulled in, Joe spotted Char's car. "That's her car, Grace. She's here."

"Maybe not. If she's in Thailand, she may have gotten a ride to the airport."

"That's true." Joe was pensive and shoveled fries into his mouth. "This is stupid, Grace! I can't beg her to like me!"

"But you have to have closure, Joe. Good or bad, you need to know so you can move on."

"Okay. You're right." Joe took a swig of his coke and opened the car door. "Wish me luck."

Grace gave her brother a hug. "Good luck, Joe. I love you. I will be waiting right here and praying."

Joe climbed the stairs to Char's third floor apartment. He apprehensively approached the door. He wanted to turn around, but couldn't face Grace if he chickened out. He put his ear to the door to see if he heard anything going on inside. Then he knocked. No answer.

He took the key from his pocket and put it into the slot. His hands were shaking as he turned the key. *What am I doing?* He slowly opened the door that led into her kitchen. Char stood nervously at the stove with her finger to her lips, warning Joe to be quiet. Joe was horrified when he saw her battered face.

"Char! What is wrong? Your face! What happened to you?"

Char was panicked and in the loudest whisper she could muster pleaded with him. "Joe, please! You have to leave right now!"

"Char, what is going on? Talk to me, please!" Joe was frantic, trying desperately to understand.

"I am begging you, Joe! Please! Go! He will kill you!" Char moved toward Joe pushing him to the door and opening it.

Joe stopped and took her gently by the arms and looked her in the eyes. "Who is *he*? Char, please answer me! Who hurt you?"

Then from the bedroom came a tall, dark eyed man with disheveled hair. He'd just awoken. He was holding a gun. It took Joe a second to realize who it was and then it registered. His heart beat in his throat.

39

This is the confidence we have in approaching God: that
if we ask anything according to His will, He hears you.

~John 14:27

"Tony, what are you doing here?"

Tony let out an eerie snicker. "This is my girl now, Joe.
Do you have a problem with that?"

Joe was shocked and confused. He looked to Char for understanding.
She was crying.

"Char, what's going on? Do you know each other?"

Tony responded for her. "Of course, we do, Joe. We've known
each other for a while, just like your sister and Will. Doesn't feel good,
does it?"

Joe was dumbfounded. He looked to Char and she returned a
look of desperation. Tony moved closer, the gun higher, aimed at Joe's
forehead. Tony had a glazed look in his eyes and spoke in a possessed
voice. It made the hair on Joe's body stand on end.

"Say goodbye to Char, Joe. And just so you know, your sister is
next." Tony laughed demonically as he put the gun against Joe's skull.

Joe realized this was the end. His body trembled in terror.

Then the door pushed open and sent Joe sideways. The gun fired
and Tony was pummeled to the floor by an officer. It was his brother,

Francesco. "It's over, Tony. No more! Do you hear me? You need help and I'm not giving up until you get it! We love you, Tony! Why can't you see that?"

Tony was in shock as his brother handcuffed him and handed him over to the assisting officer. When Tony was led out the door, Francesco sat on the floor and sobbed. He cried out, "Oh God, please save him!"

Char ran to Joe and hugged him while she confessed. "He followed me, Joe. He's been living here. He took me hostage. He said he'd kill you and your family if I didn't do what he said!" Char was weeping as she held onto Joe.

Joe was perplexed. "Did you know him?"

"He came into the restaurant I worked at while I was going to college. He asked me out several times but I was always working or going to school. We never met up and he finally stopped coming around. I had no idea that he was Grace's boyfriend!"

Francesco answered some more questions. "The gun I kept at my mother's house was missing. Tony was the only one who knew my gun was there. When Grace called to tell me she was back, I knew I had to have her followed."

And then Grace ran in. "Francesco! What is going on? I just saw Tony..." Grace was looking around as she spoke and saw her brother and Char behind the door. She ran to them sobbing and hugged them.

Joe filled her in on what had happened and Char admitted one last thing. "I prayed Joe. I remembered that you said to pray about anything and God would hear me. I was so scared! He beat me and forced himself on me, but I prayed like you said I should." Char was choking back her tears. "He answered my prayer! You came! It's over!"

Char, Joe and Grace held each other and cried tears of freedom. Francesco called an ambulance and walked dejectedly toward the door. "Grace, Char needs to go to the hospital to get examined."

"I'll take care of it, Fran. Thank you for saving my brother's life."

"You're welcome. Please pray for Tony and my family too. I'll be in touch."

And the door closed behind him.

40

For the Lord himself will come down from heaven with a loud command, with the voice of the archangel and with the trumpet call of God, and the dead in Christ will rise first. After that, we who are still alive and are left will be caught up together with them in the clouds to meet the Lord in the air. And so we will be with the Lord forever. Therefore encourage one another with these words.

~1 Thessalonians 4:16-18

Jack's birthday...

Jack's birthday fell over Labor Day weekend. Carrie decided to celebrate it with everyone at their house. Everyone made the effort to be there, as they knew this was probably Jack's last earthly birthday.

The church was filled to capacity and all of Jack's loved ones graced the front pews of the church. Jack preached from his wheelchair. His gaunt face accentuated his bright eyes and smile.

Jack read from Titus, chapter two. "Say no to ungodliness and worldly things. Live self-controlled, upright and godly lives in the present age while we wait for the blessed hope- the appearing of the glory or our great God and Savior, Jesus Christ."

Jack explained that Titus was a friend of the apostle Paul. Paul wrote to Titus from prison, teaching him how to pastor to a rebellious congregation on the island of Crete. Titus was a young leader preaching God's word.

"The best way to get rid of discouragement is to remember that Christ is coming again. The Second Coming of Christ is the most exciting, glorious truth in all the world. When we look around the world today and see all of the sadness and pessimism, we need to remember that the Bible is the only book in the world that predicts the future with complete accuracy.

"An unbeliever sees a hopeless end, but a Christian sees an *endless hope*. Death is an experience that people fear, but for the believer, fear is removed. It will be a glorious release- a fulfillment of everything you ever longed for. We have the assurance that we are going to a home where all is happy, peaceful, and joyful. We need to be willing to suffer whatever hardships given to us, for the sake of all that is to come.

"Earthly possessions should not concern us because they will pass away. But the possessions in heaven are enduring. This world is not our home. Our citizenship is in heaven. To him who is faithful, Christ will give a crown of life. Death is the Christian's coronation- the end of conflict and the beginning of glory and triumph in paradise. The first time Jesus came, he was judged by man and nailed to a cross. The second time, He will come in glory and judge man from his throne.

"So, don't hold back anything from your Father in heaven. Have a relationship with him. Let Him be the Lord and Controller of your life. That is what He wants from you."

And after the sermon, Jack baptized Achara, whose terrifying experience with Tony Russo led her to solely depend on God.

41

The revelation from Jesus Christ, which God gave him to show his servants what must soon take place. He made it known by sending his angel to his servant John, who testifies to everything he saw- that is, the word of God and the testimony of Jesus Christ. Blessed is the one who reads aloud the words of this prophecy and blessed are those who hear it and take heart what is written in it because the time is near.

~Revelation 1:1-3

After church, everyone headed to Carrie and Jack's house. Food was plentiful and church friends got together and built a ramp for Jack to get in and out of his house in his wheelchair. The tables were set up to facilitate all of the guests.

After much chatter, they all filled their plates from a smorgasbord style set-up of hot dogs, hamburgers, salads, baked beans and dessert. Then took their seats at the table, and this time, Achara led the prayer.

"Dear Lord, thank you for putting me in the path of these wonderful people. I know it was your plan and I am so grateful. I admit that I still don't understand all of the mysteries of your universe, but I do know that you are real and you hear our prayers. I accept your plans for my life. Guide all of us, Lord. Direct us, teach us, and help us to listen to you. And thank you for revealing the most important promise of all- the one we need most- eternal life with your son, Jesus. Amen."

Sniffles were heard around the room. Char's baptism was clearly the work of God. The guests congratulated Char on her baptism and shared stories of their own. Some were baptized as infants, others later in life. After a few minutes of conversation, Jack spoke.

"Thank you all for being here. Chances are this will be my last earthly birthday. Dr. Jollie said he thought a few more months. I am telling you this to prepare you and let you know that I am ready."

The silence was tangible. No one knew what to say, so they listened. Jack continued. "The day we die is the birthday of eternity. It is merely a doorway to eternal life. That brings me joy and I want it to bring you joy as well. The great adventure is what comes after death, being in Christ's presence. First Corinthians 2:9 says that no eye has seen, no ear has heard, no human mind had conceived what God has prepared for those who love him." Jack looked around the table. "This is truth."

"God commanded the apostle John to talk about his visit to Heaven, which he did in detail in the book of Revelation. Today I want more than anything for you to feel comfortable about my death. I want you to ask me any question, or speak of your fears. When God calls me home, I want you to feel peace and celebrate my homecoming."

Joe started. "If no eye has seen, how can we know for sure?"

"Because God has revealed what he wants us to know through the Bible, Joe. God commanded the apostle John to tell about it, so he wrote it down. God showed John heaven and it has been recorded. Isaiah and Ezekiel wrote about it as well in the Old Testament, hundreds of years before Jesus was even born. It will be more than our human minds can imagine. We are heading toward a glorious climax. It is fact."

Achara asked next. "What happens right after you die?"

"Good question, Char. Scripture tells us that when a Christian dies, he goes to a present heaven or paradise. This isn't our final destination, but we will be with Jesus waiting for God to bring down the new heaven and the new earth. The present heaven is up there," Jack pointed above, "And the future, eternal heaven will be down here; but redone."

Micah joined his dad in explaining. "Read Revelation, chapter

21, Char. It clearly states that John saw a new heaven and a new earth because the first heaven and the first earth had passed away. He talks about the New Jerusalem coming down out of the heavens. There will literally be heaven *on earth,* but perfect…an unimaginable blessing."

Emma smiled and joined in. "My favorite passage is verse four in Revelation 21. It says He will wipe every tear from our eyes. There will be no more death or mourning, or crying or pain." Emma knew that this was Ben's favorite scripture and it gave her peace to know that he was there, experiencing it.

Jack continued, excited that the conversation was progressing. "Heaven is 100% real. It is a city whose builder and maker is God. It will have buildings, culture, mountains and trees. John 14:2 tells us that before Christ was crucified, he told his apostles, not to let their hearts be troubled. He said, 'My father's house has many mansions; if it were not so, would I have told you that I am going there to prepare a place for you? I will come back and take you with me so you may be where I am.'"

Then John McDonald added, "That's a promise. John 3:16 says that God so loved the world that he gave his one and only son so that whoever believes in Him shall have eternal life."

"And there will be no oceans or seas. That fascinates me," James Rutherford reacted.

"That's right, James. Revelation 21, verses 15 and 16 talk about the dimensions of the new heaven. A city this size would stretch from Canada to Mexico and from the Appalachian Mountains to the California border. Heaven will encompass the whole earth, with the river of life as its source. Perfect in every way!"

"Yep! I saw it in my dream of heaven," Matthew added. "The river comes down from God's throne- down the middle of the street! It is so beautiful there!"

"And it is crystal clear," Grace joined in, "And on each side of the river stands the tree of life, bearing twelve crops of fruit every month."

"Does it really say that in the Bible?" Achara was astounded and wanted to learn more.

Jack replied confidently, "Revelation 22, verses one and two, Char."

Char kept on. "Are there really streets of gold there?"

"Yes!" Matthew shouted. "They are so shiny and beautiful!"

Jack laughed and quoted scripture once again. "Revelation 21, verses 19 and 20, Char. It states that the foundations of the city walls are decorated of every kind of precious stone. It mentions jasper, sapphires, emeralds, onyx, rubies, turquoise. There are twelve stones mentioned in all."

"And there will be no night there," Micah added. "There is no need for lamps or light of the sun because God gives the light." Micah smiled. "How cool is that? That's my favorite."

Char was on a roll. "Can you explain the tree of life, Jack?"

"Sure. The tree of life is mentioned three times in Genesis, in the garden of Eden and then again in Revelation, four times. Revelation 2:7 says 'whoever has ears, let them hear what the spirit says…to the one who is victorious, I will give the right to eat from the tree of life, which is in the paradise of God.' On the new earth, Char, we will be free to eat the fruit of the same tree that nourished Adam and Eve. The Bible begins with paradise lost, and ends with paradise regained."

Micah finished, "In Genesis, the first book of the Bible, humans gave in to Satan and brought sin into the world. In Revelation, the last book of the Bible, Satan is quarantined from God's people. Hence; a place of perfect peace and love."

"First Thessalonians, chapter 13 is a good place to read too, Char," Jack added. "Paul wrote this letter. It explains the rapture of God's people and how we will be with him forever. It is okay to mourn, but you have to believe that we will all be together again. So, when God calls me home, you will mourn for yourselves, but not for me because I'll be with my Savior- our final destination."

Then Matthew finished the questioning. "Uncle Jack, do you think we'll go to church there?"

"That is a great question, Matthew. But there won't be any need for a place to worship because Jesus will be there. Every place will be holy and perfect. We will have face- to- face companionship with Him."

"That is so cool, Uncle Jack!"

A feeling of peace came over the room. The conversation brought hope to all of their hearts. Without Christ, they knew they would have nothing. They knew that heaven was a place beyond their comprehension; whose maker and architect was God. They just had to accept and trust Him and they would find out.

And after dinner, Char announced that she would be taking a sabbatical from teaching to go back to Thailand. Joe already knew and was saddened, but he understood. She missed her parents and after all of the trauma she had been through, she needed time away to clear her mind. She would return in August. Her principal was holding her job for her.

Joe could not imagine not seeing Char for eleven months, but knew if it was God's will, they would be together. They planned to stay in touch through social media and pray for God's guidance and healing.

42

For we are His workmanship, created in Christ Jesus for good works, which God prepared beforehand so that we should walk in them.

~Ephesians 2:10

Christmas…

Thanksgiving had come and gone. Their gatherings were shrinking, as their kids married. They were starting their own traditions and sharing time between families. Jack was weakening daily and spent most of his time in his wheelchair. As Christ's birthday approached, Jack insisted they continue the tradition at their house, but his kids had another plan.

Grace and Joe kept in touch with Micah and Maggie. They all wanted this Christmas to be a memorable one, so they arranged a trip to Nashville. Grace wanted to make sure Jack could cross it off his bucket list! Max and Colleen Boone were more than happy to have everyone to their beautiful home. They were excited to meet Grace's family, the one they heard so much about; and that meant so much to Grace.

The kids set it up so that Jack had transportation from gate to gate at the airport, as well as to the baggage claim area. Mr. and Mrs. Boone would be waiting right outside when they arrived. Mitchell had rented a wheelchair accessible van so Jack would have easy access wherever they went and they all could be together.

Dr. Jollie approved the trip. He knew that Jack had God on his side. How could he lose? He had already beaten the odds and was living longer than he had ever anticipated. This holiday, Jack Finnegan would be taken care of. It was his turn.

Everything went as planned. They all flew in on Christmas Eve morning. The families meshed as if forever friends. The weather was unusually warm, so that too was on their side. They ate dinner together and went to the 7:00p.m. service at the Boone's church. Pastor Kevin welcomed all of them at the start of the service. He read the Christmas story from Luke, chapter two. He spent most of the sermon discussing verse fourteen: "Glory to God in the highest and on earth, peace to those on whom his favor rests."

The pastor explained that these words were the song of the angels to the shepherds one memorable night in Bethlehem, two thousand years ago. He said that centuries had passed, but the world still longed for peace. He addressed the congregation and asked, "Where is this peace?" He paused waiting for them to ponder.

"Peace is clearly not evident in this world with all of the fighting and hatred. But peace does live in the hearts of those who trust in our Savior's grace. On the first Christmas night in Bethlehem, God was visible in the flesh. This was Jesus Christ- the God of our universe, the creator and author of our lives. He came down from heaven in human form. *Why?*"

Jack was smiling and answering the question in his mind. He loved listening to Pastor Kevin preach. Jack had spent so many years preparing sermons. It was such a treat to be part of the congregation, instead.

Pastor Kevin paused again and then answered his question. "His ultimate purpose in coming to the world was to bring us back to His kingdom. God gave his son in this very dark world- the King of peace and love. He was born to die as the final and perfect sacrifice of our sins. He was only on this earth thirty-three years, but He transformed a civilization!

"In Jesus, we have wisdom, power, justice, mercy, love... the list goes on. Through Him, *all* things were made. He is the light of all mankind. Apart from Him, all is darkness. On that one significant night in history, God brought the light of the world. We need him to live a victorious life. There can be no lasting peace until Jesus comes to the heart of all people, but we have to let Him in.

"When the angel of the Lord proclaimed peace on earth, goodwill to men, it was for *anyone* who would accept this beautiful baby as their Savior. God's gifts are free. We just have to accept them. So tonight, let's celebrate God's perfect gift to the world."

After the service, the Boone's invited Pastor Kevin back to the house for dessert. They all sat poolside and Mitchell and his band played their acoustic guitars and led them in singing Christmas songs. Jack's family wiped tears from their faces as they saw the joy in Jack's eyes. He sang along, praising the Savior he loved and would meet face-to -face

And after a few songs, Will got down on one knee and asked Grace to be his wife. And without hesitation, she accepted. Carrie and Jack cried tears of joy, knowing that Will and his family were handpicked by God for their precious daughter. He was definitely able to do more than you could possibly ask or imagine when you were patient and waited for Him.

Christmas morning, they all slept in and then shared a breakfast of egg casserole, cheese grits, sausage balls and monkey bread. They agreed to bypass the gift-giving as they all had more than they ever needed or wanted. Both families supported needy families instead.

That afternoon they curled up and watched *It's a Wonderful Life* and right after the movie ended, the doorbell rang. Colleen made eye contact with Grace, Joe, Micah and Maggie. They knew who it was. Seconds later, in walked Jade, Beau and Jenna Walls.

Beau walked toward a very surprised Jack. "You didn't think we were going to miss Christmas with our favorite people, did you?" Beau bent down and took Jack into a bear hug. Jade was next in line.

"Merry Christmas to my favorite earthly anchor. You saw me through my storms and I'll never forget it, Jack. We couldn't imagine Christmas without you two."

Jack was thrilled. "Thank you so much for being here! This

weekend couldn't get any better. How'd you pull this one off without me knowing?"

Colleen Boone chimed in. "You just happen to have some of the nicest and *sneakiest* kids on your side." Colleen laughed and finished explaining, "Jade and I spoke on the phone and we have rooms set up for all of you."

"Will and Mitch, why don't you show them to their rooms and we'll catch up after they get settled."

Grace followed along so she could talk with Jenna. "I am so happy you are here, Jen!"

"Me too, Grace. You know Jax is in a residential facility in Utah for the next few months. He is getting some intense therapy for his gambling addiction. His parents did lots of researching and this is one of the best facilities in the country."

"Mags told me. I'm praying for him."

"Thanks, Grace. It's really bad. He's had a couple of setbacks. I pray God sees him through."

Will, Mitch, Jade and Beau met up with them in the hallway. Will stopped Jenna. "Jen, this is my brother, Mitch."

Jenna held out her hand. "So nice to meet you, Mitch. I love your music."

"Nice to meet you too, Jenna. And thank you. You are welcome any time to a concert. Just let me know."

Then Grace piped in. "Oh, don't worry, Mitch. We *will* take you up on it."

"Yep, since you asked, I'm in." Jenna teased back.

"It's a deal," Mitch confirmed. "Now let's get you guys to your rooms so we can celebrate Christmas!"

43

Each of you should give what you have decided in your heart to give, not reluctantly or under compulsion, for God loves a cheerful giver.

~2 Corinthians 9:7

After spending a couple of hours around the pool catching up, all of them piled into the van and headed to Vanderbilt Children's Hospital. One of Mitch's projects was frequent visits with his band to see the children suffering from cancer. It all started one day when Mitch received a letter in the mail from a six-year-old boy named Butch. He told Mitch that he loved his music and hoped that he could get out of the hospital one day soon to see one of his concerts.

Mitch immediately got his band together and they set up a time to meet Butch and his friends at the hospital. It became a monthly occurrence. Mitch also arranged for front row seats for him (and his parents) at one of his local concerts. Butch was a fan!

Unfortunately, Butch's cancer was winning and he would be spending Christmas in the hospital. Mitch kept in touch with his parents by phone and visited Butch weekly. Today, Mitch and his band had their vehicles stuffed with presents and they all caravanned over to the hospital.

When they arrived, the nurses had all of the children in one large room where they often got together to watch television. Thanks to Mitchell Boone Band, they had more than one TV and video game systems so all of them could enjoy. Squeals of happiness and applause came from all of the kids. Mitch introduced everyone and they had enough gifts to go around. The guests took turns visiting with the patients, and playing games with them. A true spirit of Christmas.

Butch immediately took a liking to Jack. Jack rolled his wheelchair up next to Butch. Jack extended his hand. "Hi Butch! I'm Jack."

Butch shook his hand and answered, "Hi Jack! Nice to meet you. I've been praying for you."

"Well, thank you, Butch. I will be sure to return the favor."

"Mitch told me that you had cancer too. Are you dying?"

"I am."

"Are you scared?"

Jack couldn't believe the candidness of this precious child. He felt an immediate connection.

"I am not scared at all, Butch."

"Me either. But it makes me sad that my mom and dad are so sad."

"I know what you mean. My family cries a lot too."

"My mom says Jesus will make me better, but I know I'm dying. I just don't want to tell her because it will make her so sad."

It troubled Jack that Butch was carrying this burden. "How do you know?"

"I just know. I have DIPG. It means Diffuse Intrinsic Pontine Glioma. It's an incurable brain cancer. I can feel it. I can't walk anymore and it's getting harder to swallow and breathe. That's why I'm here. My friend, Julia died last week of it. I miss her, but I know I'll see her soon." Butch smiled at Jack with sincerity, as if visualizing their reunion.

"You sure will, Butch. That's the beauty of death. It's just a passing over to a new beginning. Just think, we'll see each other again too."

Butch looked at Jack with a sparkle in his eye. "That's so cool. If you die first, will you meet me if you can?"

"Of course, I will. But if God calls you home first, you have to promise to meet me."

Butch giggled. "It's a deal. Let's shake on it."

Jack laughed and shook his hand. "I am so happy I met you, Butch. I think this is another one of God's plans. What do you think?"

"For sure!" Then Butch looked at Jack and asked curiously, "Do you have an angel, Jack?"

"Well, the Bible says we have angels watching over us, but I haven't met *mine* yet. How about you?"

"Yep. Sometimes at night when I can't sleep, he comes and sits on my bed with me. He tells me everything is going to be okay."

Jack's eyes welled with tears. "That is beautiful, Butch. How does that make you feel?"

"He makes me feel safe and peaceful."

As they were talking, Butch's parents walked up to introduce themselves to Jack.

Butch's father extended his hand first. "Hi. I'm Bob, Butch's dad and this is my wife, Annie. We've been praying for you. Mitchell asked us to."

"Well, thank you for that. It's great to meet you both," Jack said as he returned his handshake. "You have an amazing young man right here."

Annie smiled and ruffled Butch's hair. "We think so."

Then Butch reversed in his wheelchair. "See you later, Mr. Jack. I'm going to visit with Mitch. Come on, Dad. You want to play Mario?"

"You bet!" Bob excused himself and joined his son.

"Later, buddy." Jack replied.

Annie pulled over a chair from a table nearby and sat down by Jack. "You seemed to have made a real impression on Butch. We haven't seen him that full of life in a few days. Thank you."

"Well, we have a lot in common, I guess." Jack smiled nervously, not wanting to upset her by bringing up the cancer.

Annie stated to cry, shielding her face from the other side of the room. "Butch's cancer is incurable. But I'm praying for a miracle."

"I know. He told me."

Annie looked up at Jack. "He told you?"

"He did. He even told me what type of cancer he had."

"That's unbelievable. We haven't talked about it with him yet. He just knows he has cancer."

"He knows more than you think, Annie. He's a smart kid."

"I know. He's very smart. Can I ask you a question, Jack?"

"Sure."

"How do we tell him he may die?"

Jack paused pensively and then responded. "He already knows, Annie. He's not afraid to die, but he's sad that you and your husband are sad."

"He told you that?"

"He did."

"Why won't he talk to us about it?"

"Probably because he doesn't want to make you any sadder. I am someone he can relate to since we both have terminal cancer. We had a wonderful conversation. I would love to keep in touch with him. Do you mind if I call him?"

"I would love that! Mitchell and his band have been such a God-send. They have brought Butch and all of these kids so much joy!" Annie wiped tears from her face. "We have received so many blessings through all of this."

"That's how God works, Annie. He will see you through. May I suggest something?"

"Please."

"Talk openly to Butch about everything. He's ready. He just wants *you* to be ready. It's important that he has peace about how you will be when he dies. You have to assure him that you will be fine and that you will be together again one day. You'll be surprised how much comfort he will give you, too. He's got a lot to share with you." Jack smiled knowing that God had Butch covered in protection.

"Thank you, Jack. I promise we will."

Jack and Annie exchanged cellphone numbers and after a couple of hours, the Finnegan, Boone and Walls' clans headed back home.

Before Jack left, Butch came racing up to him in his wheelchair. Jack pulled up beside his and gave Butch a big hug. "I think it's time to talk to your mom and dad, okay? Tell them how you're feeling and be honest with them. Tell them you don't want them to be sad, okay?"

"I promise, Jack. Mom said you're going to call me."

"I am. Is that okay with you?"

"Yes! Can I call you too?"

"Absolutely. I will keep my cellphone with me at all times."

"Mom said I can keep her phone by me, too."

"Okay. I'll call you tomorrow."

"Yessss!" Butch answered excitedly. "Talk to you tomorrow, Mr. Jack!" Then he wheeled away to join his friends.

That night, Butch, Annie and Bob Quinn shared the best conversation since their son was diagnosed with cancer. Butch shared his concerns with his parents and told them about his angel. They prayed together that night and thanked God for their new friend, Jack Finnegan.

They all felt God's peace.

44

Today in the town of David a Savior has been born to you. He is the Messiah, the Lord…On the eighth day when it was time to circumcise the child, he was named Jesus, the name the angel gave him before he was conceived.

~ Luke 2:1; 21

That evening, the Walls, Finnegan, and Boone families shared a dinner of prime rib and all of the trimmings. Jack led the prayer before dinner.

"Lord, thank you for all of these amazing people gathered here today. None of us are here by chance. It is your perfect plan. Thank you for Butch, Bob and Annie Quinn. Be with them Lord and give them peace and comfort during this trial in their life. Thank you for that day several years ago when you sent Jade into the doors of my church on Sanibel Island. Your story had a perfect beginning, middle and end. Today we celebrate the birth of your son, Jesus. Thank you for that perfect gift to us over 2000 years ago. You sent us a tiny baby to accomplish your magnificent purpose. He is the light of our world. You sent Him to die as the final and perfect sacrifice for our sins. Help us to remember Him *not only* during the Christmas season, but *every minute* of our lives. Help us to praise Him this holy season and every day after. In your precious son's name. Amen."

During dinner, they discussed the remarkable connection between Jack and Butch. They all agreed it was a relationship that God planned from the beginning. Coming to Nashville for Christmas was perfect in more ways than one. After dinner, everyone piled back into the van and drove around the city of Nashville to take in the stunning display of lights. Jenna and Mitch took an instant liking to each other. Jenna was blown away by his generosity and sincere humility. His notoriety and fame were never discussed. His talents were quietly acknowledged as a gift from God.

That evening, Achara facetimed Joe and they all got to meet Achara's parents. With lots of translations on Char's part, everyone got a chance to talk. Her parents were full of love and laughter- just like Char.

Later that evening when everyone else had gone to bed, Mitch and Will sat poolside and discussed the holiday. Mitch confided in Will that Jenna would be someone he would be interested in dating, but knew she was in a relationship. He couldn't help but notice the way she interacted with the children at the hospital, a quality he always found endearing. He always hoped to be a dad someday. Will advised him to pray about it and told his brother that he knew that God would show him the right one when he least expected it; just as he had met Grace.

"Look at how I met Grace!" he laughed. "I rescued her from her abusive boyfriend. You just never know what God has planned, Mitch. And now she's going to be my wife."

"You are a lucky man, Will. She's a keeper."

"Thanks, Mitch. Your day will come."

That evening, Carrie and Jack prayed together in bed. They thanked God for their longtime friends and newfound family. Jack's heart was full and he felt at peace. He couldn't wait to give his new little buddy a call. They would be flying back home the next day, along with Micah and Maggie who had to return to work. Joe, too would be heading back as he had plans with friends from work. Grace had talked Jenna into staying a couple of extra days, so they could show her around Nashville. They would all fly home together at the end of the week and then Jenna would drive back to North Carolina.

They were all very grateful for their teacher vacations.

45

Faith is confidence is what we hope for and assurance about what we do not see.

~Hebrews 11:1

New Year's Eve

Jenna loved Nashville. There was so much to do and Grace, Will and Mitchell had shown her every nook and cranny of it. It was the most fun she had experienced in a very long time. That week in Nashville was just what Jenna needed. The weight of worrying about Jax and wondering if he would relapse was a distant memory. She knew that he was in good hands and it took the pressure off of her. She prayed that he would learn the skills necessary to beat his addiction; and most importantly, that he would pray for the strength to do it. The menacing thing was that she was developing feelings for Mitch. He possessed every possible quality that she could ask for in a companion. The guilt consumed her, as she knew that she had made a commitment to Jax.

Jenna stayed longer than she anticipated, but it was hard to say *no* to Grace, Will *and* Mitch. There was no hurry in getting back and the Boone's were more than hospitable. She knew that she had lifelong friends in them. She was so grateful that her family had made the trip to celebrate with their beloved Jack. It was already New Year's Eve. Her vacation was coming quickly to a close.

They all agreed to stay at the Boone house for the New Year. No one was in the mood to take on the crowds of the city, so they would stay in the safety of their own four walls. Billy Madison, Mitch's agent and his wife and two young boys would be joining them; along with members of Mitch's band and their significant others. They grilled out steaks and the kids swam in the heated pool. The adults played charades. They watched the apple drop on the television in New York and the kids banged pots and pans. Grace and Jenna called their respective families.

Their company left shortly afterwards. The Boone family, along with Jenna and Grace, sat around the kitchen table.

Grace shared the conversation she had with Jack. "My dad called Butch to wish him a Happy New Year." She smiled thinking of his thoughtfulness, but felt a simultaneous sadness, knowing this was probably his last one.

Mitch joined in. "He is an amazing guy, Grace. I can't believe the connection he had with Butch. It was uncanny."

"A definite God thing," Jenna added. "It was like they both found peace in each other."

"It changed Annie and Bob's life," Mitch continued. "I talked to Bob today and he told me that they are having the most amazing conversations with Butch. He said that Jack told them to talk to him openly. Evidently, Butch has an angel that visits him. He told Jack, but he was afraid to tell his parents. He didn't want them to be sad that he was dying."

Mrs. Boone was moved to tears. "That is beautiful, Mitch. God is so good. He plans out everything."

"It's so true," Grace continued. "It's incredible how God kept tugging on our hearts to bring Jack to Nashville, too. It was perfect!"

"I can't believe his faith!" Will responded earnestly. "He is six years old and has absolutely no fear of dying."

"That's what faith is, son. No fear- total trust in what we cannot see. That's why it says we have to be like children to get to heaven. They are so trusting."

There was a silence while everyone took in the discussion.

Then Jenna broke the stillness with her heartfelt gratitude. "Well, this was one of the most incredible weeks of my life. Thank you so much for your kindness and hospitality. It will never be forgotten, I assure you."

Mr. Boone acknowledged her gratitude. "Jenna, you are welcome here *any time*. You have been an absolute joy to have around."

"I agree," Mrs. Boone chimed in. "I hate that you have to leave. It's so nice having my kids and their friends around. It brings so much life to this quiet house."

"Well, I've enjoyed every second. You are a wonderful family." Jenna found herself fighting back tears, as she felt the reality of her words.

Mrs. Boone yawned. "Well I'm going to be the first party pooper. I'm heading to bed." She went around the table and kissed the tops of everyone's head. Mr. Boone followed her to the door.

"Goodnight, Mom. Love you!" Will and Mitch shared their sentiments.

"Love you back. Sleep tight."

46

Be on your guard; stand firm in your faith; be courageous; be strong.

~1 Corinthians 16:13

New Year's Day was football day. Mrs. Boone made a bunch of appetizers and they all hung out and relaxed. Jenna couldn't believe how comfortable she felt with them. Later that evening, Grace, Will, Jenna and Mitch went out to dinner. They listened to bands at some of the local honky-tonks. They would be flying home the following day and were all a little melancholy; especially Mitch. He had grown so fond of Grace and Jenna and enjoyed spending time with his brother. He hated to see them go. Life on the road was fulfilling, but often lonely without your loved ones around.

At the bar, Will and Grace got up to dance and Jenna and Mitch shared their feelings.

"I have had such a great time, Mitch. I'm sort of sad about leaving."

"I was thinking the same thing. It's been a while since Will and I have hung out. I miss him. And you, Grace, Joe and your families were just the icing on the cake."

"It was great how everyone got along. Jack was genuinely touched by it all. Your family is so generous. Thank you for everything."

"Anytime, Jen. At least you have Jax to go back to. It's tough being on the road and not having anyone to share it with. It's hard to date in this business. Everyone I meet seems to be fixated with my life style, not me." Mitch laughed nervously and looked to Jenna for a response.

Jenna smiled and responded with sincerity. "God has someone picked out for you, Mitch. And she will be a very lucky lady."

Mitch blushed and put his head down. "Well, thank you, Jenna. Jax is a lucky guy, too."

"Thanks, Mitch. He is a great guy, but I am worried about our relationship to be perfectly honest. He's being treated for his gambling addiction. I just hope he beats it. There's always a fear in the back of my mind. Before he went in, I found myself hiding valuable things for fear of tempting him. His family has been through a lot too."

"Do you love him enough to make it work? To stand by him even if he slips again?"

Jenna paused and nervously stirred the ice in her glass with the straw. "I don't know, Mitch. I'm scared. And his sister is my best friend. I don't want to hurt her either."

"I know it must be tough, Jen. I will pray for you both. But you can't base a relationship on the possibility of hurting his sister. This is your life that you are talking about."

"I know." Then Jenna fought back tears. "I feel so guilty talking about him to you. It feels like such a betrayal. But this week has been wonderful. I have felt so relaxed knowing Jax is in good hands. I haven't worried about anything."

"You aren't betraying him, Jen. I am just a friend listening. Please don't feel guilty. Just pray about it. It will all work out."

"I will. I'm going to go back and visit my grandpa before I go back to North Carolina. He is a retired minister. He is always an amazing voice of reason."

"They are great people to have around, aren't they? My dad is the same for me. No judgment- just sound advice."

"Exactly." Jenna smiled and looked at Mitch. "Thanks for listening and for your prayers. I'll be praying for you too."

"I have a question for you. I am going to be on tour in early March in Charlotte. That's not too far from Raleigh, is it?"

Jenna's face beamed with agreement. "About an hour and a half. Are you offering me a ticket?"

"As many as you would like. Just let me know. Will Jax be home by then?"

"I don't think so, but I'm sure I could interest Micah and Mags."

"Okay, let me see if I remember this right. Micah is Jack's adopted son. He's the doctor and Mags is your best friend- Jax's sister?"

"Wow- aren't you a good listener! That is correct."

"Well, I promise to get ahold of you as it gets closer."

"Thank you, Mitch. I will be looking forward to it. Let me write down my number for you." Jenna reached into her purse and took out an old ATM receipt. She wrote her cell number on it and handed it to Mitch.

Mitch took out his phone and called it. "There, now you have my number too."

Grace and Will returned to the table, amused by their inability to dance.

With disappointment in her tone, Grace lamented. "I hate for this week to end, but we should probably head out. Our flight leaves early tomorrow and we still have to pack."

"I hate it, but you're right," Jenna agreed.

The ride home was quiet. Everyone seemed pensive. The Nashville streets were still alive with Christmas embellishments. The streets bustled with visitors. As they drove home, you could hear the distant hum of music coming from the establishments. A sadness came over Jenna as she thought about the decisions that lie ahead of her.

47

Listen to advice and accept discipline and at the end you
will be counted among the wise.

~Proverbs 19:20

J ohn Walls was still an active part of the retirement center. He
had lots of friends and still led the Sunday service at the age of
ninety-one. Beau and Jade made weekly visits and called a couple
of days per week to see if he needed anything. His response was always
the same, "I have everything I need or want. You two need to stop
worrying about me."

Jenna visited whenever she was back from North Carolina and
would call him periodically on the weekends. He always gave her a
feeling of peace. He instilled in her God's wisdom, piece by piece.

When Jenna returned from Nashville, she did as she planned. She
knew she needed a good ole dose of Grandpa John before she made the
trip back to Raleigh. She dialed his number.

"Is this my Jen-Jen?"

Jenna giggled on the other end. John Walls always called her Jen-
Jen; and her twin brother, Ben-Ben. He said they were worth *double
the love.*

"It is, Grandpa! How are you doing?"

"Couldn't be better, Jen. I miss your grandmother, but the older I get, the closer I get to seeing her again."

Jenna mused again. *Oh, how I want love like that in my marriage one day!*

"How are you doing? I saw your mom and dad this week. They said you were having a blast in Nashville."

"I just got back from Nashville today. I am driving back tomorrow. Time to get back to teaching. We had a great time! I wanted to come visit you today. Is it a good time?"

"Any time is a good time for you, Jen-Jen. Come anytime, please! I'm just working on my sermon for Sunday."

"Okay, great! I'll be there within the hour."

When John Walls opened the door, he opened his arms, as well. Jenna ran into them. As she squeezed him tightly, she greeted him. "Grandpa, I have missed you so much!"

John kissed the top of her head twice and returned the squeeze.

"Couldn't be better, Jen-Jen. I've missed you too!"

Then he took his granddaughter into a side hug and led her to a small dinette table. His Bible lay open by his computer. The Book was worn and tattered, signs of enduring love.

Jenna took a seat beside him. She felt an indescribable love, as she looked at the ripened hands that had composed so many life-changing messages. Jenna took comfort in knowing that once he was gone, he would not be erased from the memories of all of the people whose lives he had touched. She cherished her time with him.

"What are you preaching on this week, Grandpa?"

"Grace and faith, Jen." Then he hesitated to collect his thoughts. "You know, living here has been such a blessing. You meet so many people your age; some younger, some older; and they come from all walks of life. The other morning, I was sitting at breakfast talking and someone asked me what grace meant. And then right after that, someone asked me about faith."

Jenna listened attentively. She was always blown away by how simply her grandpa could answer a question. While he spoke, she wondered how she would answer those questions.

"I must admit, Jen-Jen that I was kind of shocked. I just assumed at my age that you'd have those two words mastered, but you just never know!" John shook his head, as he pondered. "But that's how God works, Jen-Jen, because they are going to get their answer on Sunday!" John laughed and took a sip of his coffee, which jogged his memory. "Can I get you a cup of coffee?"

"I'll get it Grandpa. Can I freshen yours up?"

"Well sure. Why not?"

Jenna walked a short distance from the table to the small kitchen area. Mr. Coffee still housed several cups.

"So, what brings my beautiful granddaughter here today?"

"Well, I wanted to see you, of course. But I needed to pick your brain."

"Uh oh! The last time you picked my brain was when you were dating that football player from college. What ever became of him anyway?"

"Ugh! Grandpa, don't remind me! I've learned from that mistake…" And then she paused, "I think I did anyway."

"What is that supposed to mean?" John laughed heartily and then took another sip.

"Well, you know I've been dating Jax."

"I do. I've been praying for him, Jen. Your dad told me about his gambling addiction."

"Thanks, Grandpa. He needs it. It is a real struggle for him. He just keeps relapsing and he's hurt so many people through it all."

"Any addiction is hard, Jen. Mainly because it separates you from God. Does it scare you?"

Jenna's eyes welled with tears. "It does. Very much. I really thought he was the one I was going to marry. I truly do love him, but I know it's going to be a constant struggle in our life. Right now, he is in Utah in a residential setting. He is getting intense help, eight hours per day."

"Does he have a strong faith, Jen?"

"I thought he did, but he seems to have fallen a little bit. He feels ashamed. It's like he feels he can't be forgiven, so he's given up."

John listened and his heart felt heavy for Jenna. He knew his granddaughter's heart.

"And this week in Nashville, I met someone. I feel so guilty about it!" Jenna wiped tears from her face.

"Explain your guilt, Jen. I'm confused."

"Well, it was just one of those instant connections and we even talked about it. I told him about my fears with Jax, but I made it clear that I was committed to Jax."

"Nothing is wrong with being transparent with someone, Jenna. You're not married to Jax." John paused, trying to watch his words. He didn't want to offend her. "What exactly do you mean by *committed?*"

"Well, I can't leave him now, Grandpa! He needs me. And Maggie, his sister, is my best friend!"

"Jenna, relationships are a two-way street. There is compromise and giving on both sides. Those aren't reasons to stay in a relationship with someone. God may be leading you down a different path."

"How do I know that? How do I know when it's God's will, Grandpa?"

John Walls repositioned himself in his chair so that he was facing his granddaughter. He took both of her hands in his. "Jenna, you need to be still and know that God is in charge. You are confused and not listening."

Jenna took a deep breath and looked at her grandpa. "I know, Grandpa! I can't shut off my brain! I don't want to hurt anyone!"

"Okay, first of all, it's never a good idea to hop from one relationship to another. You need time to grieve and to talk to God. Which makes me think that this is definitely God's plan. Jax is in Utah and this other young man is in Nashville, correct?"

"Yes, sir. His name is Mitch."

"Okay. God is giving you time, Jen. What are the qualities that you like in this Mitch person?"

Jenna smiled. "Everything, Grandpa. He has a strong faith. He's kind, loving, patient, polite, and compassionate. He's very wealthy, but you would never know it. He's very humble and he gives his money away. He comes from a wonderful family. He's easy to talk to, we share the same values and…"

John smiled and interrupted. "Well those are definitely Godly qualities, Jen. Are you keeping in touch with Jax?"

"Not for the first few months, at least. The counselors don't want him to have any outside interruptions right now."

"Okay, this is what we are going to do, Jen. You are going to pray about this. Talk to God about it- just like you talked to me. Ask him to guide you and give you direction in all of this. Faith is trust, Jen. It is believing in something that is true and committing your life to it. Hebrews 11:6 explains that without faith, it is impossible to please God. Anyone who comes to him, has to believe that He exists and that He blesses those who earnestly seek Him." Jenna met her grandpa's eyes and he spoke. "Seek Him, Jen."

Jenna hugged her grandfather. "Thank you, Grandpa. Did I just get a sample of your sermon on faith for Sunday?"

John laughed. "Yes, you did, Jen-Jen. Now how about grace? What is grace, Jen?"

"I learned it from the best, Grandpa," Jenna said, laughing and leaning into him as he walked her to the door. "It's a free gift from God. One we don't deserve. He sent His son in our place to cancel out our sins and He offers it to everyone, even His enemies. And when we accept His offer and place our faith in His sacrifice, we receive His Holy Spirit and a place in heaven with Him one day."

"Wow! You really were listening to my sermons." Both of them shared a laugh and John gave one last piece of advice. "You have to put your life into His hands and trust Him, Jen. He's with you on this path, and He will show you the way down it, or off of it… I promise. I'll be praying too."

When Jenna left, she felt peace. She was so grateful for her faithful grandfather. She would commit herself to prayer and see where God led her.

48

To do what is right and just is more acceptable to the Lord than sacrifice.

~Proverbs 21:3

Spring...

Joe and Char continued to keep in touch daily by text. The last phone call they had, Char informed Joe that she and her parents were going away for a few days to an island in Thailand. She explained that the phone service there was bad. She had written him a letter and was going to be sending it express mail. He would be receiving it in two days. She told Joe that she knew she wanted to spend the rest of her life with him, but she needed to tell him some things. She told him that she did better writing them down. She asked that he take the letter to a quiet, private place to be read. Joe agreed. He loved Char and this time away made it clear to him that she was *the one*.

The letter was scheduled to arrive on Saturday, so Joe planned to take a drive to the mountains in Ellijay, Georgia. This was Pastor Jack's favorite spot to prepare his sermons. And when the letter arrived that morning, that is exactly what he did.

Joe stopped at Subway on the way and got himself a sub. He had butterflies in his stomach in anticipation of Char's words in the letter.

She was such a kindhearted person. It touched his heart that she would take the time to write him a letter, knowing she wouldn't be able to talk to him while she was away. He felt so blessed.

He found a beautiful spot and laid out his blanket. Spring was in the air. It was April and the smell of the budding flowers filled the air. Shades of emerald replaced the starkness of the trees. Joe opened the letter and read:

My loving Joe,

This was impossible for me to tell you over the phone and I always do better writing things down. It gives me time to re-read and make it right.

I will get right to the point. On March 22, I gave birth to a baby boy.

I know you are shocked right now because you obviously know it is not yours. It is Tony's.

Joe's hands shook as he read. A nausea came over him and bile rose in his throat. He let out a primal cry, "No, Lord! Please!" He took deep breaths, wiped his wet eyes and continued reading.

I left Georgia because I didn't want to burden anyone with the truth. It was all too overwhelming to wrap my mind around. I didn't think you would ever be able to look at me the same way, knowing that my first sexual encounter was with a man who abused your sister. It was a horrific experience and I want you to know that I closed my eyes and prayed every time he forced himself on me. I started feeling sick in August and I did a pregnancy test. It confirmed that I was pregnant by a man who raped me.

Before I became a Christian, my first thought would have been to abort. I always thought rape was justified. But the more I prayed about it, God made it clear to me that there were other options. There were many couples in the world, struggling to conceive. I knew the life inside of me was God's creation and perfect in every way- innocent of choices. I also knew that it would be difficult raising a child whose biological father was such a vicious man. I couldn't imagine explaining that to my son one day; and I knew lying was wrong. So, I prayed and God led me to a Christian couple in Thailand who have tried for years to conceive. Jack's words about Micah rang in my ears- "God's chosen child." They are amazing people and have cried tears of joy since they learned they were going to have a son. We haven't decided the future conversation with him yet. Right now, we are praying about it and leaving it to God. All that matters for now is that he has a happy home.

And the most amazing gift of all is that through all of this, my parents have accepted Jesus as their Savior. I smile as I write these words because I think of Jack again- he always quoted Romans 8:28: 'and we know that all things work together for good to those who love Him.' It is definitely the truth.

I want you to know that I love you, Joe. I hope you are not angry with me; but if you are, I understand. There was just no need to upset everyone's lives. It is up to you who you want to share it with and where you want to go from here. It is behind me now. I am returning to America in August to continue teaching, and I will leave Thailand knowing I did the right thing. I feel peace and I want you to feel it too.

Please contact me if and when you are ready to talk. I will be back on Saturday. Love and prayers- Char

Philippians 3:13-14: Forgetting what is behind and straining toward what is ahead. I press on toward the goal to win the prize for which God has called me heavenward in Jesus Christ.

Joe sobbed as he finished the letter. This was Char's favorite scripture because it was written by Paul, once known as Saul, who persecuted Christians. God saved him and used Paul to share His gospel. Paul dedicated his life to sharing God's word and wrote 13 books of the New Testament. He faced his last moments on earth penniless, friendless, cold and waiting to be beheaded. But he knew the heavenly reward awaiting him and he wouldn't have traded places with anyone.

Joe's body convulsed with tears of pain for Char. He cried from the depths of his soul, "Lord! Help me! *I hate Tony Russo!*" Joe caught his breath in between sobs. "Why did he have to hurt her like that? She is so brave, Lord! Help me to forgive him. Take this from me, Lord!"

Joe sat in the quiet of the mountains. When he composed himself, he opened his eyes and on the tip of his shoe sat a yellow butterfly. Joe was stunned and felt a peace come over him. He started to laugh, thinking of Jack's affirmation of yellow butterfly sightings when he prayed from his heart.

"Thank you, Lord," Joe said humbly as he wiped the tears from his face. He knew what he had to do. He pulled out his cellphone and called Char.

Char answered on the first ring.

"Joe! I was hoping you would call! Are you okay?"

"Char! Are *you* okay? You are the most selfless person I know."

"You're not angry?"

"I'm angry with *him*, not you. Char, I am ready to move on. I love you and I want to spend the rest of my life with you."

Char was crying on the other end. "Thank you, Joe. I am so grateful that you still want to be with me."

"This wasn't your fault, Char. I just wish you didn't have to go through all of it by yourself. What was it like?"

"Delivering a baby?"

"Yes."

"It wasn't bad, Joe. I promise. I thought of it as being a surrogate mother. I became good friends with Dao and Sunan, the parents.

They went to all of my doctor appointments with me. They paid for everything. When the baby was born, the doctor immediately handed it to Dao. They were so happy, Joe."

"I am so proud of you, Char. That was such a brave thing to do."

"No, it was the *right* thing to do, Joe. They named him Matthew because Dao said that it means 'gift of Yahweh.' He was a gift from God to them, Joe. Isn't that beautiful?"

Joe listened with an intense love in his heart. She found the good in everything. The glass was always half full. She made him want to be a better person. "You are a strong person, Char. I don't know how you got through it with such a positive attitude."

"I wasn't alone, Joe. God truly saw me through it. And my parents were so amazing. I am so blessed to have them. I told them everything. I told them how I prayed and how you rescued me. They wanted to learn more about God. We've been reading the Bible together. It's a miracle."

Joe told Char about reading the letter, praying and the yellow butterfly that landed on his shoe.

"I just got chills, Joe. That is so beautiful. Like Jack said, angels come in all forms."

Joe laughed. "I'm now a believer."

"How's Jack doing? I miss him."

"He's hanging in there. He's tired and weak, but has the same optimistic attitude. He has defied the odds. Dr. Jollie said he's lived longer than anyone else he's diagnosed with kidney cancer."

"God must still have work for him to do."

"You may be right. I can't imagine what else there could be. He is the ultimate servant of God. I can picture him meeting Jesus and hearing the words of Matthew 25:21, 'well done, good and faithful servant! You have been faithful with a few things; I will put you in charge of many things.' Jack has lots of rewards ahead of him in heaven."

"I agree. He truly did everything as if working for God. I learned so much from him and without judgment."

"I know. He will be missed."

"Have you decided if you want to talk to anyone about this?"

"I think for now we need to sort through it together. Like you said, it's behind us now. I don't want you to have to keep reliving it. I just can't wait to have you back in the states."

"Me too, Joe. Thanks for being you. I am blessed beyond words."

"Ditto."

49

Guide me in your truth and teach me, for you are God my Savior. My hope is in you all day long.

~Psalm 25:5

Life went on as usual. Grace and Will were back teaching, planning their summer wedding. And as Grace suggested, they incorporated a music time with their students. The changes in their attention, verbal language skills and personalities amazed both of them. *Music was good for the soul!*

Jenna fell back into a routine in North Carolina. Jax's counselors were slowly working relationships back into his life. Jax's parents, Maggie and his brothers flew to Utah for the weekend to take part in family therapy. Mags reported to Jenna that Jax seemed happy and hopeful, but he had a long way to go. The real challenge was going to be when he was dismissed from the program and he had to put what he learned into practice.

Jenna had not heard from Jax in three months. She was praying for God's guidance, as she promised her grandfather. She was feeling a renewed peace, taking one day at a time. She knew that she would eventually have to be part of Jax's therapy if they were going to spend the rest of their lives together. Maggie told Jenna that Jax said he would be contacting her soon. Until then, she would go on with life and pray.

Friday afterschool, Jenna checked her text messages on the way out to her car. Her heart skipped a beat when she saw a text message.

Mitch: Hi Jen! I'll be in NC in two weeks. Are you still interested in coming to a concert?

Jenna felt excitement and guilt at the same time. The man she had planned to marry was in rehab and she wanted to meet up with another guy. She hadn't told Maggie or Micah about the concert. She didn't want Mags to think she was betraying her brother; and if Maggie did question her about her feelings, she knew she couldn't lie. She opened her car door and sat in the driver's seat. She texted back.

Jenna: Hi Mitch! I am very interested. I'm just about to drive home from work. I will be in touch later. Thanks for the invite!

Jenna tossed her phone into her purse and started the car. The engine's roar blended with the beating of her heart and the commotion in her head. She prayed aloud, "Lord, I need you! I am *so confused*. Please make this clear to me."

When Jenna got to her apartment, she checked her mailbox. She pulled the pile out of the box and placed it in the teacher bag hanging from her shoulder. She unlocked her apartment door and put her bag on the counter. She grabbed a coke out of the fridge and pulled up a stool at the counter. She pulled out her mail. There was her first correspondence with Jax sticking out of the stack of mail.

Was this her answer?

Jenna felt her heart beating in her throat. Her hand shook as she looked at the return address…the rehabilitation center in Utah. She lay her head on the countertop and started crying. She pleaded between her sobs, "Please God! Help me through this!"

With trembling hands and a quivering heart, Jenna opened the letter.

50

The Lord gives strength to his people; the Lord blesses his people with peace.

~Psalm 29:11

Jen-

I hope this letter finds you content. I've written this letter so many times! My garbage can is filled with torn pieces of my heartfelt thoughts. I've concluded that there aren't words to express all that I really want to say to you. So, here's the best I've got... You are the best thing that ever happened to me, Jen. I never thought that I would find myself again, let alone love, but you helped me uncover both. I love you, Jen.

Jenna's shoulders shook with emotion. Her tears smeared the ink on the letter. Memories raced through her mind as she thought back to the beginning of their relationship- so fresh and full of hope. She was sure he was *it*.

Paige, Jax's previous girlfriend broke up with him because she didn't think he could meet her needs with a social worker salary. She was used to having everything. Money wasn't a priority to Jax. Helping others was his calling. Paige's decision destroyed his self-worth.

Jenna grabbed a napkin from the counter and wiped her eyes. She continued reading.

> Today is three months to the day that I've entered rehab. I've met some of the most amazing people here. This was definitely where God wanted them. They are changing lives every day. Mine too is slowing being transformed. I am learning so much about myself, and what makes me tick; why I make the choices I do. In my group therapy sessions, I meet with addicts of every nature- drugs, alcohol, pornography, gambling, shopping... we're all the same...just dependent on different things. I've learned a lot about you too, Jen. You have an amazing integrity. You are the same inside as you appear on the outside. There is no discrepancy between what you say and do. Your walk is the same as your talk. I am striving for that, Jen, but I have a long way to go! I still have a lot of demons within myself that I need to conquer. It is going to be a forever battle and quite honestly, Jenna...you don't deserve this battle. You deserve someone with the same integrity, Jen. I have been praying for you and I know that once I set you free, God will lead you to that person. I'm not writing this letter to hurt you. I know that this is God's idea. I've met someone here. Her name is Jan. She too has a gambling addiction and has hurt so many in her life, as I have. We have really bonded over these three months. She knows exactly how I feel. I find a peace with her that I've never felt. I can be so transparent with her.

Jenna's crying seized and she felt a sudden peace come over her. *Transparent*, she remembered silently, *that's what grandpa said was important in a relationship*. She read on.

You need to move on and see what blessings are in store for you. You have been a blessing in my life for sure. It's time to spread the wealth☺ I would love to remain friends and would love to hear from you; but that is completely up to you. Please don't worry about me- just keep me in your prayers and I will do the same for you. Thank you for everything, Jen. I will be forever grateful to God for putting you in my path.

Jax

Jenna finished the letter and sat in complete stillness for thirty minutes. Her mind was blank, but a serenity took her over.

Then the phone rang and snapped her back to consciousness.

51

Lord, you establish peace for us; all that we have accomplished, you have done for us.

~Isaiah 26:12

Jenna took her phone from her purse. The face of the phone read, *Mags*.

With the peace of answered prayer, Jenna answered. "Hi Mags."

"Are you okay, Jen?"

Jenna paused. "You knew?"

"I just hung up with Jax. He told me about the letter. He knew you got it today and he wanted me to check on you."

"I'm fine, Mags. I've had three months to think through our relationship. His letter was beautiful and I am so happy that he has met someone who understands better."

"Me too. It's just sad. I have to grieve the concept of no more Jenna and Jax." Maggie laughed. "But if you are okay, so am I."

"I'm okay, Mags. We'll get through it. Jax said he has been praying about it and he believes it's God's plan. I agree."

"I'm so relieved, Jen. You sound peaceful about it. Micah and I have been praying about it too. Jax has a long road ahead of him."

"I promise. I plan to keep in touch with him. I want to stay friends, for sure. He will always have a special place in my heart."

"Thanks Jen. What's going on? Other than a *Dear John* letter?"

Jenna burst into laughter and then extended the invitation. "Well, the Mitchell Boone Band is coming to Charlotte in two weeks. Would you and Micah be interested?"

"We would have loved to, but one of the doctors at the hospital is getting married and we've been invited. And quite honestly, I think it's a good idea for you to go alone."

Jenna wasn't sure where Mags was going with this conversation. "What do you mean?"

"Come on, Jen. You are my best friend. You don't think I noticed the connection you and Mitch had in Nashville?"

Jenna felt her face flush. "Really?"

"Of course. I wasn't thrilled about it at first, but now I see that this may very well be God's plan."

"I love you, Mags. There was a connection, but I told Mitch that I was committed to Jax."

"I had no doubt, Jen. I just always thought you were the one for my brother. But, I'm not in charge, God is."

"Thanks Mags. Have fun at the wedding and we'll talk soon."

"You have fun too. Say hi to Mitch for us. He really seems like a great guy. And- count us in next concert!"

"I promise."

When Jenna hung up, she thanked God and then sent Mitch a text.

Jenna: Can you talk?

Mitch: Sure. I'll call you in 10 minutes.

Jenna: perfect!

52

Speaking the truth in love, we will grow to become in every respect the mature body of him who is the head, that is, Christ.

~Ephesians 4:15

The phone rang in exactly ten minutes. Jenna answered. "You are a man of your word."

Mitch laughed. "Well, I try to be. What do you mean?"

"Ten minutes exactly."

"Were you watching the clock?"

Jenna blushed and laughed nervously. *Busted!* "I guess I was."

"Well, I'm happy that my phone call was well- awaited. So, who's coming?"

"Just me."

"What about Micah and Maggie?"

"They have a wedding to go to."

"Jax?"

"Still in rehab." Jenna thought about mentioning the Dear John letter, but changed her mind just as quickly. Her grandpa was right. She needed to mourn this break-up and not rush into anything.

"Well, I don't want you to drive alone. I'll book a flight for you and

I'll pick you up at the airport. Can you come in on Thursday night? The concert is Friday."

"Sure- I can go to the airport right from work on Thursday. I'll have to take off, but I can use a personal day. But, please, let me book it."

"Nope. My mother raised me better than that. I invited you, so I'll take care of it."

Jenna laughed. "Well, if you insist."

"I insist. When do you have to be back? Can you take off Monday too?"

"I think I can manage that."

"Then do it! We can hang out in Charlotte the rest of the weekend. I've never been. It's supposed to be a great city."

"Okay. As long as I'm back Monday night."

"I'll get on it and get back to you."

"Thanks, Mitch. I'm looking forward to it."

"Me too, Jen. I'm happy you are coming."

When Jenna hung up she got a pad of paper and a pen out of her desk drawer. It was time to write Jax back. The words flowed like lava.

Jax,

Thank you so much for your kind words. You and your family were easy to be around. You guys made it easy to "walk my talk." ☺ I felt no hurt at all when I read your letter. I, too believe that this is God's plan. I felt myself drifting after I found my jewelry in your coat pocket. I have totally forgiven you, but it was difficult for me to understand. I am so happy that you met someone that you can be transparent with. There shouldn't be any secrets in a relationship. That is so important. It seems that being with someone who understands your addiction would make it easier, but your counselors know better than me. I will be praying for you both. And, yes, I want to remain friends. Your family will forever be a big part of my life.

I wanted to tell you that I met someone too. His name is Mitch. It is Will Boone's brother (Grace's fiancé). I met him in Nashville when we celebrated Christmas there with Jack. I'm sure Mags gave you the details of the celebration. It was perfect! Jack met a new friend, Butch. He is a six-year-old with cancer. They have been keeping in touch. Butch has the same spirit as Jack- keeping his eye on eternity☺

Anyway, your letter did find me content and I appreciate your prayers. Since I've read your letter, I've decided I am going to pursue my friendship with Mitch. I am going to take it slow and see where it leads. I know you both can conquer this battle. Remember that all things are possible with Him. Just keep God the center of your life and trust Him even in your weakness.

Philippians 3:13-14 says it all- let go of the past and look forward to what God wants you to become. You are forgiven and have a clean slate. Move on to a life of faith and obedience and everything will fall into place.

Much love and lots of prayers- Jenna

53

Hear my prayer, Lord; listen to my cry for mercy. When
I am in distress, I call to you because you answer me.

~Psalm 86:6

Jack spent more and more time in bed. The cancer was taking over
his body, but not his spirit. He talked to God daily, sharing his
excitement of meeting Him and asking that He watch over his
family and friends; and see them through the loss. The Finnegan house
was a revolving door. Family and friends came by daily to visit Jack and
get filled with the hope that he shared so well.

One afternoon, Jack called Carrie into the room. I need you to take
me somewhere and I don't want you to argue with me. Carrie sat at the
side of the bed and took her husband's hand.

"Where?"

"It's a secret."

"Jack Finnegan! You know I hate secrets!"

"You'll find out soon enough. You're my driver. I'm the GPS."

"Okay, you win," Carrie said suspiciously. She helped Jack into his
wheelchair and down the ramp from the front door to the car. Jack got
in the passenger side and Carrie folded the chair and put it in the back
seat. About fifteen minutes later, Carrie was pulling into the driveway
of the state prison.

Carrie stopped the car. "Jack, what are you doing?"

"I've got to give it one more try, Care. It's tugging at my heart."

"Jack, you have got to be kidding me! That man is a monster!"

"Please, Carrie. Just do it for me."

And fifteen minutes later, Carrie and Jack Finnegan sat across from Tony Russo, the man who beat their daughter and abused Joe's girlfriend.

This time Tony accepted the visitation. Jack had been writing him letters telling him that it wasn't too late. He told him that God still loved him and could heal his sinful ways. Francesco had called Jack that morning and told him that Tony wanted to see Jack. Jack knew this was an answer to prayer.

When Tony was led out by the guards into the visitation room, he saw Jack and sobbed. The realization of Jack's final days was evident. Tony knelt down before him and cried at his feet.

"Why aren't you giving up on me?" Tony wailed, choking on his tears. His sobs echoed off the cemented walls. "I don't deserve this love!"

Jack smiled and reached his hands to Tony's shoulders. "Look at me, Tony."

Tony slowly looked up at him, revealing his moistened face.

"Tony, before I leave this earth, I need to know that I am going to see you again. Please do this for me."

Tony continued weeping. He looked down, embarrassed by the memories. "How could God ever forgive me?"

"Philippians 1:6 says that God, who began a good work in you will carry it on to completion. God completes his work, Tony. This is it. He loves you. He alone is your joy. He will meet your every need. Just ask for forgiveness, Tony! Tell Him you need Him. He'll give you a clean slate if you mean it. Tony, without Him, you can't do *anything*! You should know that by now!"

Tony listened and wept. "I don't deserve forgiveness!"

"None of us do, Tony! But God wants you to be the son he designed you to be. Second Peter 9 says that God is patient with you, not wanting *anyone* to perish, but *everyone* to come to repentance."

Tony was curled in a ball, his hands wrapped around his ankles, rocking back and forth. Raucous cries erupted from his body and then he did it.

"I am so sorry, Lord! I am so ashamed! I have done such evil things! I don't even know who I am anymore! Please forgive me! Help me, Lord!"

Tony's pleas were so loud and heartfelt that the guards in the room were moved to tears. Carrie felt the Holy Spirit in the room, as the hair on her body stood on end.

Jack kept on. "That's it, Tony. Do you accept Him? Do you promise to follow Him and allow Him to change you?"

"Yes! Lord, please! I need you to change me! I hate myself!" War cries of emotions erupted from Tony. Then his sobs turned to sniffles. His body stopped jerking…his tears subsided. He looked up into Jack's eyes and his vacant eyes revealed life.

Tony stated softly and adamantly, "I felt Him. I felt Him, Jack." Then Tony put his head on Jack's knees and they cried together.

Carrie couldn't believe she had forgiveness in her heart for this man, but God had moved her to pity. She came from behind the wheelchair and knelt down with both men. Tony looked up at her. "I am so sorry I hurt your family! Please forgive me."

Carrie hugged Tony. "I forgive you, Tony. I'll be praying for you."

Then Jack preached. "I forgive you, Tony. Remember to trust Him for everything. You have a lot of time in here. Pray without ceasing. Listen to Him. Tell Him your every thought and need. You have a lot more apologies to make, but God will see you through. Pour your heart out to Him and thank Him for the answers that are on the way."

54

Those who walk uprightly enter into peace; they find rest as they lie in death.

~Isaiah 57:2

That evening, Jack and Carrie lay in bed discussing their visit with Tony.

"I can't believe it, Care. God is so good! That was my final work for God on earth."

Carrie paused and thought about what Jack had said. "What do you mean, Jack? You don't know what God has planned."

Jack let her words sink in, thoughtful of his response. "It's almost time, Care. The cancer is winning."

Carrie's heart skipped a beat and she immediately started weeping. A desperation came over her as she snuggled up against her husband with her head on his gaunt chest.

"Oh no! Please, Jack! I'm not ready!"

"You have to be, Care. Everything in God's perfect timing. We're not in charge, He is."

Carrie said nothing else. She sobbed in Jack's arms until he fell asleep. She knew the signs, but didn't want to face it. She noticed the change in his breathing, the exhaustion, loss of appetite and continued weight loss.

She knew it was the time to call the Hospice nurse. It was Jack's desire to die at home comfortably.

Carrie called Micah next. Jack made Micah promise that he would go on with his life. He called his dad daily while he finished his work at the hospital.

Micah answered with angst. "Hi Mom. Everything okay?"

"Hi Mike. Your dad says the time is near."

There was a perceptible silence on the other end. "We'll be there tonight. Is he awake?"

Carrie carried the phone with her toward the bedroom. "In and out. Let me check."

Carrie sat on the side of the bed and put her hands on Jack's stomach. "Can you talk, honey? It's Micah."

Jack's eyes opened immediately at the sound of his son's name. A smile spread across his face. "Of course."

Carrie handed the phone to Jack. It amazed her how quickly he had weakened. His voice was labored and he had difficulty holding the phone. He was surrendering his will to live and seemed more than content with it.

"Hi, son. I believe today is the day that I meet my Savior."

Micah was crying. "I'm jealous, Dad. Be sure to tell Him I said hello."

Jack and Micah shared a tear-filled laugh.

"I'm coming as soon as I get a flight, Dad. Do you think you can hang in there for us?"

"I'll try, Mike. A hug from my boy would be an amazing departure."

Micah stifled his sobs. "Well, just in case God has another plan, I want you to know that you were the best earthly dad ever!"

Tears streamed down Jack's face as Carrie held the phone for him. She could hear Micah through the phone and shared in the weeping.

"I love you, Micah. You were such a gift from God. I am so proud of you. Remember- do everything for His glory and celebrate my life."

"I promise, Dad. You rest, okay? Mags and I will see you soon."

Carrie took the phone from Jack. "You okay?"

"I couldn't be better, Care. I have an eternity of peace and happiness ahead of me. What could be wrong? I need to call one more person, though."

Carrie sat at the side of the bed. "Who?"

"Butch."

"Are you sure it won't upset him?"

"I know it won't. He's ready, Care. It's hard to explain, but when you surrender it to God, it's just this peace you can't explain. Butch has it."

"Okay." Carrie took Jack's phone and scrolled to Butch's number. She held the phone to Jack's ear.

"Hi Jack!"

"Hey Butch! How's it going?"

"Great! It's time, isn't it Jack?"

"It is, Butch. How did you know?"

"I just know. I'm getting close too. I'll see you there, right?"

"Absolutely, buddy. You know I'll be waiting for you."

"I know you will. Tell my friend, Julia I'm coming soon if you see her, okay?"

"It's a promise. I love you, Butch."

"Love you, too, Jack."

Carrie wiped tears from her eyes as she listened to the conversation. She hoped and prayed that she would be this ready when God called her home. The faith of Jack and Butch made her desire to grow in her faith.

Jack dozed back to sleep in seconds. Bev, the Hospice nurse arrived and checked Jack's vitals. Jack opened his eyes and smiled at her. "Are you my angel?"

Bev let out a comforting laugh. "Hi Jack! Sorry to disappoint. I'm Bev, your nurse. I'm here to make you as comfortable as possible. Are you in any pain?"

"A little bit."

"Okay. Well, I am going to give you some medicine to help with that."

While Bev was tending to Jack, Carrie called family and close friends. Before they arrived, Carrie climbed in bed with the love of her life for the last time.

"I love you so much, Jack. Thank you for being the most wonderful husband and father. I am going to miss you *so* much." Carrie sobbed.

"I love you too, Care," Jack replied with all of the energy he could muster. "Remember, you promised me- celebrate."

55

Blessed are those who mourn for they will be comforted.

~Matthew 5:4

Within the hour, Jade, Beau, Grace, Will, Joe, Emma, John and Matthew arrived. Katie and Chloe stayed with their grandparents. Carrie prayed that Jack would hold on long enough to say goodbye to Micah and Mags.

The nurse explained that although Jack was not responsive, they should assume that he could hear everything they said. She also explained that it wasn't uncommon for him to have a sudden burst of energy before he passed.

Everyone took their turn holding Jack's hand and speaking calmly, sharing stories and thanking him for his friendship and love.

Matthew climbed on the bed and kissed Jack on the cheek.

"Say hi to my dad for me. Okay, Uncle Jack?"

A smile formed on Jack's face and a tear rolled down his cheek. Jack lifted his arm and squeezed Matthew's leg.

The nurse continued to check on Jack. She explained that his blood pressure was dropping and his breathing was becoming irregular. This usually indicated a matter of hours.

Everyone sat around Jack's bedside and shared stories of their times together; and prayed. And in between, they assured Jack that they were there and he was loved.

And then Micah and Mags arrived an hour later. When Jack heard his son's voice, that sudden burst of energy showed itself and shocked everyone. He sat up in bed and said, "What'd you do? Grow wings?"

The room burst into laughter as Micah and Maggie approached his bedside. "God is good, Dad. There was a direct flight just waiting for us when we got to the airport. Thanks for waiting for us."

"You are welcome. I wanted you to meet my parents." Jack looked to the opposite side of the bed and said, "Mom, Dad, this is Micah."

Everyone in the room had chills. Jack unmistakably saw his parents.

The nurse winked at Micah, indicating a common occurrence.

Micah didn't miss a beat. "Nice to meet you, Grandma and Grandpa. You take good care of my dad, okay?"

Jack smiled. "And look at my good-looking angel over there. He's been here the whole time just watching over me."

No one spoke. The room was silent as everyone took in the divine introductions.

Jack carried on a conversation with the opposite side of the room. "Okay. I'm ready. I can't wait to meet Him face-to-face! The best is yet to come!"

And just as quickly as his sudden burst of energy came, Jack's breathing pattern quickened. He closed his eyes and a light from the window illuminated his smiling face, as he raised his arms to the heavens.

And then the gates of heaven opened up and Jack Finnegan entered them.

Bev was crying joyful tears as the rest of the group stood awestruck.

"He's passed to the other side," Bev said as she took Jack's pulse.

Then out of the mouth of a babe, Matthew shouted, "That was awesome! I wonder if he saw my dad yet!"

Emma picked up her son and hugged him tightly. "I bet he was waiting for Jack, don't you?"

"I know it!" Matthew alleged excitedly.

Carrie sat on the side of the bed and looked one last time at her husband's serene face. And with an unnatural calmness, she spoke. "I feel peace." Then, she looked to Bev. "Is that a typical passing?"

"Very typical, Carrie," and then she added, "For a believer. An unbeliever is very different. Your husband is in paradise."

Then John McDonald spoke up. "The same thing happened with Molly." John smiled as he remembered it. "She was smiling and talking to someone. She had her arms raised too, as if following the light."

Bev continued. "I'm going to step into the other room and do some paperwork. You can spend as much time as you need. If you know what funeral home you will be using, I can call them when you are ready. Do you have any questions?"

Carrie answered immediately and stood up from the bedside. "Jack and I decided on Murphy's Funeral Home. I'd like for you to call them, please. I don't want to sound harsh, but I know where he is. Jack told me that for a believer, death is to be away from the body and at home with the Lord. He's with his Savior. I have no doubt."

Jade and Beau walked toward Carrie and put their arms around their friend. They led her toward the door. And hand-in-hand, the guests walked out of the room, convinced that eternity existed; and their beloved Jack was beginning a new life there. They would all be together again someday.

56

For to me to live is Christ and to die is gain.

~Philippians 1:21

The celebration of Jack's life...

Grace and Joe spent the night with their mother. Grace slept with her mom and they cried themselves to sleep. Joe called Char in Thailand to share the news.

The next morning, Carrie woke feeling empty. She saw Grace sleeping next to her, but knew eventually, that place beside her would be forever vacant. She went into the shower and sat on the shower floor. She put her arms around her ankles and rested her forehead on her knees. She rocked, sobbing aloud, as her tears washed down the drain... along with the earthly finality of Jack Finnegan's presence.

Jack was interested in every aspect of her life and he was gone. Life wasn't always understandable and Carrie knew she would have to wait to get her questions answered. Then, and only then, would she have complete clarity. But for now, she promised Jack that she would celebrate his life and that is what she planned to do.

As Carrie dressed, she held onto Joshua 1:9, be strong and courageous. Do not be afraid or discouraged for the Lord your God is with you wherever you go. She said it repeatedly in her mind, and then spoke aloud. "Okay, Lord. I'm listening. Please, help me through this!"

The funeral service was scheduled for the following Saturday. Jack was loved by so many that Carrie wanted to allow enough time for them to arrive. Jenna flew in on Friday night after work. She had been keeping in touch with Mitch. He told her that he and his family would be at the service for Jack. She would see him again the following weekend at his concert in Charlotte. The service was going to be held at the Gwinnett Braves Stadium, as was Jack's beloved *Surrender* sermon; the sermon that brought together the most unlikely: the drunk driver, the widow and the heart recipient.

News spread throughout Georgia, Florida, Tennessee and North Carolina, so Jack's church, once again, could not hold the throngs. The memories flooded back as Carrie, Micah, Joe and Grace made the arrangements. Carrie found herself crying as she thought back. Jack was such a giving person and she knew that the giver always got more than the receiver. Giving was what brought Jack joy. Carrie often stopped and wondered what Jack was doing in heaven. That brought a smile to her face. She knew God had big plans for him.

The morning of Jack's service, the stadium was once again filled to capacity. Carrie wondered if Jack could see the crowd from heaven. Daniel Bar- the driver under the influence that killed Ben Walls- led the service. He had completed his seminary courses and was now a practicing minister; only the work of a mighty God! His life was transformed through tragedy.

Mitch and his family joined the family and friends of Carrie, Grace, Joe and Micah at the service. Even Dr. Jollie shared in Jack's celebration of life. Will never left Grace's side. It was becoming evident to Jenna that love and faith were a Boone family trait. And as promised, Mitch arranged for Jenna to be picked up afterschool on Thursday of the following week, to be taken to the airport for their long weekend in Charlotte.

Micah would perform the eulogy. He was strong and encouraging like his dad; even though they didn't share the same genes. A stillness came over the crowd when Micah walked to the pulpit. The crowd was silent waiting for Jack's tribute. Micah began:

"In Second Timothy, verse seven, Paul writes his last words to Timothy, a man he loved like a son. Paul was a prisoner in Rome, about to be executed. He wrote, 'I have finished the race. I have kept the faith. Now there is in store for me the crown of righteousness, which is the Lord, the righteous judge will award to me on that day. And not only to me, but to all who have longed for his appearing.'

"This made me think of my dad. He has finished the race and kept the faith and now he is with his Savior. The first time I stood at the pulpit was to celebrate the joining of my dad and my beautiful mom, Carrie, in marriage. Today, we celebrate my dad joining his heavenly Father.

"First Corinthians 9:24 states, 'do you not know that in a race, all the runners run, but only one gets the prize? Run in such a way as to get the prize.'" Micah paused, smiling, and then went on. "My dad ran to win. I have no doubt that he has walked through the gates of heaven and met his Creator. My dad served God every single day of his life and I know that when he met Jesus, Jesus said, 'Well done good and faithful servant. You have been faithful with a few things. I will put you in charge of many things. Come and share your master's happiness.' These are the words of Matthew 25:23."

Carrie wiped joyful tears from her eyes. She thought the same thing about her husband. The Bible promised this and they knew Jack earned it.

"I feel peace knowing that my dad is in paradise working joyfully for his Creator, alongside his parents, who were killed on a mission trip in Africa. They too served God with an undying faith. God has set before us a race and we have to run it. It will involve effort, commitment and endurance, but God wants us to finish strong! With joy!

"Follow His footsteps in the race of life. Jesus doesn't ask more of us than He Himself has experienced. He knows exactly what we are going through because He was God in human flesh, sent by God from heaven to save us from our sins.

"My dad never asked *why* he got cancer. He never questioned his

Savior. He used to tell me that the world was God's classroom and everything in it- all that we possess, belongs to Him. No matter what the disaster, my dad saw it as an opportunity to grow. He saw it as a challenge, that together he and God could handle; an opportunity to seek God, and depend solely on Him.

"My dad taught me that being grateful in all things was seeing the world through God's eyes. He told me to appreciate the hard times as much as the good so I would be constantly aware of God's presence in my life. He taught me to lean on Him and to focus on the word of God because His word was perfect. He told me that God didn't make mistakes. My dad's Bible was the channel to his soul."

Micah paused and pulled an envelope from his pocket. "I wanted to read an excerpt from a letter my dad left me after he died. As he lay in bed at night waiting to be called home, he wrote letters to all of his loved ones. I will cherish mine forever." Micah unfolded the letter and read:

"Micah, go to God with confidence because there is absolutely nothing that He can't provide. Your earthly father has been called home, but your heavenly father is with you wherever you go. There is nothing too big for Him, Mike. Don't get caught up in the *what-ifs* of life. Wanting to undo decisions you regret is wasted time. See your failures as a blessing. They will humble you and help you to be empathetic to others and their weakness. They make you depend on God.

"Move on with gratitude knowing that God keeps giving you chances. Life holds endless opportunities when you have Christ as the center of your life. He is all you need to live your life. He holds all of the answers to life because *He is life…the way, the truth, and the life.*"

Micah swallowed back his emotion, breathing heavily into the microphone, but pressed on. "It's not the failures in life, but the choices you *didn't* make that you will regret. If God opens a door for you, He'll walk you through it, even if it's the wrong one. It's time to fly, son! Don't give into fear! Go live your life and I'll be waiting for you in paradise."

Micah folded the paper as he cried tears of mixed emotion. Then he addressed the crowd with one more point. "I challenge you today to live like my dad, Jack Finnegan. I was named after the prophet, Micah in the Bible. I stand by Micah 7:7: 'As for me, I watch in hope for the Lord. I wait for God, my Savior. My God will hear me.'

"Hope is the anchor of the soul. The rougher the weather gets, the more we need our anchor. I am going to run the race set before me. I promise to live my life on earth to the fullest, loving God's people. I am going to laugh a whole lot more and hope for a future in eternity by clinging to God's promises.

"Make your relationship with God the center of your lives and lock your eyes on the goal- life forever with Jesus in heaven. God bless all of you and thank you for being here today to celebrate my dad. Let's keep his legacy alive."

A thunderous applause erupted once again throughout the stadium, followed by Jack Finnegan's favorite hymn, "Amazing Grace." It resonated through the stadium and out onto the streets; and then rose into the heavens to honor God's precious child, Jack Finnegan.

57

Whoever sows sparingly will also reap sparingly and whoever sows generously will also reap generously. Each of you should give what you have decided in your heart to give, not reluctantly or under compulsion, for God loves a cheerful giver.

~2 Corinthians 9:6-7

The goodbye…

After the service, friends and family stopped by Carrie and Jack's house. Several women from Jack's church left the service early and had everything ready for their arrival. Food of every category decked the countertops. The conversations were a blur, but Carrie made it through the day with her best friend, Jade right by her side. When the crowd thinned, Carrie, Beau, Jade, their children and significant others sat on the patio reminiscing. It was then that Pastor Mark from the Sanibel Island church and Pastor Gary, Jack's assistant pastor from the Georgia church presented Carrie with an envelope.

Pastor Mark began, fighting his tears. "Where do I start? There are no words to describe how much Jack was loved. He changed lives one day at a time. The standing- room- only stadium was just a small testament of that. When Jack was getting weaker, Pastor Gary and I were receiving *hundreds* of phone calls a week from parishioners, asking what they could do. So, we decided to take up a collection for your family. We thought everyone could use money- especially a pastor and a teacher!" The room burst into laughter and Pastor Mark continued.

"Anyway, we knew that Jack wanted his ashes spread on the gulf, by the condo he lived in when he was the pastor on Sanibel."

Carrie nodded in agreement, dreading the finality of that day. She stared straight ahead in a daze as if reliving the conversation with him. "He said that when I retired, it would force me to go to the beach more."

"Well, I think his wish came true. As a gift for Jack's service, all of the members of Jack's churches on Sanibel and in Georgia collected enough money to *buy* you that condo." Pastor Mark handed Carrie the envelope. "Here is the deed. It's all yours, Carrie. Paid in full."

Everyone in the room gasped and then started clapping out of sheer appreciation of the charity. Carrie held the envelope in her quivering hands and sobbed. Her body shook with a cacophony of emotion- heartbreak, gratitude and joy, all rolled into one.

After she collected herself, Carrie rose and hugged both pastors with silent embraces. Then she sat back down and addressed the room. "How can I ever thank these loving people enough? I am so humbled by their generosity."

"By accepting it, Carrie," Pastor Gary responded. "They were so excited about it! It was done in love and they are getting as much joy out of it as you are."

58

For you O Lord, have made me glad by what You have done. I will sing for joy at the works of your hands.

~Psalm 92:4

Afterschool on Thursday, Jenna excitedly headed to her car to get her luggage. While she was getting it out of the trunk, a car pulled up.

"Jenna Walls?"

Jenna turned around to acknowledge the driver and started laughing as Mitch got out of the rental car.

"What are you doing here? Aren't you supposed to be practicing music or something?"

Mitch laughed, as he went in for a hug. "That comes later. I thought you'd be more comfortable driving to the airport with someone you knew. It will give us time to talk since we didn't get much of a chance at Jack's service."

Mitch took the suitcase from Jenna and put it in the back seat, while Jenna got in the passenger side.

"Thank you, Mitch. To be honest, I wasn't sure what or who would show up to get me. I didn't ask because I didn't want to sound ungrateful."

Mitch laughed. "Did you expect a stretch limo?"

Jenna laughed out loud. "Like I said, I wasn't sure."

"Well honestly, I like these little economy cars. Good on gas and easy to drive."

"I agree. I'm pretty simple myself…and honestly very relieved that it wasn't a stretch limo!"

Mitch laughed and continued the conversation. "What an amazing celebration of Jack's life!"

"Wasn't it? I can't stop thinking about it! My mom and dad are flying to Fort Myers this weekend to spread his ashes."

"Yeah, Will is going too."

"That's right! I keep forgetting you are brothers. Sorry!"

"That's okay. Are you sure you didn't want to go?"

"I'm sure. It's just immediate family. My parents fall under that category. My mom and Carrie are best friends. Carrie met Jack through my mom. Did I ever tell you that story?"

"No, but Grace did. Definitely a God thing."

"No doubt."

The ride to the airport was non-stop conversation and laughter. Jenna shared stories about Ben and all of the blessings that came out of his death. Mitch was incredibly easy to be around. Jenna was overjoyed to be spending the whole weekend with him.

When they landed, Mitch and Jenna headed to baggage claim. Mitch wore a baseball cap at eyebrow level, concealing himself from prospective fans. After getting Jenna's suitcase, they headed outside where Billy Madison, Mitch's manager was waiting in a black Escalade SUV. Billy hugged Jenna and welcomed her.

"Where we headed?" Billy asked as he put Jenna's suitcase in the back.

"To the Hilton, Bill. Jen can drop off her stuff and then we can head to the PNC." Then Mitch turned toward Jenna for approval. "Is that okay with you, Jen?"

Jenna laughed. "I'm just along for the ride. Whatever you think."

When they arrived at the hotel, they walked straight to the elevators. Mitch already had her room key. They headed to the fifth floor and stopped at room 515. Mitch opened the door and put her luggage on the king-sized bed. The curtains were open, revealing a stunning lake view.

"Does this work?" Mitch asked with smiling eyes.

"It is beautiful, Mitch! Thank you so much!"

"You are so welcome. I am right down the hall with the rest of the band- room 525. I am going to go freshen up. I will be back in about an hour. We'll grab something to eat and head to the PNC."

"What exactly is the PNC?"

"I'm sorry. The PNC Pavilion. It is the amphitheater we are performing at tomorrow night. We are going to do a couple of sound checks to make sure we're ready."

"Sounds awesome!"

"Great. I'll see you soon."

Mitch headed out the door and Jenna sat down on the bed to collect her thoughts.

"Thank you, Lord! This is too good to be true!"

59

He will fill your mouth with laughter and your lips with shouting.

~Psalm 92:4

Jenna took a shower and changed into a casual sundress and flip flops. An hour later, a friendly rap graced the door. Jenna opened the door, trying so hard to stifle her unspeakable excitement.

"Hi!" She bellowed, louder than normal.

Mitch burst out laughing. "Hi! Are you always this happy on vacation?"

Jenna joined in the laughter. "I'm sorry, but I am so excited that I am going out to dinner and to a sound check with you!"

Mitch opened the door. "After you," he smiled as he met Jenna's joyful eyes. "I am so happy that you are so easy to please."

Jenna grabbed her purse and a jacket off of the bed and headed out the door with Mitch following behind.

"Where we going to eat?"

"I thought we'd eat right here at Edgewater Bar and Grille. We ate here last night and it was great. Great steaks and seafood. How does that sound?"

"Perfect! I love them both!"

They headed downstairs and the waitress led them to a table by the lake. The sun shimmered off the water like diamonds, while music played in the background. They enjoyed a dinner of medium rare ribeye and lobster tail. They enjoyed a laugh over the fact that they both liked ketchup on their steak.

Jenna confessed with a chuckle, "My dad was horrified that I put ketchup on my steak. He said it was an insult to the chef!"

"My mother too! She used to forbid me to ask for it when we went out to eat as a family."

"How about your hamburger? Ketchup, mustard or mayo?" Jenna probed.

"Mustard and onions." Mitch affirmed.

"Me too! Miracle whip or mayo?" she continued.

"Definitely mayo."

"Me too! I hate miracle whip! Mexican or Chinese food?"

"Ahhh, that's a tough one. I love them both. It depends on my mood. You like sushi?"

"Love sushi!" Jenna lamented with a groan of adoration.

Mitch laughed. "You just love to eat, don't you?"

"Definitely one of my top five favorite things to do!" Jenna chuckled.

"Oh yeah," Mitch agreed. "Top three for me. How 'bout favorite movie?"

"My Best Friend's Wedding!"

Mitch choked on his coke, laughing. "What? I never even heard of it! Second favorite?"

"Forrest Gump."

"Now you're talking!"

"What's yours?" Jenna asked

"The Good, the Bad and the Ugly. I'm a big Clint Eastwood fan."

The conversation continued until the sun set in front of them. Hues of pink and purple covered the sky, a masterpiece only a perfect artist could create. When they noticed, they both fell silent for a few seconds.

"Wow!" was all Jenna could muster.

"Majesty." Mitch added.

"Amen." Jenna concluded.

"You ready for some sound checkin'?"

"Can't wait!"

Mitch paid the bill and pulled Jenna's chair out for her. He took her hand and they walked to the parking lot to find the economy sized rental car. Neither said a word, but both had never felt happier.

When they got to the car, Mitch opened the passenger side door for Jenna and asked one more question. "Favorite band?"

"Mitch Boone Band, silly."

"Good answer."

60

You make known to me the path of life; in your presence, there is fullness of joy; at your right hand are pleasures forevermore.

~Psalm 16:11

The concert Friday night was more than Jenna could have imagined. From the dressing room hang-out before the show, to the introduction of the Mitch Boone Band by Billy Madison. Jenna felt pure exhilaration!

Jenna sat with Billy's wife, Susie for the concert. She was as kind and loving as her husband. They had two boys, Josh and Joey who joined them on the front row. Jenna couldn't decide who she enjoyed watching more- Mitch or the boys. Josh and Joey danced the whole time, belly laughing over each other's moves, never sitting down. Every so often, they would make their way over to hug their mom or grab her hands to dance with them. About halfway through the concert, the youngest boy, Joey started grabbing Jenna's hands to dance with him. It was one of the most enjoyable nights that Jenna could remember; and all the while Jenna met Mitch's gaze. They both sensed trust and respect for one another, no words were necessary. Jenna had confided in Mitch about Jax's letter, and her desire to get to know him better. Mitch's prayers were answered. They both knew this was heading from friendship to relationship.

After the concert, they all headed back to the hotel and ordered pizza in the band's adjoining rooms. Jenna drove back with Mitch in the infamous rental car. It was a quick and successful escape from the overzealous teens gathered outside the back door of the pavilion. No one paid attention to the economy car. Jen wondered if it was a planned decoy.

"Did you have fun?" Mitch asked as they fled the parking lot.

"It was amazing, Mitch! You guys are awesome!"

"Thank you! And thank you for being here. It means a lot."

"Thank you for having me! This has been the best weekend I have had in a while."

"And it's not over yet!" Mitch answered excitedly.

"I know! I don't want it to end." Jenna said smiling into Mitch's joyful eyes.

"Me either." And with that, Mitch took Jenna's hand and held it all the way to the hotel. At the end of the evening, Mitch walked Jenna back to her room to ensure she was safe.

"I thought tomorrow we could check out Charlotte. I'll come down and get you about nine o'clock. We'll go to breakfast and check out the sights. How does that sound?"

"Sounds like a perfect plan to me. Isn't the Billy Graham Library in Charlotte?" Jenna always wanted to go there.

"It is! I had that on my list. Would you like to go?"

"I would love it! My mom and dad visited and said it was great. You know, I read that Mr. Graham was totally against a library having his name. He didn't want anything taking away from the name of Jesus. In order for him to agree to it, they had to present it to him as a ministry, with the intention of communicating the message of Jesus."

"My parents went and loved it, too. Mr. Graham was brought up on a dairy farm, so the library is styled after a dairy barn. The entrance is in the shape of a cross."

"I can't wait!"

"Me either, Jen. See you at nine."

Jenna fell asleep with a smile on her face, thanking God for putting Mitch Boone in her path.

61

Are not all angels ministering spirits sent to serve those who will inherit salvation?

~Hebrews 1:14

Saturday, Carrie and her family, along with Beau and Jade, flew into Fort Myers airport. They were going to break in the condo and spread Jack's ashes, as he requested. Carrie clung to the urn as if it were Jack's hand. Grace, Will and Joe walked ahead to the baggage claim and when they arrived, Joe's knees buckled. Like an angel, there stood Achara with a smile as bright as God's promises.

She ran to Joe and leapt into his arms. The rest stood back and enjoyed the reunion. Char had been in touch with them for details. She let them know she was surprising him.

Joe was stunned and speechless but held Char tight, like it was for his life.

Carrie had rented an SUV to accommodate everyone. Beau drove the short trip to Sanibel Island. The conversation was steady, but solemn; a disharmony of emotion. Joe had so much to talk to Char about, but avoided conversation, not to arise suspicion of her trip to Thailand. Carrie was quiet, contemplating the new beginning of her life on Sanibel Island and the finality of Jack's earthly life.

When they arrived, everyone exited the car, leaving their luggage for the moment. Jade took charge. She put her arm around her best friend and walked toward the stairwell of the condo, that would soon be Carrie's home. "You ready?"

Carrie lay her head on Jade's shoulder as she clutched Jack's ashes. Grace, Will, Joe and Char walked hand-in-hand behind them. Beau brought up the rear.

"I'm as ready as I'll ever be," Carrie said as she whispered a silent prayer for strength. Memories and regrets raced through her mind. *Jack and I wanted to retire here together,* she lamented in her mind. *Lord, help me through this pain!*

Carrie left the grip of Jade as they approached the door of her new home. She unlocked the door and before opening it, looked back at her loved ones who were with her through thick and thin. "Ready?"

"Ready!" They responded in feigned, joyful unison.

When Carrie opened the door, balloons escaped the door bringing amusement to all. They entered and shut the door behind them. Balloons, signs, and banners filled the space proclaiming sentiments of welcome and love. The blinds were open presenting a glorious view of the ocean as Carrie walked toward the light. She opened the sliding glass door and set the urn down on the patio table. She found her place in a patio chair, looking out at God's masterpiece. She covered her face, lowered her head and sobbed tears of gratitude *and grief.* Her friends and family gathered around her and wept with her.

That evening, they ordered pizza. The refrigerator was already stocked with drinks, cold cuts, and everything they would need to get through the long weekend. They sat on the patio and listened to the roar of the waves rushing in to meet the shoreline. They shared their favorite memories of Jack. They watched the sun lower into the horizon. The sky darkened, bringing light to another area of God's perfect world. They retired to bed shortly afterwards. They had an early morning ahead of them.

At six o'clock a.m., Pastor Mark pulled one of the parishioner's boats up to the shore to pick up Carrie and her family and friends. Carrie clenched the urn and they walked silently down to meet him. Seaweed and shells littered the shoreline. Birds pecked the sand like fingers on a keyboard. The ebb and flow of the tide moved rhythmically as it had since the beginning of time. The rumbling of the current energized them, filling them with hope.

Carrie met Pastor Mark's embrace and held on tight. "Thank you for doing this for us."

"My pleasure. It was always Jack's wish. And what Jack wants, Jack gets."

Everyone laughed and got into the boat. Pastor Mark headed out a couple of miles toward the skyline. The spray of the salt water hit their sun kissed faces. When the boat stopped, Pastor Mark prayed aloud with his face toward the vast sky:

"Holy Father, we find solace in the fact that Jack is with you, but we still mourn his absence. He was an amazing friend, father, and husband. Oh Lord, we miss him. Thank you for that time with him. We don't grieve hopelessly, but we mourn with hope, just as your holy words tell us to do. We know that this is just a temporary absence. We understand that we will live eternally with him; and most importantly with you, when you call *us* home. Lord, this is where Jack came when he was your servant here. He found comfort and assistance from you when he worked on his sermons. This is where he wanted his body to rest until you resurrect it. Help us to triumph over the sadness and troubles of this life with faith and trust in you. We want to face death with joy and anticipation…just like Jack did."

Pastor Mark motioned to Carrie indicating it was time. Everyone placed their hands on Carrie and prayed as she removed the top from the urn. And just as the sun peeked over the horizon; under God's expansive sky, they spread Jack Finnegan's ashes over the ocean. And seconds later, a yellow butterfly fluttered in front of Carrie's face. A peace that surpassed all understanding came over her once again. Joe and Grace smiled with understanding as tears streamed down their faces.

"I've never seen a butterfly out this far," Jade observed as she met Carrie's joy-filled eyes.

"Angels take all forms, Jade."

62

God is our refuge and our strength, an ever-present help
in trouble.

~Psalm 46:1

As promised, Mitch arrived at nine o'clock on the nose. When
Jenna opened the door, it took a second, but they both burst
out laughing. They both sported khaki shorts, navy t-shirts
with baseball caps and tennis shoes to boot.

"Good minds think alike," Jenna managed.

"I guess so!" Mitch said in shock. "I'm thinking you should at least
change your t-shirt. This is a little too cutsie for me. What do you
think?"

"Awe, come on Mitch! I love cutsie!"

Mitch looked at Jenna, trying to gauge her response. Jenna couldn't
contain herself and laughed out loud. "I agree!" Jenna headed to her
suitcase and pulled out a t-shirt. "Be right back."

Jenna headed into the bathroom to change, as Mitch took a seat
on the bed.

After a few seconds, Jenna appeared in hot pink. "Better?"

"Much. Thanks, Jen. I hope I didn't sound self-absorbed, but I never
understood couples who dressed alike. It's just not my thing. I guess I
like a little individuality."

"I totally agree. My mother felt the same way. She never dressed Ben and me alike."

"I forgot you are a twin! Good for your mom!"

Jenna laughed and continued. "Ben was the worst about it! If we were going out somewhere together and even resembled each other *a little*, he'd say, "Okay, which one of us is changing?""

Mitch laughed and took Jenna's hand while they walked to the door. "I wish I could have met Ben. It sounds like he was a great guy. I want to hear all about him."

Jenna smiled and looked at Mitch with tears in her eyes. "Thanks, Mitch. He was the best. I really miss him."

"I bet you do. I can't imagine my life without Will in it."

"It was a tough time in our life, but God always brings good out of tragedy."

"Absolutely," Mitch agreed. "And you'll be together again one day. That's the best thing."

Jenna wiped tears from her face. "That is what I hold onto *every day* of my life."

"Let's go have some fun, Jenna Walls!" Mitch said as he pulled Jenna toward the elevator door.

Jenna giggled. "Let's do it!"

They had breakfast at a local IHOP and talked non-stop. They covered everything from childhood to their faith. It was clear that they were on the same page with almost everything; with the exception of favorite movie. It was refreshing for both of them.

Next stop was the Billy Graham Library. Jenna and Mitch enjoyed the *Journey of Faith* tour that included the library and the home that Billy Graham lived in from age nine until he left for college. They took time in the Memorial Prayer Garden beside the burial site of Ruth Graham, Billy's wife, and finished at the Graham Brothers Dairy Bar for some ice cream. While they sat and ate their ice cream, they reminisced. Jenna shared a story she remembered from a devotional of Billy Graham's.

"I remember when I was a little girl, probably about eight or nine, I was going through a time of doubt. I remember my mother coming into my room one night to say bedtime prayers with me and I asked her if she was sure that we went to heaven when we died. She assured me and then told me she would be right back.

"When she came back, she was holding Billy Graham's devotional book called, *Unto the Hills*. I will never forget it. I still have the book. It's worn from being read so much! The devotion was called "The Dying Words of Christians" and in it, Billy Graham shared how right before his grandmother died, she sat up in bed, smiled and said she saw Jesus and he was reaching out his hands to her. Then she said she saw her husband. His name was Ben- which I'll never forget because it is my twin's name. He had lost his leg and eye at Gettysburg. She called out excitedly that he had both of his eyes and both of his legs! And then she took her last breath. It was life-changing to me. I will never forget it."

Mitch smiled and shared his favorite. "We had the same book, Jen. The one I remember is "A Gull from God." It was about a captain and his crew that ran out of fuel and crashed their B-17 into the Pacific Ocean during World War II. They were missing for weeks and all of New York City was praying for them. They returned and the captain told the news that a gull came out of nowhere and landed on his head. He reached up, killed it and divided it between them. They ate every bit, even the bones. The gull saved their lives and the captain came to know Christ because of it. He said there was no other explanation except that God sent one of His angels to rescue them.

Then Mitch's phone rang.

63

I am sending an angel ahead of you to guard you along the way and to bring you to the place I have prepared.

~Exodus 23:20

Mitch looked at the face of the phone and answered immediately. "Annie, hi! Does my buddy need to talk?" Jenna smiled, knowing it was Butch's mom. Jenna watched Mitch's joyful face turn to sorrow. She rubbed his back acknowledging her support. When he hung up, with tears in his eyes, he announced that Butch was gone.

They sat in silence for a few seconds as they tried to wrap their minds around the enormity of what had just been told to them. Then Mitch divulged the conversation.

"Annie said he died peacefully." He paused letting those words sink into his mind. "She said that just as the sun was rising, he took his last breath." Tears streamed down his face as he recalled the conversation. "He called out to Julia and Jack before he died, Jen." Mitch looked to Jenna for reassurance. "Annie said his hands were raised and he had total joy on his face."

Jenna was sobbing, but gathered her breath to respond. "Mitch, that is so beautiful!"

Jenna had met Butch on Christmas Eve when they went to Vanderbilt Children's Hospital to visit him. Jenna had an instant connection with

Butch. She recalled him telling her about his friend, Julia who had just died the week before. He told Jenna that he couldn't wait to see her again.

"Isn't it amazing, Jen? Annie sounded sad, but peaceful. I think she knows he's *home*."

Jenna knew the feeling and shared it. "We felt the same way when Matthew, Ben's son, had his dream about heaven. It was that divine peace."

Then Mitch looked at Jenna with urgency. "Will you go to Tennessee with me, Jen?"

"When?"

"Now. Let's go to the airport and get a flight. I want to be with Annie and Bob."

"Okay. Sure."

Mitch took Jenna's hand and lifted her from the bench. They drove back to the hotel to get their things and Mitch called for a flight.

On the way to the airport, Mitch shared more of the conversation. "Annie said Butch wanted me to sing at his funeral." Mitch smiled, recalling the conversation he had with Butch at the hospital Christmas Eve. "Butch told me the same thing. He said he wanted all of his friends to know I was his friend."

Jenna laughed. "Spoken from the mouth of a six-year-old."

"I want to make it perfect for him, Jen. I feel so bad that I didn't get to say goodbye."

"Don't beat yourself up, Mitch. You talked to him before you left for Charlotte. He knew how much you loved him."

Jenna was lost in thought thinking back to her twin's funeral service. Her family's peace didn't come right away. Ben was in a car accident and they harbored hate for the irresponsible drunk driver. It wasn't until they forgave him and then met Ben's heart recipient, that they felt peace. They knew God was working everything for the good. And now Emma was married to John MacDonald. Only by the grace of God!

At the airport, they returned the rental car and boarded their flight. Jenna shared details of Ben's death and her family's redemption through it all. Mitch listened with full attention, mesmerized by her family's strength; and God's redeeming love.

64

I am the resurrection and the life. The one who believes
in me will live, even though he dies; and whoever lives
by believing in me will never die.

-John 11:25-26

Max and Colleen Boone picked up Jenna and Mitch at the airport. On their way, Mr. and Mrs. Boone delivered dinner to Annie and Bob Quinn's house. They visited with them and shared stories about little Butch. They headed to the Boone's house first to drop off luggage and get freshened up. Then Mitch and Jenna hopped in Mitch's Hummer and headed to the Quinn's house.

Annie and Bob were overjoyed to see them. They were both only children whose parents were deceased. Their family was comprised of numerous friends from all walks of their lives.

People came and went, offering hugs, condolences and lots of food. Jenna fell right into fix-it mode, answering the phone calls and finding room in the refrigerator and freezer for all of the food. She remembered her mom doing the same thing at Carrie's house after Jack died. She learned it from the best.

When things settled down, Annie, Bob, Mitch and Jenna sat in the living room and talked. Annie started the conversation with heartfelt gratitude. "Thank you so much for being here. It means so much to us. You know, Butch watched your concert on UTube last night."

Mitch felt humbled and saddened. Butch was his biggest fan.

Annie continued, sensing Mitch's uneasiness. "We have an appointment with the funeral director tomorrow morning. We would love your help with planning the service. You know that all that Butch cared about was that you would sing at his service."

Mitch smiled respectfully and responded. "Well, his wish is my command. We are here for you. Whatever you need."

The conversation continued. Bob and Annie took turns sharing the last hours of Butch's death. "There was never a moment of sadness," Bob admitted. "Butch was joyful the whole day. He told us the time was near and kept referring to the angels that were gathering."

Annie joined in. "He kept telling us how excited he was to see Jesus, Jack and Julia. He kept kidding around and calling them 'the Js.' He told us not to be sad because we would be together again and he would be fine. And he kept telling us that we were having another baby... a baby girl named Joy.

"Just before he died, we were all laying on his bed. We put a picture window in Butch's room so he could watch the sun rise and set over the pond in the backyard. He said it gave him peace." Bob was deep in thought, remembering every instance.

Annie stared ahead as if reliving every moment and finished the story. "First, he called out, Jack! And then, Julia!" Annie started crying wiping the tears as quickly as they fell, but didn't miss a second of the story. "And then he was actually giggling! His face had pure joy on it." Annie looked to Mitch and Jenna with marvel in her eyes. "And then he raised his arms to heaven as if someone was going to take him into their arms. The room filled with this brilliant light *just* as the sun rose over the pond." Annie's shoulders shook as she took in the reality of their loss.

Bob finished for her. "Then Butch said, 'I love you Mom and Dad!' And he took his last breath."

Mitch and Jenna cried along with them. Then Jenna recognized the reality. "Well, there is no doubt where he is! Pastor Jack used to say that when an unbeliever dies, we mourn for them. But when a believer dies, we mourn for ourselves. We'll all get to hug him again one day, but for now, Butch is right- he is just fine!"

Jenna shared Matthew's dream of heaven and all of its details, straight from the book of Revelation. Annie and Bob were so grateful for Jenna's openness. It felt uplifting to talk to someone who experienced similar grief. It gave them hope that they too would get through it.

Later that evening, Jenna called her mom. She knew that today was the day that they had spread Jack's ashes on Sanibel Island. She also wanted to tell her mom about their detour from North Carolina to Tennessee; and to tell her about Butch's passing.

Jade answered on the first ring. "Hey Jen! I've had you on my mind. How was the concert?"

"It was fantastic, Mom! We've taken a little detour. We are now in Tennessee."

"What are you doing in Tennessee?"

"Butch died, Mom. We were at the Billy Graham Library when Mitch got the call from Annie. He wanted to come here to support them, so I came with him."

"That's great, Jen. You know how much we appreciated the support when Ben died. How are Annie and Bob holding up?"

"Surprisingly well. Butch died an amazingly peaceful death, Mom. It's a beautiful story. You'll have to share it with everybody. Butch called out to Jack right before he died. His parents said he was giggling with joy and had his hands raised to heaven. He took his last breath just as the sun rose over the pond in his yard. He can see it from his bedroom window."

Jenna waited for her mom to respond, but all she heard was sniffling. "Isn't that a beautiful story? Are you okay, Mom?"

"I'm fine, Jen. I just have something to add to that beauty."

"What do you mean?"

"Well, we got up at 6:00 a.m. to meet Pastor Mark on the beach. We wanted it to be private, so we went when no one was around. He borrowed one of the parishioner's boats. We went out on the ocean a little way and stopped. Pastor Mark said a beautiful prayer and just as Carrie was spreading Jack's ashes, the sun rose."

Jenna felt the hair on her arms stand on end. "Mom! That is beautiful! Maybe Jack met Butch when the sun rose! He promised Butch he would if he could."

"I wondered the same thing, Jen. And right after the sun rose, a yellow butterfly fluttered in front of Carrie's face! When was the last time you saw a butterfly out on the ocean?"

"No way, Mom! Jack always saw yellow butterflies when he was praying!"

"I know! Carrie and the kids told me. They said they felt that peace that…"

Jenna joined in, "surpasses all understanding. God is great, Mom."

"Always, Jen."

"Well, I'll be back Monday night. Tell everyone that I said hello and be sure to tell them the story. It is a definite God wink!"

"I promise. They'll know right when I hang up with you. We are meeting on the beach tonight."

"I'm heading upstairs to tell the Boone family, too!"

"I love you, Jen. Tell them we said hello."

"Love you too, Mom. Will do."

65

Truly I tell you, unless you change and become like little children, you will never enter the kingdom of heaven.

~Matthew 18:3

Sunday, Mitch and Jenna met with Annie and Bob to plan Butch's ceremony. Before they started, Mitch asked to see Butch's room.

"Annie, I can't explain it, but I've had this tugging on my heart to see Butch's room. When I spoke to him last, he was laying in his bed looking out at the pond in your backyard. I asked him to tell me about his bedroom. I want to see if it is the way I pictured it." Mitch smiled thinking back to their conversation. "He was so detailed in his descriptions."

Annie and Bob agreed and they all headed toward Butch's sanctuary. On the way, Annie made a confession. "We haven't been back in his room since he died. We just weren't ready. Thank you for asking."

Bob grabbed his wife's hand and they led the way to the closed door- closed to hide the reality of what was missing behind it. Jenna took Mitch's hand and they followed humbly behind. When Annie opened the door, the sun from the plate glass window illuminated the sky-blue walls. Covering the walls were drawings of heaven that Butch had created since his diagnosis. For what seemed like a full minute, the four of them stood in silence taking in the splendor of Butch's faith.

"Wow," was all that Mitch could muster, his voice cracking. "This is unbelievable."

Jenna let go of Mitch's hand and in a trance walked the room, mesmerized by the detail in his artwork. She looked over at his sobbing parents and established fact. "He's with Jesus." Jenna wept joyful tears and sat down on Butch's bed. "My nephew, Matthew drew similar pictures. This is clearly God's intercession. I feel so much peace."

Jenna continued to spy the circumference of the room. "I love the way you framed and displayed his drawings, Annie. You need to use these pictures to share hope."

Annie composed herself and smiled. She walked toward her favorite picture hanging on the wall right beside Butch's bed. "This is my favorite one." Annie stared through the drawing without blinking. She spoke her memory, as if present in it. "Bob and I had been praying for a miracle. This one told us, without a doubt, that he was going to be with the Lord."

Bob moved beside Annie and took her hand for support. He too remembered the moment vividly and continued. "We brought Butch his dinner that night. We would all eat on TV trays in his bed. Butch called it a 'Winner's Dinner.'"

Annie laughed and sat down beside her husband. "Yes, a dinner for conquerors. He said Jesus conquered death at his resurrection and so would we."

Bob kept it going. "When we brought dinner in, Butch led the prayer. He thanked God for his bravery in dying on the cross. He told Him that he was ready, whenever God called him home."

Mitch had chills all over his body. He sat down on the other side of the bed to join Jenna, never breaking concentration. Annie continued the conversation.

"When we finished praying, he told us he had drawn his favorite picture yet. He said his angel told him about heaven and how Butch wasn't going to believe its beauty." Annie pointed to the picture. It hung majestically on the wall. "This is the river of life coming down from

God's throne. He even gave us the scripture, Revelation 22:1." Annie stared ahead remembering every second. "We felt a divine calmness. We knew Butch was ready *and willing* to meet his Savior; and we were convinced of his destination."

Mitch broke the silence with a God-given revelation. "You have to display these pictures in church! You can use Revelation 21 as your scripture and share Butch's legacy! This will change lives!" Mitch looked at Bob and Annie. "Would you be able to do it?"

Annie, with joy in her eyes, looked at Bob. They smiled in confirmation. "We'd love to," they responded in unison.

Mitch added, "I was thinking I could end the ceremony with "On Eagle's Wings.""

"That is perfect, Mitch! That was one of Butch's favorites!" Annie sat back down on the bed and grabbed Butch's pillow. She inhaled the last, earthly scents of him. As she did, Bob spotted an envelope under the pillow with Mom and Dad sketched on the outside. Bob picked it up and met his wife's tear-filled eyes.

Jenna motioned to Mitch to leave the room. They stood to exit. "We will give you some privacy," Mitch expressed as he took Jenna's hand.

"No, please," Annie declared. "Don't leave. There is a reason you are here. Please stay."

Mitch and Jenna sat back down on the bed. Bob took the envelope as Annie anxiously awaited beside her husband. Bob read it aloud:

> Mom and Dad…as you read this leter, jus piccher me with Jesus. My angel red scrptur with me tonite. He said it is tru that no eye has seen or ear has herd what God has prepaird for those who love him. I am not scard at all! I promis! Plez don't be sad. I will see you agan. And I don't have cancr anymore! Take gud care of my baby sistr. I think Joy wuld be a butiful name for her becuz she will bring you so much hapines. Thank you for being the best earthle parents! I love you!
> PS, plez give this to Mitch and let him no that God protecs him even at his concertz. Love, Butch

Bob opened the other folded piece of paper and handed it to Mitch. The drawing was of Mitch and his band on stage. They had joyful smiles and guitars strapped across their bodies. At the four corners of the stage were angels. Tears splashed on the drawing as Mitch took in the detail. "This is the best gift I have ever received!"

"Are you pregnant, Annie?" Jenna asked elatedly.

"Not that I know of," Annie smiled, looking toward Bob with confused joy. "But I think I am going to take a pregnancy test because Butch certainly sounds convinced!"

Annie went on to explain that she was diagnosed with endometriosis after Butch was born. The doctor told her that her scarring was significant and it would be impossible to conceive again. She added that if she was indeed pregnant, it was a miracle from God.

Mitch took Jenna to the airport that evening. The plan was for her to return the following weekend with Grace and Will for Butch's celebration of life service.

66

Those who hope in the Lord will renew their strength.
They will soar on wings like eagles; they will run and
not grow weary. They will walk and not grow faint.

~Isaiah 40:31

Saturday morning, family and friends gathered at the church for Butch's ceremony. The altar was a celestial gallery of Butch's artwork; whimsical and colorful depictions of Butch's forever residence; autographed by the artist himself, in child-like scrawl.

Annie and Bob stoically stood at the front of the altar greeting people and sharing their son's life. When the pastor climbed the steps to the altar, the guests took their seats. The aisles were lined with wheelchairs, occupied by the patients from the Children's Hospital; Butch's brothers and sisters in Christ. Their faces glowed with delight, the realization deep in their hearts that their buddy, Butch was with his Abba- his heavenly daddy.

The mood and atmosphere in the church were like nothing Mitch had ever encountered. A peaceful sensation was felt throughout…the usual melancholy, somehow sheltered in tranquility. God was surely in this place. His almighty presence filled the audience with solace and hope. It was one of celebration, not mourning; the joyful acceptance of eternal life.

The pastor began the service. "Welcome everybody! We are here to celebrate Butch's union with Jesus today." Some of Butch's friends started to clap, drawing the others in. The thunder of applause sent vibrations of certainty throughout. The pastor's uninterrupted smile spoke more truth. "Just saying the name 'Butch' gives me that Christmas feeling! Amen?"

A resounding "Amen" filled the room. The congregation smiled and nodded in agreement. The pastor continued. "You know what I mean, right? Butch made me want to be a better person. He made me want to pray more, read my Bible more; love more. Butch got it! He understood the whole trust in God thing! He *knew* Jesus. His cancer was insignificant because he knew that meeting his Savior was the ultimate! He knew his suffering on earth was temporary. Butch crossed the finish line!"

"The scripture today comes from Revelation, chapter 21, verses 18 through 27: The wall was made of jasper, and the city was pure gold, as clear as glass. The wall of the city was built on foundation stones inlaid with twelve precious stones. The twelve gates were made of pearls— each gate from a single pearl! And the main street was pure gold, as clear as glass. I saw no temple in the city, for the Lord God Almighty and the Lamb are its temple. And the city has no need of sun or moon, for the glory of God illuminates the city, and the Lamb is its light. The nations will walk in its light, and the kings of the world will enter the city in all their glory. Its gates will never be closed at the end of day because there is no night there. And all the nations will bring their glory and honor into the city. Nothing evil will be allowed to enter, nor anyone who practices shameful idolatry and dishonesty—but only those whose names are written in the Lamb's Book of Life."

Pastor Lou stopped and looked out to the crowd- all there to honor Butch. "This is where Butch is right now! When you get sad, just think of that! Butch is in paradise with Jesus!" The pastor paced the altar with excitement. "Can't you just see Butch holding Jesus' hand, walking the golden streets; and drilling him with questions?" Laughter and sniffles filled the room. The crowd nodded in jubilant agreement.

"This scripture is God's truth! John, Jesus' beloved disciple, was rescued by God from the Island of Patmos. John was sent there by the Roman soldiers for preaching the gospel. Jesus gave this message to John. He allowed John to see and record future events in order to encourage us! John is describing what Jesus showed him!" Pastor Lou paused to let the words sink in. "We have nothing to fear, friends. Our final destination will be glorious. And Butch is basking in that glory, as I speak."

Next, Pastor Lou introduced Bob and Annie. They read the letter that Butch left them and then Annie shared their miraculous news. "By the grace of God, Bob and I are having another child. And if all goes as Butch says it will, her name will be Joy."

When the congregation quieted, Bob concluded: "We only had Butch six, short years, but they were the most fulfilling years of our lives." Bob lingered, collecting himself. "Romans 8:28 says that God works everything for good and I am here to tell you, that is truth. We will miss Butch, but we know that we will be together again. God used Butch's illness to change lives. We have no regrets or anger. God has blessed us beyond words and we will continue to Trust Him in all things- good or bad."

The ceremony concluded with Mitch Boone's rendition of "On Eagle's Wings."

After the ceremony, Bob and Annie let the kids pick out a couple of favorite drawings to bring back to the hospital with them. The rest of the drawings would adorn Joy's nursery. She would know at a very young age who her brother was; and most importantly, her Savior.

67

For if you forgive other people when they sin against you, your heavenly Father will also forgive you.

~Matthew 6:14-15

Grace got home from work and checked her mailbox. She walked toward her apartment door as she flipped through bills and advertisements. Then she stopped dead in her tracks.

On the bottom of the pile was a letter addressed to her and a return address from the state prison- Tony's current residence. Grace's heart raced, her mouth parched. She felt faint and grabbed the door handle for balance. She entered the apartment and dropped all but Tony's letter at the entrance. She walked to the living room in a daze. She dropped to the couch, staring at the letter in her hands- as if it would speak. She knew that the only way to get the message was to open it.

Thoughts swirled through her brain; gymnastics of the mind. *Should I throw it out and leave it in the past where it belongs?* Grace breathed deeply, pensive. *Should I open it and trigger those dysfunctional memories?* As she considered, the phone rang. Grace was startled back to reality- out of her trance. She rose with hope to see who was calling. She needed some support right about now. She looked at the face of the phone. It was Char. Grace answered immediately.

Char questioned Grace without a greeting. "Did you get a letter?"

Grace's heart skipped a beat, remembering instantly that Char, too had a torrid past with Tony.

"Yes. You too?"

Grace heard sniffling on the other end. "Char, please, tell me what is wrong! Should I open it or throw it out?"

"It's a letter of apology, Grace. You need to read it, but then we need each other to discuss it." Char spoke calmly and deliberately. Grace listened. Her pale eyes danced as she remembered every detail of her tumultuous past with him. She knew Tony's good side; sin took him over.

"Grace, are you there?"

"Yes, I'm sorry, Char. I was just thinking. I will read it and call you back."

"No, I will be over in 30 minutes."

Grace smiled. "That is better yet. Thank you for calling, Char. I love you."

"Love you too, Grace."

Grace headed back to the couch and picked the letter up, off the coffee table. As she opened it, she spoke a word of prayer. "Lord, please help me to see these words through your eyes." Then she opened it and read.

Grace and Char,

I am writing this letter to both of you because my message is the same...I am so sorry! I have had a lot of time sitting in the darkness of my prison cell. Before Jack died, he and Carrie came to visit me. I accepted Jesus as my Savior and I felt cleansed and renewed. I feel like I have a new life. When I think back to the person I was, I am both sickened and ashamed. I have cried many heartfelt prayers, begging God that one day, you would both forgive me. If you don't, I understand. I want you both to know that I am not the same person anymore. I was consumed with sin and evil. I lost control of myself. Satan controlled me, instead. That person is nailed to the cross now. I am a new creation in Christ. Francesco keeps me informed. My family has forgiven me and visits me often. I am so blessed to have them! I am happy that you have both found happiness. I pray that one day, I will get another chance; but I know it is God's will- not mine. I will be praying for you and your families. If you have it in you, please do the same for me.

In Christ, Tony

There was a rap on the door and Grace answered. Char embraced her and they cried together. Then hand-in-hand, they walked to the living room and sat down on the couch. Char faced Grace squarely. "How do you feel?"

"I feel peace, Char. That door is closed and I am so grateful that Tony found God. I saw that good side of him when I first started dating him, but sin took him over."

"Do you forgive him?"

Grace hesitated, but responded with certainty. "Yes. It will take time to forget, but we have to forgive, or we aren't forgiven." Grace looked at Char. "How about you, Char? You saw Tony at his absolute worst! Are you able to forgive?"

Char, too hesitated, trying to collect her thoughts. "I agree with you. I believe we have to forgive to have closure and move on." Char stared ahead, lost in the past. "Those days with Tony in my apartment were chilling. When I looked in his eyes, I was looking into a dark hole. He had no soul, Grace. He was possessed." Char squeezed her eyes shut, shuddering in remembrance.

Grace took Char's hand and squeezed it for support. "That must have been horrific. I am so sorry, Char." Grace wept, wishing she could take it from her. Joe had confided in his sister about Char's pregnancy and her choice to give the child up for adoption. Grace was awed by her bravery.

"I was scared, Grace, but God really does work suffering for the good. Think about it. I found the Lord through your family. I found your brother as my forever partner. I've gained amazing family and friends. An infertile couple got a baby. I choose to be grateful. I choose joy!"

Grace hugged Char. "I love you, Char! I am so happy my brother found you!" Then she paused and added, "Now, how do we forgive Tony?"

Char looked pensive. "Well, I'm not ready to run to the prison and hug his neck, are you?"

Grace laughed. "No! Oh Char, I am *so* far from that day. But maybe a simple letter back to him for closure. Hold on."

Grace ran to her teacher bag by the door and pulled out a pad of paper and a pen. She sat down on the couch, looked at Char and asked, "Are you ready to close this door?"

"Slam it."

Grace proceeded to write back to the enemy, simple and to the point. She read aloud as she wrote it:

Tony,

>Thank you for your apology. Char and I are so grateful for your fresh start. We forgive you and will be praying for you.

Grace signed her name and handed the pen to Char. "Done," Char announced as she slammed the pen down.

"I will mail it tomorrow," Grace stated matter-of-factly.

"That door is officially closed, Grace."

"Yup. Done. Now, let's go get some ice cream and celebrate!"

Epilogue

I will be your God throughout your lifetime- until your hair is white with age. I made you and I will care for you. I will carry you along and save you.

~Isaiah 46:4

Sanibel Island -five years later...

J ade and Carrie got up early and tiptoed down to the beach. Carrie's condo was carpeted with sleeping bodies- big and small, young and aging...their children and grandchildren...God's exquisite gifts of love.

The breeze was warm and soothing as they stood looking out at the place where Jack's ashes were spread- just five years earlier. The wind swept wisps of hair off of their bronzed faces, as the first signs of sunlight danced toward the horizon. The low tide exposed treasures of the ocean floor. They unfolded their beach chairs in unison. This behavior was becoming a habit...a good one. The friends sat reminiscing the past- the year they first came...

Char and Joe were engaged at the time. Now, they were married with a beautiful, two-year-old daughter, Isabella. Her name meant, *devoted to God.* She was a miniature version of her faithful, courageous mother.

Grace married Will and God filled their home with now, three-year-old Travis- Will's clone. And like his dad and Uncle Mitch, he went everywhere with his guitar…even the bathroom.

Micah and Mags had four-year-old, John… who, of course, went by Jack, in honor of his gramps.

Jade felt especially reminiscent that morning. "It is amazing how God works, Carrie. I think back and I can see clearly how God strategically placed specific people along my path to fulfill his plan for me." Jade hesitated and swallowed back tears. "Who would have thought that my husband's affair would have led me to Pastor Jack, who would become my best friend's husband?" Then Jade laughed and added, "and our marriage counselor!"

"I know!" Carrie agreed, "and Jack came at the perfect time in my life!" She paused and took a breath. She had one of those moments; a moment that takes your breath away for a second…an intense sadness. But then it's gone and the moments are fewer and shorter, but still they come. "I miss him daily, Jade," Carrie admitted with raw honesty.

Slowly, but surely, the rest of the crew made their appearances. First down was Jenna and Mitch. They were married three years and were the proud parents of Charlie and Chase…two-year-old twin boys. Jenna thought twins skipped a generation, but no such luck!

Both boys were squirming in their parents' arms, wanting to get loose. Jenna emptied the beach bag, exposing every vehicle known to mankind into the sand. The boys plopped down and got to work. Mitch joined them, building roads and playing dad. He told his family often that their twins beat country music any day of the week.

"Mom, you really should have warned us before we had kids."

Jade laughed out loud. "Whatever do you mean, Jen?"

"Will we ever sleep?" Jenna asked with exasperation.

Mitch piped in. "Will these two ever sleep?" He pointed to his boys, laughing, then tickling them until they pleaded for him to stop. Their contagious cackles filled their hearts to overflowing.

Jenna smiled and bent down to hug her husband. "Well, just so you know, there is no one I would rather lose sleep with."

Mitch kissed her. "Agreed. Let's wear them out! The sun and sand are good sleep aides!"

Within the hour, everyone was camped out on the beach- a circle of tents, coolers, toys; and a whole lot of love. The only ones missing were Bob, Annie, and Joy, but they were on their way. Jenna acknowledged Annie's text.

"Bob, Annie and Joy should be here any minute!"

"Yessss!" little Travis celebrated. "I wuv Joy!"

About that time, Joy came barreling down the beach, yelling, "Hi guys! I'm here! Wait for me!"

Everyone within earshot stopped what they were doing to watch the female version of Butch making her grand entrance. Butch's choice in name for his baby sister was spot-on. Joy exuded happiness and it spread like wildfire!

Five-year-old Joy was dropping her beach toys, stepping out of her flip-flops and hugging her "cousins" all in one clean sweep. Bob and Annie were out of breath, trying to keep up.

"She may be female, but she is Butch made over!" Bob was laughing as he unpacked their goods.

Everyone hugged and pulled their chairs into a circle so they could catch up. The kids played on and off all day, in between naps and lunch. They played hard until their sun-kissed faces exposed sleepy eyes. The mood calmed and they sat waiting for the sun to escape beyond the horizon.

Carrie felt a twinge of sadness as she thought of Jack again. She turned to Jade and shared her thoughts. "I always wonder if Jack can see his grandchildren from heaven. He would have loved this, Jade."

Jade smiled, thinking of Jack smiling down. "I bet he does... but if not, he will someday...live and in person."

Carrie smiled and stared out to the water. The sunlight glinted off of the brilliant, sapphire sea. "I know. Sometimes, I just can't wait until that day."

Seconds later, little Jack stood before Carrie's chair and startled her out of her lonesome stupor. "Wook Mimi! A yewo buttefwy."

Carrie and Jade looked down to Jack's little hand and balancing on the end of his pudgy, little finger was a yellow butterfly... a Jack Finnegan original.

Jade gasped and with tears in her eyes said, "Care, I think you just got your answer- straight from the heavens."

Carrie looked to the heavens and yelled, "I love you, Jack Finnegan! I'll see you on Glory's side!"

Acknowledgements

To my husband, Bob for loving me and supporting me in all of my ventures. He edited for me and shared great male insight. He is the one who pushed me to finish this book and to continue in completing the trilogy. And the handy, 'Who's Who' at the front of the book was his creation!

We lost my mom in December 2017, and my precious dad lives with us now. In order for me to write, I need Bob to help care for my dad and he does an incredible and self-less job. I am so blessed to do life with him! I love you, Gibby!

To my sweet, multi-talented, friend, Dezi De Hart! She was one of the editors of my book and gave me incredible, constructive feedback. She even convinced me to change my title from "The Best is Yet to Come" to "Angels Take All Forms." It is amazing how God puts people in your path! I met her while vacationing in Florida (before our official move). I walked into a random hair salon and the rest in history. She is my hairdresser and her dad, Vinny is our mechanic. Her sister, Brittany and her mom, Cheryl, complete this God-loving family! They are people of integrity. They "walk the talk" and we are so blessed to call them friends.

To Pastor Greg Freeze, our pastor at Spring Life Church in Spring Hill, Florida. My husband and I have learned so much about God's word from him! Many of the sermons in my book are from lessons that I learned from him. His genuine mission in life is to bring people to Christ. We are blessed to be a part of this amazing church family.

And to all of you who have read my books! Thank you for giving me a chance!

And finally, to my Lord and Savior, Jesus Christ who leads, directs, forgives, and loves me- even when I am terribly unlovable! I cannot imagine doing life without Him! Thank you, Abba!

CPSIA information can be obtained
at www.ICGtesting.com
Printed in the USA
BVHW081000161219
566813BV00001B/173/P